Dear Reader,

It's that joyful time of year again! And Santa has some wonderfully festive books coming your way this December.

Bestselling author Marie Ferrarella brings you our THAT'S MY BABY! for December. This holiday bundle of joy is still a secret to his or her dad…and Mom is sure to be a *Christmas Bride.*

And the patter of little feet doesn't stop there. Don't miss *A Baby for Rebecca* by Trisha Alexander, the latest in her THREE BRIDES AND A BABY miniseries. *Holly and Mistletoe* is Susan Mallery's newest title in the HOMETOWN HEARTBREAKERS miniseries, a tale filled with Christmas warmth and love. And for those of you who've been enjoying Tracy Sinclair's CUPID'S LITTLE HELPERS miniseries, this month we've got *Mandy Meets a Millionaire*—with the help of some little matchmakers.

December also brings Diana Whitney's *Barefoot Bride*—the heroine is an amnesiac woman in a wedding dress who finds love with a single dad and his kids at Christmastime. This is the second book in Diana's wonderful PARENTHOOD miniseries. *The Sheriff's Proposal* by Karen Rose Smith is a warm, tender tale that takes place during the season of giving.

I hope you enjoy all our books this month. All of us here at Silhouette wish you a happy, healthy holiday season!

Sincerely,

Tara Gavin
Senior Editor

Please address questions and book requests to:
Silhouette Reader Service
U.S.: 3010 Walden Ave., P.O. Box 1325, Buffalo, NY 14269
Canadian: P.O. Box 609, Fort Erie, Ont. L2A 5X3

DIANA
WHITNEY
BAREFOOT BRIDE

Silhouette®

SPECIAL EDITION®

Published by Silhouette Books
America's Publisher of Contemporary Romance

To our family's most recent bride, my beautiful daughter-in-law, Jennifer Gilstrap, a sweet, charming and indisputably intelligent young woman of whom we are all extraordinarily proud.

 SILHOUETTE BOOKS

ISBN 0-373-24073-2

BAREFOOT BRIDE

Printed in U.S.A.

Books by Diana Whitney

DIANA WHITNEY

says she loves "fat babies and warm puppies, mountain streams and California sunshine, camping, hiking and gold prospecting. Not to mention strong romantic heroes!" She married her own real-life hero over twenty years ago. With his encouragement, she left her longtime career as a municipal finance director and pursued the dream that had haunted her since childhood: writing. To Diana, writing is a joy, the ultimate satisfaction. Reading, too, is her passion, from spine-chilling thrillers to sweeping sagas, but nothing can compare to the magic and wonder of romance.

Deer Santa

It's me agin, Rory Morgan.
Last Christmas I asked for a
new mommy. Maybe I was not
good enuf. This year I was beter.

But I still fite with my sister
She boss me around because
she is 10 and I am only 8.

I no you have alot of work
and maybe there are not enuf
mommys but Daddy and Shawna
have bin sad for a long time.
I have bin sad too.

P. S. My speling is not good.
I will do beter if I have a
mommy to help me.

Thank you
Rory Morgan

Chapter One

Tucking her knees up, eight-year-old Rory Morgan scooched sideways on the narrow rear jump seat of her father's King Cab pickup. Issuing an eager sigh, she gazed out the back window for the tenth time in as many minutes to admire the freshly chopped fir tied in the truck bed. "This is the best-est Christmas tree in the whole wide world, isn't it, Daddy?"

"Sure is," Reed Morgan agreed, casting an amused glance in the rearview mirror.

His youngest daughter, who was positively fried with excitement, had pressed her nose against the back window until the glass was clouded with happy breath. "Do you think Santa will like it?"

"He'll love it," Reed assured the child, then slowed to steer around a mud puddle. "Santa's a classy guy."

Rory spun around, her eyes huge. "How do you know, Daddy? Did you ever meet Santa?"

"Well, ah..." Reed's gaze shifted to the sullen thirteen-year-old seated beside him. He'd hoped that a family outing to select their holiday tree would cheer his oldest daughter. Instead, Shawna seemed even more bored and depressed than usual. Sighing, Reed refocused on the rutted rural road. "Let's just say that Santa and I go back a long way."

"Wow," Rory murmured, apparently awestruck by the notion that her father had more than a passing acquaintance with the beloved Christmas Claus.

Shawna suddenly leaned forward, staring at what appeared to be a distant crumple of white fabric heaped on the shoulder of the puddled road. "What's that?"

"I don't know," Reed murmured. "Looks like someone's laundry."

As they drew closer to the peculiar pile, which resembled a wad of wrapped linens that may have bounced from the bed of a neighbor's pickup, Reed noted that even in the gray light of a winter dawn the fabric emitted an odd, distinctly uncottonlike sheen.

Rolling down the window for a better look, his booted foot instinctively touched the brake, slowing the truck to a crawl. He squinted against the rush of frigid wind, pulled down his brimmed work hat and scrutinized the glimmering fabric.

"It looks like satin," Shawna announced, confirming her father's observation.

"It sure does." Reed grinned, wondering which of his ranching neighbors harbored a secret yearning for satin sheets, a sensual luxury that most residents of their earthy rural community would consider laughably frivolous.

"We can't just leave it there." With that authoritarian pronouncement, Shawna zipped her quilted jacket against the chill wind that continued to whistle through the open window. "We have to take it home until we find out who it belongs to."

Despite a perverse desire to tease any red-faced owner who stepped forward to claim the bundle, Reed shook off his daughter's suggestion. The fir tree filled the entire truck bed and he certainly didn't want to drag a pile of muddy linens into the relatively clean cab of his pickup.

"Whoever lost it will be back," Reed told the disappointed teen, and would have kept on driving had he not spotted a sprig of dark hair poking from beneath the satin folds.

He jammed the brake so hard that the truck fishtailed in the mud, then he steered to a complete stop and sat there, staring in disbelief.

At first Reed feared the woman was dead, but when the fabric vibrated, he realized that she was curled forward, hugging her bent knees. Her face was buried in her lap, and the back portion of her voluminous white satin skirt, which had been pulled forward as a hood and to enfold her upper body, provided scant protection from the bitter cold. She was shivering violently.

Shoving the truck into park, Reed flipped off the ignition and opened the driver's door. "Stay here," he told his curious daughters, both of whom were preparing to exit the vehicle.

Ignoring the disappointed whines of his children, Reed approached the hunched figure cautiously. "Are you all right, miss?"

The satin slid down to her shoulders as she looked up, blinking in bewilderment.

Reed's breath backed up in his throat. Despite a few mud smears and abrasions marring an otherwise flawless complexion, she was without doubt the most exquisite woman he'd ever encountered, with hair as black as midnight and eyes bluer than a field of spring cornflowers.

That gorgeous hair was piled atop her head in an intricate if somewhat disheveled style into which tiny white blossoms and seed pearls had been woven along with a presumably unintentional scattering of leaf debris. A neat teardrop of matching pearls dripped from each of her perfect earlobes, and when her spine straightened, her shoulders automatically squared into an aristocratic posture to expose the sheer bodice of what Reed surmised to be an extravagantly elegant wedding gown.

Lifting her chin, the woman spoke with a genteel courtesy that under the circumstances seemed particularly bizarre. "Yes, thank you," she murmured, despite a dazed expression that quite clearly indicated otherwise. "I'm quite well, thank you."

Squatting, Reed sat back on his boot heels to scrutinize the purplish bruise above the woman's left brow and a reddened scrape at her jawline. "Have you been in an accident?"

"Accident? I, ah..." Her gaze darted sideways, then lowered demurely as she issued a nervous laugh. "Gracious, I must have fallen asleep. Isn't that the silliest thing?"

Reed was too startled to answer. Instead, he studied her expression, noting a faint panic in her eyes. "Do you know where you are?"

She frowned, absently smoothing the soiled satin over her lap while glancing at the fenced pasture beyond the road. "Actually, I am feeling a bit lost at the moment. What is the name of this place?"

Reed followed her gaze beyond a split-rail fence studded with Christmas lights. "That's Harland McKenzie's ranch. Are you a friend of his?"

"I don't think so. The name doesn't ring any bells." Her frown intensified. "We *are* in California, aren't we?"

"Yes," Reed replied slowly, his heart sinking like a stone. "We're just south of Grass Valley."

"Is that close to Los Angeles?"

"No, it's in Northern California, in the Sierra foothills." Responding to her bewildered stare, he added, "You know, Gold Rush Country, home of the old forty-niners."

"Oh." Her expression indicated that the description meant nothing to her, yet she managed a polite smile. "So, are you some kind of gold miner?"

He laughed. "No, ma'am. I guess you could call me a full-time cherry farmer and wannabe rancher."

The smile finally sparkled its way into those gorgeous blue eyes. "A wannabe rancher?"

"I'm running a couple dozen head right now, but I wannabe running a hundred."

"Ah. Well, I certainly admire a man with ambition." She stared across the field for a moment, then her eyes widened. Shivering, she hugged herself, rubbing her upper arms, which were protected from the chill wind only by a sleeve of translucent lace extending from the puffy satin shoulder caps to the center of her slender, perfectly manicured hands.

Wishing he had a jacket to wrap around her trembling shoulders, Reed skimmed a glance at her satin gown, the hem of which was frayed and muddy. Not surprising, considering that the nearest pavement was two miles away—as was the nearest church.

As if reading his thoughts, she laid a self-conscious hand on her lace-clad bodice. "Under the circumstances, my attire must seem a trifle peculiar."

"Well, now that you mention it."

She returned his thin smile, then licked her lips and avoided his gaze. "I wish I could explain, but the truth is that I haven't a clue why I'm wearing this." Heaving a worried sigh, she pressed a fingertip to her temple, eyeing a soiled smear on the shimmering skirt. "It's ruined now. I suppose I'll have to pay for it." She glanced around the ground, her brows puckered. "But I seem to have lost my purse."

"What does it look like?"

"My purse?"

Reed nodded.

"It's ... it's ..." Dazed, she rubbed her upper arms, ignoring the violent shiver that suddenly vibrated her slender frame. "A purse is a purse," she said finally. "Who pays attention to details?"

Plainly, she was having trouble recalling more than the details of a handbag. The woman's memory appeared to be seriously impaired, leaving Reed to struggle with something, anything, that might jog her mind for a clue as to what had happened to place her in such a precarious situation.

"You mentioned Los Angeles," he said kindly. "Is that where you live?"

"To tell you the truth, Mr.—" She slid him a quizzical glance.

"Morgan, ma'am, Reed Morgan."

"Pleased to meet you, Mr. Morgan."

"Likewise." Acutely aware that she hadn't returned the introduction, he nonetheless tipped his Stetson hat and silently berated the absurdity of carrying on politely nondescript conversation with someone who could be an escaped mental patient. The fact that his children were watching from the truck added to Reed's concern, yet despite the woman's obvious confusion there was something inherently normal about her, and strangely appealing.

"As I was saying, Mr. Morgan, I've been sitting here wondering the answer to that question myself." Sighing, she lifted her face, absently wiping a wind-whipped curl of hair from her eyes. "I'm sure this will sound absolutely insane to you, but the truth is that I'm not exactly certain where I live, or what in the world I'm doing here." A flash of white teeth nervously scraped her lower lip. She angled an apologetic smile. "I must appear quite foolish."

"Not at all," Reed lied.

"If I could just get rid of this rotten headache—"

Reed reached out, cupping her icy hands between his palms. "Why don't you come with us, miss? We can get you some help."

To Reed's surprise, her eyes narrowed. "What kind of help?"

"There's a hospital up the hill—"

"No!" She yanked back her hands. "No hospital."

Startled by her sudden vehemence, Reed stood, automatically reaching down to help the woman, who was struggling to her feet. "You've got a nasty bump on your head," he told her. "You really need to see a doctor."

"I'll be fine," she whispered as a rush of tears dampened her exquisite porcelain cheeks. "You were kind to stop. Thank you."

"Well..." Frustrated, Reed released her elbow, rubbed his jaw and jammed his hands into his pockets. "I can't just leave you here."

"Of course you can. I'm not your problem." She spun to face him, clearly panicked. "Please don't call the authorities. I'll confess to feeling slightly confused at the moment, but I can assure you that I'll be quite all right. It's just—" the color drained from her face "—this darn—" her eyes glazed "—headache."

Reed caught her as she swayed forward.

As the woman crumpled into his arms, Shawna ran from the car. "What's wrong with her, Dad?"

"I don't know," he mumbled, struggling to maintain his grasp on the slippery satin. After a moment, he lifted the fragile woman in his arms and turned to his oldest daughter. "Get in the back with your sister."

As Shawna hurried toward the truck, Rory poked her head out the window. "Are we taking the lady home, Daddy?"

Since Reed didn't know what else to do, he responded with a clipped nod.

Surprisingly the little girl seemed elated by the prospect. "Wow, that's so cool. Can we keep her, Daddy? She's real pretty."

"Don't be stupid," Shawna snapped, crawling into the narrow back seat beside her sibling. "She's a person, not a puppy."

Stung, Rory folded her pudgy arms, skewering the teenager with a withering stare. "I just meant we should let her, you know, stay for a while, just until she feels better. It would be almost like—" Biting off the final words, Rory turned away, her lip quivering.

"Mama's dead," Shawna whispered, her voice thick with pain and anger. "She's not ever coming back, no matter how hard you wish, or how much you pretend."

As Reed helped the weakened woman into the front passenger seat, his daughter's comment clenched his gut and tightened his chest with an all-too-familiar ache. Neither of his children had recovered from their mother's loss. Although Reed had spent the past four years trying to help them through it, the girls remained bitter, each blaming the other—and possibly themselves—for a loneliness and loss that they simply couldn't understand.

"That's enough, Shawna," he said quietly.

As usual, his parental reprimand was greeted by sullen silence, so Reed focused his attention on the task of gathering the satin train from the ground, then piling it on the floor of the truck until the shiny fabric had completely engulfed the woman's bare feet.

She blinked rapidly, as if trying to orient herself. "This is so embarrassing. I never faint. At least, I don't think I do." Shaking her head, she extended her hand in a helpless gesture that touched Reed deeply. "I feel so silly."

"Don't worry about it," Reed mumbled, fastening the seat belt around her slender, almost childlike frame. "You just relax. We'll have you warm and comfy in no time."

As he withdrew, she laid a hand on his forearm, forcing him to gaze into eyes that seemed to swallow him whole. "You're very kind," she whispered. "I won't forget that." After a moment, a mischievous smile tugged at her lips as she added, "Even if I have to tattoo a reminder on my wrist."

An amused giggle emanated from the rear seat from Rory, who was obviously tickled by the wry remark. Even Shawna managed a smile.

Reed straightened, scrutinizing the lovely woman who, despite having found herself in a situation that would terrify the hardiest soul, had chosen a facade of humor to disguise fear and alleviate tension. He appreciated that. He even admired it. But the fact remained that no matter how brave this young woman was, no matter how likable, her presence created a serious problem. Another problem was the last thing on earth that Reed needed.

Images crowded her mind, slipping like faded specters from some dark recess she couldn't quite grasp. She understood that she was dreaming, yet continued to watch the procession of surreal faces with an odd sense of detachment. There was a rotund, mustached man arguing with an angry blond woman. She floated by them, unable to hear their heated conversation, although disturbed by the knowledge that somehow she'd been the cause of it.

As the couple faded, another face appeared, a man's face, weathered and heavily lined, with smiling eyes that regarded her fondly. She wanted to speak with him but couldn't find her voice. She wanted to shake his hand but couldn't move her arms. Still, she was overcome by a sense of deep relief and gratitude.

He seemed to understand. Nodding slowly, the old man simply floated away. Just before he disappeared, a profound sadness settled into her heart, along with a feeling of tremendous loss. She didn't know the man, yet she instinctively understood that he was a good person with a pure heart and a loving soul. She'd felt protected with him. Now that he was gone, she suddenly felt vulnerable and alone.

Only she wasn't alone.

A chill slid down her spine. Her heart raced. She turned, scanning the darkness, sensing a hazy presence that was frightening beyond reason. She saw nothing but knew that he was just beyond view, watching her, stalking her.

Her throat tightened; blood pulsed cold in her veins. She knew he was there. She knew.

He was there.

"Miss . . . are you awake?"

The voice was deep and mellow, resonating with reassurance. But she was still in the dark place, lost in a portal link between slumber and sentience.

"Damn. I know better than to let a person with head trauma fall asleep. I just turned my back for a minute. . . ."

Something touched her shoulder, something warm. Firm. Frightening.

She bolted upright, gasping, her terrified gaze darting around the vaguely familiar room.

Although the area was sparsely furnished, cheery shafts of sunlight poured through a pair of lace-trimmed windows to illuminate the soiled satin wedding gown that was now draped over a wooden chair. Two men were leaning over the bed, one of whom she recognized as her rescuer, Reed Morgan, the man with the mellow voice.

"Easy," he murmured, still grasping her shoulder. "Everything's all right now. You're safe."

"Goodness." Pressing her palm over her pounding heart, she licked her lips and waited for the adrenaline surge to abate. As her fingertips rested on soft fleece, she was reminded of the sweatsuit's owner, a lovely teenager with long, honey blond hair. Glancing up, she saw the same girl standing in the doorway beside a younger, chubbier child whose short, boyish bob hugged her little head like a shiny brown skullcap.

She smiled at the youngsters, both of whom relaxed visibly. The youngest one—Rory, she thought—offered a cheery wave.

Reed Morgan released his grip on her shoulder. He stepped back, looking decidedly uncomfortable. "I didn't mean to startle you."

"It's all right," she told him. "I know you wanted me to stay awake, but the bed just felt too delicious to resist. I'm sorry if you were concerned."

"No problem." He shrugged, shuffling his feet like a nervous adolescent, a gesture she found oddly endearing. Despite a face that was sharply planed and rugged, his eyes revealed a whimsical quality with liquid fudge softness that reminded her of a gently curious puppy. An untidy thatch of blondish brown hair sprang from his scalp, perhaps the ruffled results of having just yanked off the cowboy hat he'd been wearing earlier.

She was still eyeing that hair when he bobbed his head, startling her. Following the abrupt gesture, she turned toward the second man, an older, gray-haired gentleman sporting a plaid shirt, wire-rimmed bifocals and a really bad comb-over hairdo.

"This is Donald Stivers," Reed was saying. "He's a neighbor, and a good friend. He's, ah, also a doctor. I was hoping you'd let him check you out, just to make sure everything's okay."

Dr. Stivers leaned forward, his eyes twinkling kindly. "So, Reed tells me you've got a bit of a bump on the head, Miss...?" His expectant pause hung in the air like an unpleasant scent.

She glanced at Reed, then at the solemn girls who were crowded in the open doorway. Obviously she had a name. The problem was that she simply couldn't remember what it was. That was absurd, of course, not to mention totally humiliating, so she fixed the doctor with a cheery smile and avoided the subject completely. "A small goose egg," she told him. "Nothing serious. I probably ran into a door or something."

The doctor's eyes filled with knowing compassion. "But you can't remember how it happened?"

She felt the subtle slump of her shoulders. "No, I can't remember."

Dr. Stivers exchanged a telling glance with Reed, then laid a gentle hand on her shoulder. "I wouldn't be too concerned if I were you. Temporary amnesia is more common than most people believe."

"Temporary?" Buoyed, she wiped away a trace of moisture seeping onto her lashes, threatening to reveal just how frightened she really was. "You mean this, ah, mental fuzziness will go away?"

"It usually does."

"Usually?"

"Almost always." The doctor gave her shoulder a reassuring pat, then straightened. "There are rare cases, of course..." He shrugged, allowing the words to evaporate before adding, "Very rare."

If that was meant to encourage her, it didn't. There was something horribly ominous about the feeling of having just popped out of a pumpkin patch without a discernible past only to face a future that was dubious, to say the least. Even worse than not knowing who she was or where she came from was the prickly sensation of not really wanting to know. On a visceral level, she was perfectly comfortable with her present anonymity, which was in itself pretty scary stuff.

She cleared her throat. "I, ah, was having an odd dream when you came in. There were people..." Angling a glance upward, she absently plucked the bedclothes. "Perhaps I'm remembering something."

The doctor smiled. "Perhaps."

"But you don't think so?"

"It's hard to tell," he said, patting her hand. "A memory-deprived mind frequently creates fantasies, so it may be difficult to weed out real memory from illusion. We'll just have to wait and see. However, I would like to examine you."

A protest was forming on her lips, but Dr. Stivers waved it away.

"A formality," he assured her. "Just to make certain there's no evidence of other injury."

The implication was unnerving. "I—" Her gaze darted from her handsome host to the blatantly curious girls standing in the doorway. "I'm afraid I won't be able to pay you. I seem to have misplaced my purse."

"Ah, well, that's the lot of a country doctor," he said, chuckling. "Despite the economic uncertainties, I must admit that my pantry has always been filled with local delicacies, and as you can see—" he patted an ample stomach "—I've never gone hungry."

Despite her nervousness, she smiled at the charming man who reminded her of a doting grandparent. "Actually, my headache is nearly gone and I honestly don't think I'm hurt, but if it would make you feel better..."

"It would indeed." The doctor nodded at Reed.

"Hmm?" Reed blinked, then his eyes widened. "Oh, sure," he mumbled, crossing the tiny room. "We'll just wait out here."

He hustled the girls into the hallway, shutting the door behind him.

"How awful," Shawna murmured, casting a compassionate glance toward the closed guest room door. "I can't imagine what it must be like not to know who you are."

Little Rory's nut brown eyes were as big as pie plates. "How come she can't even remember her family, Daddy?"

Plainly irritated, Shawna glared at the younger sibling she considered the bane of her life. "Maybe the poor woman has a nuisance sister she's trying to forget, one who karate-chopped a picture of their mother."

Reed rolled his eyes. "Shawna—"

"It was an *accident!*" Rory shouted, jamming her hands on her hips. "I didn't mean to break Mommy's picture. *Sensei* told us we had to practice *uchi*s." She leapt into a ready stance, raising a hand to demonstrate the various *uchi*s, which her previously enlightened father understood to be striking techniques. "It's not my fault the stupid table got in the way."

Before Reed could intervene, Shawna shot back. "You shouldn't have been doing your dumb *uchi*s in the house. Every time I turn around, you're smashing something. You've broken Mom's favorite vase and the only casserole dish we had, the cat is scared to death of you, and now there's a great big dent in the bathroom door—"

"*Keage!*" Rory chortled. Aiming a swift snap kick at thin air, she belted out an earsplitting screech, then went absolutely rigid, pressing her palms prayerfully together as she bent forward in a reverent bow. "*Sensei-ni-rei.*"

Unimpressed, Shawna tossed up her hands and turned a pleading gaze on her father. "You see what I have to put up with? She's impossible, Dad, absolutely impossible."

Rory beamed.

Reed rubbed his forehead. "Let's keep it down to a dull roar, shall we? It would be a shame to add nerve deafness to our houseguest's other problems." He turned to Rory. "Your sister is right. If you can't be more careful, you won't be allowed to practice karate in the house."

"But Daddy—" The protest died on her tongue. Folding her fat little arms, Rory glared at the hardwood floor. "Okay, but my *sensei* is gonna be real mad at you."

"I'll take my chances."

Clearly insulted by the perceived slight to her respected karate master, Rory flounced down the hall and disappeared into her bedroom, leaving Reed to shift his focus to his oldest daughter. "You'd make me the happiest dad in the world if you'd cut your sister some slack."

"When is she going to cut *me* some slack?" Shawna replied, obviously upset. "*I'm* the one who does all the work around here. All Rory ever does is throw clothes on the floor and break stuff, and leave me to clean up the mess. It's not fair, Dad, it's just not fair."

With that, the frustrated adolescent spun on her sneakered heel and stomped into the kitchen. A moment later, the clunking of cookware signaled that she was starting breakfast, and the slamming cupboards indicated that she was not a happy camper.

Reed sighed, realizing that there was more than a grain of truth in Shawna's complaint. Rory was a handful at home, and judging by teacher notes that arrived with disturbing regularity, her behavior at school wasn't much better.

It wasn't that Rory misbehaved deliberately or out of malice, but she was definitely a hyperactive child who tended to act without thought of consequence. Shawna had once characterized her younger sister's minuscule attention span as a facial tic of the brain, an unflattering depiction that was more accurate than Reed cared to admit.

Lord, how he wished the children's mother had been there. Whereas Reed was frequently at a loss to figure out the always intricate, if occasionally illogical, function of the youthful female mind, Bonnie had intuitively understood exactly what their girls needed. Shawna and Rory had adored her; so had Reed.

After Bonnie's death, the grief-stricken family had spiraled completely out of control. Rory had become an insufferable whirlwind of energy who'd do anything for attention, and poor Shawna, who'd abandoned her own childhood to become lady of the house, had developed what Reed feared would become a permanent chip on her shoulder.

As deeply and desperately as he loved both his children, he couldn't help but feel that their problems were his fault, that he'd failed them somehow. That broke his heart.

Wiping his face with his palms, Reed wandered through the cluttered living room to gaze out the front window. Beyond the once-lush lawn that had disintegrated into a dry thatch of weeds after Bonnie's death, he focused on a small fenced pasture populated by twenty head of purebred Angus. He automatically searched the grazing herd until he spotted Fagan, the little mahogany red bull that had cost the entire profit of last year's cherry crop.

Reed didn't doubt that Fagan was worth it. Although less than a year old, the baby bull had bloodlines to die for, and Reed was counting on its offspring to be the cornerstone of a future herd. Once the cattle venture became profitable, Reed hoped to give up seasonal work at the feed store and spend more time at home with his girls.

The squeak of an opening door caught his attention as Dr. Stivers emerged from the guest room.

"How is she, Don?"

"Physically, she's in remarkably good shape. A few minor bruises on her back and upper arms consistent with having fallen, but otherwise, she seems unhurt." The doctor entered the living room, carrying a battered leather bag that seemed left over from another era. "I'd prefer to run a few more tests, including an MRI just to assure myself that there's no intercranial seepage, but ..." Sighing, he set the bag on a lamp table and rubbed the back of his neck.

"She doesn't want any tests, right?"

Donald shrugged. "No, she doesn't, and she's quite adamant about that. Besides, she's not exhibiting any symptoms of brain contusion, and without proof of insurance or other financial means, I doubt the hospital would cooperate."

"Aren't there state programs available? I mean, this *is* America. We're not supposed to let people die in the street just because they're poor."

The doctor raised a fuzzy gray brow. "She was wearing a designer wedding gown with a Beverly Hills label."

Puffing his cheeks, Reed blew out a breath. "Yeah, I know. Weird, isn't it?"

"A unique situation," Donald agreed, scooping up his bag and pulling his car keys out of his pocket. "Unfortunately, there seem to be more questions than answers at this point." As he spoke, he walked out onto the front porch, pausing until Reed had joined him. "What do you plan to do with her?"

"I haven't thought about it." Reed absently tugged his earlobe as he glanced back through the open front door. "I kind of promised not to call the authorities so I suppose she can stay here for a day or so. Maybe by tomorrow, she'll have figured out who she is and where she's supposed to be."

"Maybe."

"But you don't think so."

Heaving a sigh, Donald absently smoothed the few thin strands of graying hair that had been stretched sideways to conceal his balding scalp. "No one can tell, Reed. As I told the young lady, she might remember everything all at once, or the memories might slip back slowly in the form of odd little snippets, or her mind might even create false memories until the real ones reappear to take over. One never knows."

That was not what Reed wanted to hear. "Well, I'll have to worry about it tomorrow. Right now, I have more pressing issues to resolve."

Donald, who was ambling down the porch steps, angled a knowing glance over his shoulder. "Lost another housekeeper, did you?" When Reed didn't answer, the old man shook his head and continued toward the serviceable old sedan parked in front of the house. "Don't envy you, Reed. It's hard enough for a man to support his family nowadays, but trying to be both a mama and a papa, well, that's tough."

"I'll manage." The statement was issued firmly, with a conviction Reed didn't feel. Still, he dared not speak his doubts aloud, fearing that to do so would give them more credence.

But all the stoic silence in the world couldn't change facts, and the facts were that not one of the bushel of housekeepers he'd hired over the years had been able to tolerate Shawna's relentless criticism or Rory's unmanageable behavior. Even worse, Grass Valley was a small town, a place where everyone knew everyone else's problem. Finding a replacement wouldn't be easy.

Still lost in thought, Reed absently escorted Donald to his car and was startled when the old man suddenly turned. "You know, Reed, Shawna's thirteen now, old enough to watch her little sister for a few hours until you get home from work."

"Age has nothing to do with it," he replied sadly. "They'd kill each other. Besides, they're both on Christmas vacation next week. There's no way on earth I could leave them alone all day."

Puffing his cheeks, the doctor blew out a breath. "You might consider taking a short vacation. Lord knows, you could use some time off, hard as you've been working lately."

"Yeah, well, much as I'd like to, my checkbook has become an incorrigible nag."

"Ah, the reality of financial need," Donald muttered. "Do you have any leads on a new housekeeper?"

"No, Patty Hargrove has offered to watch the girls at her place if I'm ever in a real bind. I'll give her a call this afternoon."

Donald's head snapped around. "Pastor Hargrove's wife?" When Reed nodded, the doctor shook his head. "Guess you haven't heard."

"Heard what?"

"The pastor was in an accident last night."

Reed stiffened. "A bad one?"

"Bad enough. Looks like he suffered a heart attack while driving up the interstate and swerved into a guardrail. He's alive, but barely. I understand that Patty refuses to leave his bedside."

"Good Lord," Reed mumbled. "The poor woman must be sick with worry. Their daughter lives up in Nevada City. I'll give her a call, and see if there's anything I can do to help."

"I'm sure the family would appreciate that." After a hearty slap on Reed's shoulder, Donald slid into the worn driver's seat. "As for your other little problem—" he nodded toward the house "—I'll stop by tomorrow and see how she's doing."

"Thanks." Stepping away from the car, Reed waited until the doctor had driven onto the main road before sucking a deep breath and trudging back into the house.

He'd barely reached the front door when he was greeted by the delightful strains of childish giggles and feminine laughter. Overwhelmed by sudden nostalgia, he realized that it had been way too long since the house had been warmed by such happy sounds.

As a renewed round of giggles floated from the guest room, Reed moved cautiously to the hallway. He peeked inside, stunned by the sight of his daughters perched cross-legged on the bed, flanking their lovely houseguest. All three were hunched over, perusing a what-to-name-baby book.

"Here's a good one," Shawna said, snickering madly.

"Hildegarde?" The woman's mouth puckered into a comical grimace. "I don't think so."

Rory poked a pudgy finger on the page. "How about Hortense? That sounds kinda neat."

"Yikes, it sounds like something you shovel off the stable floor," Shawna replied, emphasizing her distaste with a disgusted shiver.

The young woman chuckled. "Let's just forget the *H*s and *I*s and move on to the *J*s."

"But Isabel's a pretty name," Rory insisted. "I think we should put it in the hat."

Shawna and the woman exchanged a glance, then both nodded in agreement, whereupon the teenager scrawled something on the nightstand scratch pad. She'd just dropped the folded note into Reed's work hat, which was sitting upside down in the middle of the bed, when she spotted him lurking by the open door. "Hi, Dad. We're picking a name for, uh..." She slid a wary glance at the amused woman beside her.

"It's okay," the young woman assured her. "You may refer to me as 'she who dropped from the sky,' but only until we draw a name, okay? After that, I expect to be addressed with all due respect as '*so-and-so* who dropped from the sky.'"

Rory hugged herself, snorting with tickled laughter, and to Reed's astonishment, Shawna reached across the woman's lap to give her sister an affectionate pat. "Heads up, squirt. If you don't do your part, we'll be here all day. Now, let's get on with the *J*s."

Clamoring back into a cross-legged position, Rory grabbed the book and began reciting names. Since reading was definitely not the child's strong suit, she phonetically butchered the more complicated monikers, which set off repeated rounds of good-natured hoots and teasing from the remainder of the tiny group.

Despite their antics, however, the cheery gaggle of females continued to toss favorite names into the hat while Reed leaned against the doorjamb, stunned. He couldn't remember the last time his daughters had worked together as a team, let alone given the appearance of actually enjoying each other's company.

It had been years since his children had seemed so happy and so...well, normal. Yet in a matter of minutes, their houseguest had brought the feuding youngsters together in the spirit of complete cooperation and, even more startling, apparent affection. Since there seemed no rational explanation for such a stunning turn of events, Reed decided that this beautiful, raven-haired creature must have been blessed with a secret power that neutralized hostility and created love out of resentment.

He wondered if the United Nations knew about this.

"Okay, this is it," Shawna suddenly announced, shoving the name book aside and reaching for the hat. "The big moment."

"Yea!" Rory chirped, clapping her hands. "The biggest moment in the whole entire world!"

Fanning her face, their lovely houseguest pretended to be overcome by anxiety. "Hurry," she whispered with a theatrical gasp. "The suspense is killing me."

Shawna held the hat up over her head. "Dad, do you want to do the honors?"

"Me?" He hooked a thumb inward, pointing toward his chest, then waved the suggestion away. "No, no, you guys have done all the work. One of you should do it."

"We want you to," Rory whined, raising her clasped hands. "Please?"

The woman, who'd laid a dramatic hand across her brow, opened one eye. "If someone doesn't draw a name in the next five seconds, my heart will give out and I'll end up with a blank tombstone." She fixed Reed with a narrowed stare. "Do you really want that on your conscience?"

Heaving a weary sigh, Reed crossed the room and plunged his hand into the hat.

"Moosh 'em up real good," Rory said.

"I'm mooshing," Reed replied, wiggling his fingers through the folded papers before selecting one.

He offered the slip to Shawna, who pulled her hands away. "You read it, Dad. I'm too nervous."

"Me, too," said Rory.

"I hope it's not 'Tina,'" the woman muttered, raising two sets of crossed fingers. "It sounds so... I don't know, little girlish, I guess."

Shawna whipped around, clearly horrified. "If you didn't like that name, how come you let us put it in the hat?"

She shrugged. "I don't know. It seemed like the thing to do at the time."

"We can pull that one out, if you want."

"Nope. I'll take my chances." With a stoic expression, she lifted her chin and nodded at Reed. "Okay, partner. What's the verdict?"

Getting into the spirit of the occasion, Reed made a production of unfolding the tiny slip, then puckered his brows as he silently read the name.

Three tense forms leaned forward.

Reed glanced up. "Ready?"

"Yes!" came their simultaneous reply.

Smiling, he emulated a British knighting ceremony by touching first the woman's right shoulder, then her left. "With the power vested in me by my screwy but lovable children, I now christen thee..." Pausing for effect, Reed held up the tiny scrap as reverently as if it were one of the Dead Sea Scrolls. He maintained the tension until all three females seemed ready to explode, then he tucked the paper into his pocket and reached out to shake the woman's hand. "Welcome to Morgan Ranch, Kate."

She lit up with a brilliant smile that did peculiar things to the inside of his chest. "Kate! I like that."

"So do I," Reed murmured, reluctantly releasing her soft palm. "It suits you."

In the flurry of hugs and giggles between Kate and the excited girls, Reed slipped out of the room, needing a moment to reflect. Something had happened in the past few minutes, something that filled him with a sense of wonder. But along with that came a wariness, a subtle anxiety that slipped like a silent warning in his mind—a warning that the very fabric of their lives had been inexplicably altered. He didn't know how, he didn't know why. He knew only that from this moment on, he and his children would never be the quite the same.

Chapter Two

"Daddy! Shawna won't let me put on the kitty-cat ornament. She knows it's my favorite, and she took it just to be mean."

The childish whine filtered up from darkness, rousing Kate from a dreamless sleep. Stretching, she sat up in bed, focusing blurry eyes on the wedge of light peeking beneath the closed door. Beyond that door was a collage of sound, Christmas music punctuated by muffled voices belonging to the generous family that had taken a total stranger into their home.

With a sleepy yawn, Kate glanced at the clock radio's glowing display and was stunned to realize that despite regular wake-up checks by various family members, she'd nonetheless managed to sleep the entire day away. It was actually dark outside.

She leapt out of bed and instantly smacked into the corner of the nightstand. Stifling a startled howl, she hopped around the room holding her stubbed foot and wondering if clumsiness was a side effect of amnesia or if she'd simply been born a klutz.

Dropping back on the bed, she cursed under her breath and felt around for the lamp that was on the nightstand just behind the clock radio. A moment later, a pool of soft light allowed her to inspect her bruised toe. It hurt like the devil but still wiggled quite nicely, so she thankfully decided that no bones were broken. That was a major relief. A fracture would certainly slow her down if she needed to make a quick getaway.

Kate's hand froze against her ankle. *A quick getaway?* What an odd thought. She would have spent some effort considering where it could have come from except for the distraction of an agitated voice beyond the closed bedroom door.

"Give that back! I had it first!"

Was that Shawna's voice?

"Losers weepers," Rory responded angrily

"You are such a brat."

"Takes one to know one—"

The diatribe was interrupted by a firm male voice. "That's enough from both of you," Reed said in a tone that from Kate's perspective was admirably even. "If you can't work as a team, we'll put the decorations away and wait until you can treat each other with a modicum of respect."

After a silent moment, Rory spoke again. "What's a modicum?"

"It means a little bit." Shawna's matter-of-fact reply was delivered without rancor, which Kate took as a positive sign that the teenager had taken her father's warning seriously.

Curious, Kate limped over to open the door and found herself at the end of a hallway that was presumably the bedroom wing of the one-story house. Across the hall, an open door allowed a glimpse into a large room where moonlight from an undraped window revealed the silhouette of a king-size bed. The master bedroom, perhaps.

But the voices were coming from her left, emanating from a cheerfully lit opening across from the two open doorways that she assumed led into the girls' darkened bedrooms.

Following the sound, Kate emerged into a roomy living area cluttered with cardboard boxes, tangled tree lights and wads of discarded tissue paper. The Christmas tree was positioned on the far side of the room, in front of a large picture window. Reed was standing on a step stool, holding a tiny twinkle bulb in one hand, and using the other to fiddle with a wire that was bound around one of the fresh green limbs. Little Rory was kneeling on the floor rooting through one of the cardboard boxes while her big sister, who was shifting a sparkling glass orb from one hand to the other, studied the heavily ladened limbs as if searching for a vacant spot.

An old-fashioned wood stove crackled in the corner, while soft Christmas music floated from a radio situated atop a plain pine bookcase on which an ancient television—the remoteless kind with fat tuning knobs—had also been placed. Throughout the room, a delicious pine scent filled the air, mingled with the delicate aroma of spicy potpourri and holiday candles and . . . fried chicken?

She sniffed appreciatively, reminded by her rumbling stomach that it had been sorely neglected. She absently pressed a palm to her sunken midsection just as Shawna glanced up.

"Hi!" A welcoming smile lit the teenager's pretty face. "Are you feeling better?"

"Yes, thank you." Encouraged, Kate moved farther into the room, pausing beside a plaid sofa that, along with the rest of the furnishings, had seen better days.

Rory rushed over to show off the sequined Santa Claus ornament nested in her hands. "Look at this one, Kate! Isn't it neat?" When Kate allowed that the ornament was quite lovely, the child immediately offered it to her. "You wanna put it on the tree? It's okay, really."

"You're doing such a good job," Kate murmured, indulging an overwhelming urge to stroke the girl's shiny brown hair. "I'd much rather watch you."

Grinning broadly, Rory spun around, emitted a startling shriek that sounded something like "E-e-e-yah!" then leapt up and snap-kicked a cardboard carton that was blocking her way to the Christmas tree. Reed, who was poking the tiny bulb into an empty wire socket, ignored the startling display, although Shawna issued a pained sigh and rolled her eyes.

A moment later, the sequined Santa dangled from an already crowded branch and Rory beamed with pride. Reed stepped down from the stool. "Are you hungry, Kate? There's plenty of chicken left."

Kate's mouth watered at the thought of food. "That sounds wonderful . . . if it's not too much trouble, that is."

"Oh, it's no trouble," Rory replied, her eyes wide and solemn. "We already fixed your dinner and put it in the oven so it would stay nice and hot. And we've got chocolate chip cookies for dessert!"

"Mmm, I can hardly wait."

"The kitchen's over here," Shawna said, nodding toward a doorway off the L-shaped dining room. "I'll show you."

As the older girl dropped the sparkly ball into the dented cardboard box, Rory issued an immediate protest. "No, I wanna show her!"

Shawna's eyes narrowed, but before she could respond, Kate spoke up. "Why don't you both show me? I'd love the company, and the truth is, I hate to eat alone."

The sisters glanced at each other, exchanging a "sure, why not?" shrug as their father's tension softened visibly. Kate watched, fascinated, as Reed Morgan regarded his daughters with affection, along with apparent relief that the conflict had been resolved without bloodshed.

The poor man looked tired, Kate thought, at least in comparison to the way she remembered him this morning when he'd bundled her into the pickup truck. He'd seemed much more energetic then, despite a few tense wrinkles creasing his tawny brow. Now, however, purplish circles had appeared under eyes that were dulled by exhaustion.

She was studying him openly when he suddenly met her gaze, and a strange thing happened. His dark eyes sparkled to life with a soft amber glow that sent a peculiar tingle skittering down her spine.

He smiled. She smiled back. Deep inside her, something warm and wonderful was happening.

"Are you still hungry?" Shawna asked, when Kate finally pushed her plate away. "There's lots more chicken in the fridge."

"Oh, no, thank you." Washing the last bite down with a long drink of deliciously cold milk, Kate set the glass aside and patted her tummy. "I'm full to the gills, but it was absolutely wonderful."

"Fried chicken is Dad's specialty," Shawna replied, carrying the empty plate to the sink.

Kate leaned forward, startled. "Your father cooked this?"

"Sure." Flipping on the faucet, Shawna glanced over her shoulder. "Dad's a great cook. He makes a pot roast to die for."

Rory, who was sitting across the table from Kate, held a hand beside her mouth and issued a stage whisper that could be heard in the next county. "And Shawna makes one that'll *really* kill you."

To her credit, the teenager simply shook her head without comment and finished washing the plate.

"Do you know how to cook?" Rory asked suddenly.

"Me? Well, ah—" Kate covered a cough. "Doesn't everyone?"

Rory slid her sister a sour look. "No."

Pushed too far, Shawna threw down the dishrag and spun around. "Now look, toad, I've had just about enough—oh, hi, Dad."

Kate spun in her chair as Reed sauntered into the kitchen, his weary gaze sweeping from one daughter to the other.

"The lights work," he announced, pulling out a chair and straddling it backward. "Who wants to do the honors?"

Rory leapt up. "I do!"

"The honors?" Kate asked.

"Flipping the switch to light up the tree." Reed rubbed the back of his neck, angling a questioning glance at his oldest girl. "Do you want to flip a coin?"

Shawna shrugged. "No, Rory can do it."

"Yea!" The child gleefully clapped her hands, and would have dashed into the living room had her father not stopped her with a look.

"In a few minutes," he said. "We'll do it as a family."

As a family.

The words rolled through Kate's mind, raising a lump in her throat. She didn't know why the quiet statement affected her so, although in the truck this morning, one of the girls mentioned their mother's death and Kate had been struck by a sense of loss so acute that it had brought tears to her eyes.

Rory's voice broke into her thoughts. "What's wrong, Kate? Are you sick or something?"

"Hmm?" Blinking, she realized that her eyes were moist. "No, I'm fine, really."

Apparently her assurance wasn't particularly convincing, because the child screwed up her little face, regarding her with great concern. "Are you worried about your own kids?"

"My own—? Oh, no, heavens, no." She shook her head with more force than necessary, oddly distressed by the question. "I don't have any children."

"How do you know?" Rory asked innocently. "I mean, you can't remember your name or anything, so maybe you can't remember your kids, either."

"People don't forget having children. It's . . . it's just not possible." Feeling flushed, Kate grabbed her milk glass and drained it, acutely aware that Reed was watching closely.

"Quit bugging her," Shawna said sharply. "Kate can't have any kids yet. She only just got married."

"Married?" Setting the glass down with a thud, Kate cast a frantic glance at her left hand and issued a relieved sigh as she held up her bare finger. "No ring. No marriage."

Shawna sat at the table, frowning. "So what about the wedding dress?"

"I don't know," Kate replied honestly.

"Maybe you were just trying it on because you're a world-famous model," Rory suggested. "You're real tall, and I think you're pretty enough."

Kate smiled.

"Or," Shawna added dramatically, "Maybe you were standing at the altar when a chandelier dropped from the chapel ceiling—"

"And boinked you on the head!" Rory chirped, getting into the speculation spirit.

The possibility that she could actually have been preparing to marry someone made Kate shudder, as did Shawna's next suggestion.

"Maybe you were whisked from the altar by a scorned lover," she said dreamily. "You know, like in *The Graduate*. That's so-o romantic."

Kate slumped forward with a grimace. "Let's go back to the world-famous-model scenario."

Rory was all for that. "Like, you were having your picture taken for the cover of *Vogue* or something, and then you were kidnapped by terrorists—"

Shawna issued an incredulous snort. "Oh, pul-eese."

Undaunted, Rory continued to spin her wild tale with fevered enthusiasm. "And they were gonna hold you for a billion dollars' ransom, only you escaped by jumping out of the helicopter—"

"Helicopter?" Flipping her blond hair behind her shoulders, the teenager leaned across the table, laughing. "That's ridiculous. If she'd jumped out of a helicopter, she'd have been squished flat."

Crossing her arms, Rory fixed her sister with a squinty stare. "Not if that big ol' satin skirt flooped out like a parachute."

"'Flooped?'" The comical image made Kate chuckle, despite Shawna's coldly unamused expression.

Beside her, Reed thoughtfully stroked his chin. "I hate to admit it, but there's a certain cartoonish logic to her theory. Very imaginative."

Rory flashed a proud grin.

"I give up." Pushing away from the table, Shawna marched across the room and began pulling things out of the refrigerator. "No wonder she's so incorrigible. You're always taking up for her."

Reed blinked. "I'm not taking up for anyone, honey. I was just giving your sister credit for creativity."

"Well, I wish she'd get creative with the laundry once in a while, or use that sterling imagination to keep her room from becoming a toxic dump." Sullen and obviously hurt, Shawna pulled a loaf of bread out of the pantry and flopped it onto the counter. "Do you want some leftover chicken in your lunch, Dad?"

The question, which seemed harmless enough to Kate, caused Reed to stiffen visibly. "You don't have to do that, Shawna."

She tossed a puzzled glance over her shoulder. "But I always pack your lunch."

"I know, sweetie, and I always appreciate it." He looked away. "But I won't be going to work tomorrow."

"How come?" Rory asked, although she appeared thrilled by the prospect of having her daddy stay home.

If Rory was pleased, however, Shawna seemed unduly upset by the news. She threw the bread back in the drawer as she issued a sharp answer to her sister's question. "Because Mrs. Collier quit," she snapped. "Dad doesn't trust us enough to leave us alone."

Rubbing his eyes, Reed heaved a weary sigh. "Trust has nothing to do with it, honey."

"Then give me a chance, Dad." The girl spun around, pleading. "Mrs. Collier didn't do hardly anything, except sit on her fat butt eating chocolates and watching soap operas."

"Yeah," Rory added helpfully. "And Shawna can do that."

Reed raised his hands, palms out, as if shielding himself against further argument. "We've already discussed this. I'm not comfortable leaving you two unless there's an adult in the house." As soon as the words left his mouth, he must have regretted them, because all eyes turned toward Kate.

It was Shawna who pointed out the obvious. "Well, Kate's an adult."

A red flush spread along Reed's jawline. Kate was painfully aware that he couldn't look at her.

She cleared her throat. "If I were in your father's shoes, I'd be pretty leery about leaving my children in the care of a complete stranger."

"You're not a stranger," Rory said. "At least, not anymore."

Smiling, Kate patted the girl's chubby hand. "Think about it, sweetie. How can your daddy know what kind of person I am if I don't even know myself? Besides, I haven't memory of caring for children. I wouldn't know what to do if you or your sister got hurt or sick."

"It's easy," Rory said emphatically. "All you hafta do is pick up the phone and dial 9-1-1 . . . right, Daddy?"

Reed managed a thin smile. "There's more to it than that, squirt."

As Rory's face twisted in preparation for what promised to be an unpleasantly protracted argument, Kate took pity on her clearly distressed dad. "Listen to me," she told the unhappy youngster. "There's nothing in the world I'd rather do than take care of you and your sister. Even though we've just met, I feel as if I've known you all my life." Which was certainly true enough, since the only life she remembered had begun this morning. "The point is that I can't stay."

Rory went rigid. "Why not?"

"This is your home, Rory, yours and Shawna's and your father's. I don't belong here."

Tears squirted into the eight-year-old's dark eyes. "Where *do* you belong?"

"At the moment, I'm not sure." A frisson of pure panic skittered down Kate's spine. She swallowed hard, trying to ignore it.

"But where would you go?" Shawna blurted, clearly upset. "You don't have any money, or even anything to wear. You can't just live on the streets!"

"Oh. Well, ah, I guess I'll have to get a job, won't I?" Of course, she had no idea what skills she had, if any. And who on earth would hire a woman with no name, no employment history, and no social security number? Kate tried to cover her fear with a smile, straining to stretch cheeks as stiff as sun-dried leather. "See? I'll be just fine."

Reed cleared his throat. "You realize, of course, that your family is probably looking for you."

She doubted that, although wasn't sure why. Pursing her lips, she chose to remain silent in the hope that Reed wouldn't carry the comment further.

The hope was a vain one. Leaning forward, Reed fixed her with a piercing stare. "The sheriff's department could research missing person reports—"

"No!" She licked her lips, surprised by her own vehemence even as she secretly wondered why she felt no urgency to locate her own people—assuming she had any. "I mean, the doctor said I could regain my memory at any time. I'd really prefer to wait a few days and see what happens."

A thick silence shrouded the room. Rory, bless her, finally broke it. "So why can't you wait here?"

Smiling, Kate patted the child's hand. "Because I can't continue to impose on your family."

"But you're not 'posing," Rory insisted, clutching Kate's icy fingers. "Tell her, Daddy, tell her she's not 'posing."

Reed, who'd been listening intently, now rested his crossed arms on the back of the chair he was straddling. "You're welcome to stay as long as you want, Kate."

"You're very kind," she murmured, lowering her gaze. There was something about Reed Morgan that clouded her reason. Every time she looked deeply into those all-consuming, cognac-colored eyes, her heart fluttered like a wounded butterfly and the breath backed up in her throat. "But it's not right to take advantage of your generosity when there's no way I can ever repay it."

Shawna brightened. "If it makes you feel better, you can help with the chores."

"Yeah," Rory agreed, although with less enthusiasm than her older sister. "There's always lots of stuff to do, like feeding the cows and cleaning out the stable."

"Stable?" Kate's head snapped up. "You have horses?"

"Only two. We used to have more, only Daddy had to sell 'em after Mommy—" Skimming a chagrined glance at her father, Rory swallowed hard, then stared down at the polished pine tabletop. "After Mommy went away."

Kate felt rather than saw Reed shift uncomfortably.

"So you like horses?" he asked.

"Yes," Kate murmured, although she didn't have a conscious clue as to what experience she might have had with the magnificent beasts. "I love horses."

Reed studied her for a moment before swinging his leg over the chair seat. He stood, flexing his shoulders as if they ached. "Well then, it's settled."

Startled, Kate, too, pushed away from the table and stood. "What's settled?"

"You need work, and we've got plenty of that around here. You'll be able to earn your keep while you're—" He paused, a cautious smile working its way to his eyes. "While you're waiting to see what happens."

Since an immovable lump was inexplicably wedged against her larynx, Kate agreed with a jerky nod, to which the girls replied with matching whoops of delight. In less than a heartbeat, Kate was flanked by the happy youngsters, who were both talking at once as they dragged Kate into the living room to view the tree-lighting ceremony.

Reed hung back, waiting for his daughters to escort their mysterious houseguest into the other room. As soon as they'd disappeared from view, he used a paper napkin to move Kate's empty milk glass from the table to a brown lunch bag, which he tucked into the pocket of a jacket hanging on a peg by the back door.

Then he took a pained breath, plastered on a fake smile and went to join the cheery group of tree-lighters.

Passing through the open door of what turned out to be a relatively small and drafty stable, Kate emerged into a dirt training ring abutting a fenced green pasture. An older chestnut mare was grazing in that pasture, along with an Appaloosa gelding that appeared to be in his prime. Reed, who was closing the pasture gate, glanced over his shoulder as if psychically alerted to Kate's presence.

As he crossed the training ring, she snapped a smart salute. "Reporting for duty, sir. Lead me to a shovel, then stand out of the way."

Smiling, Reed used the tip of an index finger to tilt back his hat. His gaze slid from her oversize Bon Jovi T-shirt to the stone-washed jeans that were a size too big. "I see Shawna's been digging through the back of her closet again."

"Beggars can't be choosers. I'm just thankful we're so close to the same size." Kate glanced down at the furry pink slippers she wore. "Unfortunately, my feet are bigger than hers. This is the only footwear I could pry on."

"Stylish but understated," Reed said with admirable solemnity. "Who knows, you might start a new fad."

"Stranger things have happened." Shading her eyes, Kate gazed out at the pasture. "Those are gorgeous animals. The mare has an especially nice topline, with good withers and perfectly sloped shoulders. The Appy is nice, too. His hocks are a little weak, but a well-muscled gaskin keeps him from winging in too much. I'd keep an eye on him, though. When he gets older, his gait may slacken, and lameness is always a concern."

"Do tell," Reed responded dryly.

Embarrassed, Kate lowered her hand, wiping her palm on her thighs. "Sorry. I didn't mean to sound like such a condescending know-it-all. In fact, I don't have a clue as to where that pompous drivel came from."

"My first guess would be that it came out of an extremely thorough knowledge of equine anatomy. Everything you said is absolutely correct."

She shrugged. "Maybe I was a veterinarian in my other life."

"Hmm, there's a thought. What are the major symptoms of folliculitis?"

"Folly-que-what?"

Reed's smile broadened into a genuine grin. "So much for the vet theory."

"Pity," she said with an exaggerated sigh. "It's a noble profession, and the money's great."

"Not around here. As often as not, country vets are paid with tack, feed and boarding."

Kate slid him an amused look. "For themselves or their animals?"

"Whichever," Reed replied with a laugh. "Ranchers are by nature a cash-shy lot, so most consider the barter system as currency of choice."

"Hmm, I wonder what a strong back and an empty mind will buy me?"

"Besides room and board, and unlimited access to the very latest in used fashions?" Reed's gaze slid down to the furry slippers. "I think we're going to have to do something about those. Around here, sturdy shoes are a must."

Feeling guilty about his continued concern, Kate shifted uncomfortably. "These are fine," she murmured, absently raking her fingers through her loose hair. "Please don't worry about me." When he didn't respond, she glanced up and saw him eyeing her strangely. His gaze sent a peculiar ripple down her spine. She touched her face. "Do I still have mud on my nose or something?"

He shook his head with a smile she thought was a bit stiff. "You look different today."

"I, ah, washed my hair in the shower. It dried a little straight." She caught herself fiddling with a shoulder-length strand and forced her hand back to her side. "I probably should have tried to curl it, or something."

"It looks lovely." He cocked his head, continuing to stare at her until she was so nervous she had to suppress an urge to sprint. "It's your makeup," he said suddenly.

"But I'm not wearing any."

"I know. That's why you look so different, fresher and more natural." A frown creased his brow. "And about five years younger than I would have guessed."

"Younger?" She smiled. "Well, I suppose that could be a plus someday. Actually, I'm twenty-four."

Seeming startled by that bit of news, his frown deepened. "When is your birthday?"

"It's . . . ah, wait a minute. I've almost got it." Covering her eyes, she concentrated so hard that her head began to ache. "Lost it." She heaved a frustrated sigh. "I think it's sometime in the spring, but I'm not sure."

Suspicion sharpened his gaze. "But you *are* certain about your age?"

"Yes. I mean, I think I am." She rubbed her upper arms, fighting another surge of panic. "I don't know. When we started talking about age, the number just popped into my head as if it were the most natural thing in the world, but as soon as I tried to focus on it, everything got all fuzzy again. I wonder what Dr. Stivers would say about that."

"Looks like you'll have the chance to ask him," Reed said, nodding toward the dented coupe smoking up the driveway.

Before Reed finished speaking, Kate spun around and dashed through the stable to greet the doctor as he emerged. "My," he said jovially. "You're looking considerably more chipper than the last time I saw you. How do you feel?"

"Fine." Tossing a frantic look over her shoulder, she saw that Reed had emerged from the stable and was striding quickly toward them. "Can I talk to you? In private, that is."

He adjusted his eyeglasses. "Certainly."

It was all he had a chance to say before Reed joined them. "Morning, Don."

The two men shook hands, then Reed rocked back on his heels. "Got a minute?"

"Well, sure." Frowning, the doctor slipped a sideways glance at Kate, who took a nervous step back.

"I'll, ah, just wait for you inside," she said, pausing for the doctor's confirming nod before she trudged back to the house.

Once inside, she parted the sheer curtains to watch Reed and Dr. Stivers, both of whom were engaged in quiet conversation. When the doctor glanced toward the house with a surprised expression, Kate's heart sank. Her hunch about the subject of their furtive discussion seemed to be confirmed when Reed hurried to his pickup truck and drove away.

A moment later, Dr. Stivers entered the house with a perplexed smile. "So, Reed tells me that your memory is improving."

"Hmm? Oh, I remembered my age, or at least, what I think is my age. Twenty-four."

"That's a good start," he said kindly. "The rest will come soon enough."

Distracted by the driveway dust settling in the wake of the departing pickup, Kate blurted, "Where did Reed go?"

The doctor looked up, startled. "I'm not sure. He said he had an errand."

Kate released the sheer curtain, turning away from the window. "He asked you to keep an eye on me, didn't he?"

"Well, ah..." Dr. Stivers cleared his throat.

"And he probably even asked you not to leave until he got back, right?" Without waiting for a reply, Kate sighed. "The poor man thinks I'm some kind of ax murderer. The worst part is that he might even be right."

Chuckling, Dr. Stivers shook his head. "Highly unlikely, my dear, although that does sound like a theory that Rory might have come up with. An ingenious child, Rory. Bit of a challenge, but quite bright." He glanced around. "By the way, where are the girls?"

"Rory's practicing karate behind the hay barn, and Shawna's in her room, working on a book report." Clasping her hands, Kate squared her shoulders and sucked in a fortifying breath. "Can you tell if I'm a mother?"

Stivers looked up so quickly that his glasses slipped down his nose. He pushed them back into place, blinking madly. "Excuse me?"

Closing her eyes, Kate blew out a breath. "I know this sounds crazy, but I've been frantic wondering if I could possibly have children somewhere who are feeling frightened and abandoned. I keep telling myself it's not possible, that a mother simply can't forget about her children, but..."

The words drifted away like so much steam. How could she explain the unexplainable? It all seemed so hopeless.

Dr. Stivers laid a comforting hand on her shoulder. "You're in a difficult position," he said kindly. "I can only imagine the frustration you're suffering, and the fear. Unfortunately, I can't tell you if you're an adoptive parent or a stepmother. I can, however, examine you to determine whether or not you've physically given birth. Is that what you want?"

Kate shivered, terrified by what she might learn. If she did have children of her own, what might they be going through right now? Were they feeling isolated and abandoned, as were the motherless Morgan children? The thought was chilling. What kind of mother could forget about her own children? What kind of person was she, anyway? And why did she have this onerous sense of dread at the thought of returning to something she couldn't even remember?

The answers might be even more terrifying than the questions. Still, Kate had no choice but to seek those answers and pray that the consequences wouldn't be as dire as she feared.

A lanky young deputy looked up as Reed leaned across the sheriff's department counter. "Hey, Reed. I was just about to give you a call."

"What did you find out?"

"Not much. We've got a fourteen-year-old runaway out of Manteca, and a middle-aged grandmother with a gambling problem who disappeared on her way to the beauty parlor.'' Dale Matthews, whom Reed had known since high school, dragged a computerized list from a nearby desk. "I didn't find anyone in here matching the description you gave me over the phone, but you're welcome to look through it again, if you want."

"I've got a better idea." Reed opened the paper bag he'd set on the counter.

Dale peered inside. "Let me guess. You want us to run this for fingerprints, right?"

"I, ah, thought you could, you know, check with the FBI or something."

Reclosing the bag, the deputy gave Reed a tolerant smile. "You've been watching too many cop shows," he drawled. "Budget constraints being what they are, not every little dog-and-pony law enforcement office has access to national computers."

An invisible vise tightened around Reed's chest. "You mean you can't do anything?"

"I didn't say that." Retrieving the paper bag, he slipped a furtive glance over his shoulder. "Lucky for you I just happen to have a brother-in-law with a bonafide S.F.P.D. gold shield."

Reed didn't understand the connection and said so.

"Big cities like San Francisco have hookups with national," the deputy explained. "I'll FedEx this over, and we'll see what pops up."

"Thanks, Dale. I appreciate it."

"No problem. Just let me know when you've got a side of beef to spare."

"A side of beef?" Reed let out a low whistle. "That's highway robbery. I'd be willing to go a couple of steaks."

"Toss in a roast, and you've got a deal."

After they shook on it, Reed glanced at his watch and hurried to his truck, wanting to get back to the ranch before Donald left. The entire incident left a bad taste in his mouth. On the one hand, he was relieved that the search for Kate's identity had been put into motion. On the other, he felt guilty as hell for having deceived her. He tried to soothe himself with the reminder that by the time he'd promised not to report her to the authorities, he'd already spoken to Dale Matthews. Pilfering her fingerprints, however, could only be defined as downright sneaky.

Still, he'd had little choice. His girls were already enamored of Kate. If there was a grief-stricken family searching for her, it was best to learn that quickly, before the children became more attached to her than they already were.

But there was another, more sinister possibility. Reed was ready to deal with that, too.

Chapter Three

"Are you sure?" Tying the sash of her borrowed robe, Kate fought a queasy surge, along with the unpleasant, light-headed sensation symptomatic of sudden shock.

"I'm quite sure," Dr. Stivers replied, snapping off his latex gloves.

"Even doctors make mistakes sometimes. Maybe—?"

"There's no doubt, Kate, absolutely none at all." He dropped the gloves into a small trash container and glanced over his shoulder. "Is it really so tragic?"

"Well, no, of course not." Kate swallowed hard, still struggling to grasp the surprising implication of what she'd just been told. "It's just that...I mean, I never even dreamed..." She rubbed her face, muttering into the palms of her cold hands. "Oh, Lord. There must be something terribly wrong with me."

"Wrong?" A hearty laugh died on his lips as he realized that she was truly distraught. "Oh, my dear, there's nothing wrong with you. You're a perfectly normal, healthy young woman, who simply happens to be a virgin.''

Kate flinched at the word.

As relieved as she was to determine that there were no heartbroken children grieving for their lost mother, the last thing she'd expected to discover was that she was a twenty-something spinster who'd never experienced a serious relationship with a man.

She looked up, horrified. "Do you think I could be gay?''

"Well, gracious." Nervously adjusting his spectacles, the startled man peered over the wire rims, regarding her warily. "I really couldn't say. Are you, ah, attracted to women?''

As Kate considered that, the image of Reed Morgan floated through her mind. Her body reacted instantly, with a flutter in her chest and a liquid warmth spreading low in her belly. Absently touching her abdomen, she shook her head. "No, I definitely like men." She sighed. "But apparently they don't like me."

"Nonsense." Retrieving his leather case, Dr. Stivers snapped the clasp, struggling to control an amused smile quivering at the corner of his mouth. "My guess would be that you are simply a highly moral young woman who made a conscious decision to save herself for marriage. Quite admirable, if you ask me, and far too rare."

"*Rare* is the operative word here." Kate sat heavily on the bed, slumping forward with her elbows propped on her thighs. "I don't want to be rare. I want to be normal."

"You *are* normal." Clucking like a concerned grandpa, Dr. Stivers laid a firm hand on her shoulder. "I've found that a surprisingly large segment of society holds itself to a much higher standard than that portrayed by the media."

Unimpressed, she glumly stared at her knees. On the one hand, she agreed with the doctor's assessment and couldn't figure out why a lack of sexual experience should be so distressing to her. On the other hand, however, she couldn't help but wonder if her chastity could be the result of psychological trauma rather than moral choice.

Maybe she was frigid.

Once again she envisioned Reed's muscular body rippling beneath his clothes, particularly the delicious curve of his firm, round rear rolling under a cloak of tight denim—

Puffing her cheeks, Kate shook off the arousing image before her body temperature soared to the boiling point. Frigidity, she decided, was definitely not a problem.

She glanced up as Dr. Stivers opened the bedroom door, preparing to leave. "Doctor?"

He turned, smiling pleasantly.

"I'd appreciate it if you wouldn't, uh, mention this to anyone."

His smile broadened into a paternal grin. "It will be our secret, my dear."

Reed climbed out of his truck just as Donald Stivers was descending the porch stairs. They met in the driveway. "So how is she?" Reed asked.

"Physically, she's fine." Shifting his leather case from one hand to the other, Donald Stivers slipped a quick glance at the timepiece on his left wrist. "Vital signs are normal, abrasions and bruises are healing nicely, and she seems fully cognizant and mentally alert."

Reed glanced up. "How alert?"

"As alert as you or I," he replied with a shrug. "But if you're asking about her memory impairment, I didn't note any improvement there."

Disappointed, Reed shoved his hands into his pockets and pushed a dusty pebble with the toe of his boot. He squinted sideways, angling a glum glance at his friend. "Just between you and me, Don, do you think she's faking?"

"Just between you and me?" Pursing his lips, the doctor rocked back on scuffed heels, shaking his head. "No, I don't think so. In fact, I'd be willing to bet that she isn't. Even if

she were the world's most gifted actress, certain physiolog-
ical responses can't be consciously controlled.''

"You mean heart rate, blood pressure, things like that?"

"Yes. Not that I'm a human lie detector, mind you, but I
did make a point of posing some very specific questions
during the examinations in order to observe her reactions."

"And—?"

"And I saw no indication that she was being less than
candid with her answers." Giving a restless turn, Donald
angled another longing glance at his wristwatch. "Actually, Reed, I do have another call to make before rounds at
the hospital."

"Oh, yeah, sure. Sorry to have held you up," he added,
falling into step as the doctor hurried across the driveway.
Reed opened the car door for him. "By the way, have you
heard anything else about Pastor Hargrove? I haven't been
able to get through to anyone in the family."

"They're at the hospital," Donald replied, tossing his case
onto the back seat. "None of them have left since the night
of the accident." He straightened, frowning. "It's not
common knowledge yet, but I believe the family is planning an announcement this afternoon."

Reed straightened, not liking the ominous tone of his
friend's voice. "Oh, Lord, he hasn't died?"

"No." Heaving a troubled sigh, Donald leaned heavily
against the vehicle's open door. "But the poor man has
slipped into a coma. The prognosis isn't good."

"Damn." Pushing back his hat, Reed gazed toward the
verdant pasture dotted by grazing cattle. Once, he'd viewed
life as an endless highway to be traveled and retraveled as the
whim struck. Bonnie's death had punctured that illusion.
Reality, he'd discovered, left a bitter aftertaste. Human existence was fragile and fleeting, beyond control of mere
mortals. The painful lesson had sorely tested his faith.

Reed knew that he'd failed that test. He knew because he
couldn't control the fury swelling in his chest at the sight of

his motherless children, or the aching loneliness of his cold, empty bed. He knew because the joy had seeped out of his life, replaced by the silent terror that at any moment, the icy hand of fate could reach out again, perhaps for one of his daughters.

At the thought, Reed broke out in a cold sweat. If anything happened to his children, he wouldn't be able to bear it; yet destiny carried a power far beyond human control. It was that power of fate, or more precisely a personal lack of power that left him feeling angry, impotent and riddled by guilt. It wasn't logical, it wasn't reasonable, but deep down, Reed couldn't help but feel that his own failures had cost Bonnie her life. Maybe ranch life had been too difficult for her. Maybe Reed had expected too much. Maybe she'd withered away from secret unhappiness. All Reed knew for sure is he should have done something. He just didn't know what.

During her illness, Reed had tried to strike a deal with the Big Guy. *Take me,* he'd prayed. *The children need their mother. Take me.*

As it turned out, God hadn't wanted Reed. He'd wanted Bonnie, and He'd taken her, ripping her from the arms of a grieving husband and two heartbroken babies.

Eventually Reed had accepted his wife's loss because there'd been no other choice. But he'd never forgiven it, and was still haunted by the heresy of his own unyielding anger.

After squeezing between the decorated Christmas tree and the windowsill, Kate had been observing the conversation between Reed and Dr. Stivers, fretting that the elderly physician might rethink his vow of silence and reveal the results of his examination. She'd just about convinced herself that Dr. Stivers was much too professional to violate doctor-patient privilege when Reed suddenly tossed a startled glance toward the house. Kate's stomach dropped as if it had been tossed into a bottomless pit, but Reed's gaze was fleeting and a moment later, the two men shook hands.

After the doctor left, Reed remained in the driveway with an expression so poignant that it touched Kate to the marrow. What was it, she wondered, that could bring such profound anguish to those soft and loving eyes?

Curious contemplation dissipated when Reed suddenly looked toward the house and stared right at her. Kate smiled. He gave a curt nod of acknowledgment, then tugged his hat down over his head and strode toward the hay barn with a slightly bowlegged gait that Kate found oddly endearing. What hadn't been so endearing was the blank expression on his face when he'd spotted her.

But what had she expected? Kate was, after all, a complete stranger who'd invaded his home, imposed on his family and intruded on their privacy. Despite the fact that Reed had invited her to do so, she was painfully aware that as a staunchly moral humanitarian, the poor fellow hadn't had much choice in the matter.

She leaned against the sill, wishing for a way to repay his kindness, when Rory suddenly sprinted into view. Chubby legs churning, the child dashed across the yard to grab her father in a bear hug around the waist.

Then an amazing thing happened. Reed's entire countenance miraculously changed from one of brooding contemplation to the grinning expression of unbridled exuberance. Hoisting the laughing girl over his head, he swung her around until her face glowed and her jubilant squeals vibrated across the yard to permeate the walls of the house.

After he'd set the gasping child back on her feet, he gave her boyish bob a final ruffle, then they clasped hands and practically skipped toward the pasture. Leaning over the low fence wire, Reed put two fingers to his mouth and emitted a whistle loud enough to startle passengers of low-flying aircraft. In response, several head of cattle lumbered toward the fence, apparently in search of the alfalfa chips that Rory was retrieving from a nearby bin.

Rory tore chunks from the flat, green hay chips, which were about the size of an average shirt box. She hand-fed some of the animals and tossed tempting morsels to those choosing not to venture as close as their gutsier brethren.

Although each cow was given a share of the treat, Kate noticed that an adorable brick red baby bull received most of Reed's attention. As he fed the special little guy, his expression softened and he appeared to be talking to the tiny animal the way doting parents coo to feeding babies.

Rory, too, was enamored of the baby bull. From Kate's perspective, both father and daughter were in their element, comfortable with themselves, their surroundings and each other. The loving interaction between Reed and Rory fascinated Kate and touched her deeply; yet beyond that was a peculiar sadness, a profound sense of loss that shook her to the soles of her feet.

As Kate pondered those unsettling sensations, Shawna entered the room with a limp gray-and-white cat draped around her neck. "Book reports stink," she announced, rubbing her eyes. "It wouldn't be so bad if we could pick what we wanted to read, but who's interested in a bunch of stuff written over a hundred years ago?"

"Ah, the classics. Definitely an acquired taste." Kate smiled at the snoozing animal on the girl's shoulder. "And who have we here?"

"This is Gulliver." Leaning her head to one side, Shawna slipped a finger under the cat's chin. "Say 'hi' to Kate," she coaxed. Gulliver opened one yellow eye, a relatively benign feline function that for some unfathomable reason seemed to tickle Shawna immensely. "Isn't he just the most adorable thing?"

"He does have a cute face," Kate agreed, stroking the animal's furry gray head. "I haven't seen him before. Does he usually stay outside?"

"That pretty much depends on where Rory is," Shawna muttered, moving the cat from her shoulders to the back of the sofa. "Ever since she took up karate, Gulliver gives her a wide berth."

Kate looked up, horrified. "Surely she wouldn't use martial arts on a defenseless little cat."

"Oh, no, Rory doesn't practice on Gully. Gosh, she'd never do anything to hurt him. It's just that all her jumping around and screeching drives him nuts. Of course, it drives *me* nuts, too, but I can't afford the luxury of hiding out in the barn whenever she goes on a tear."

"Ah." Sharing an empathetic nod, Kate glanced back out the window, where Rory and her dad were still at the pasture fence with the little red bull. "Your sister does seem to have been blessed with more than her share of energy."

"You can say that again." Shawna moved toward the window, following Kate's gaze. "Oh, good grief, Dad spends so much time with that silly calf you'd think they were genetically related. He has this ridiculous notion that Fagan's bloodlines are going to turn this place from a struggling cherry farm into a million-dollar cattle ranch."

"Fagan?"

"That little red Angus," Shawna explained, wrinkling her adorably stubby nose. "Dad actually plunked down a cash deposit when Fagan was nothing more than some yucky you-know-what in a bottle. Can you believe that?"

"Actually, I do believe it," Kate replied, startling herself. "Not that I know anything about cattle, of course, but artificial insemination is frequently used to breed thoroughbreds and if I'm not mistaken, it's not uncommon to establish ownership of the offspring before insemination even takes place."

Shawna's shoulders rolled in a lackadaisical shrug. "I still think it's stupid to buy something you can't even see, but Dad—" She sighed, turning away from the window. "Mom always said Dad was a dreamer. For whatever reason, she seemed to think that was a good thing."

"But you don't?"

A now-familiar sulk marred her youthful freshness. "Dreams don't pay the bills. You can't cook them, you can't wear them, and they don't—" her voice broke as her gaze fell on a cracked picture frame propped on an end table "—they don't cure cancer."

Touched, Kate lifted the portrait of a smiling, dark-haired woman, while carefully supporting the broken frame with her palms. "Your mother?"

Shawna nodded.

"She was very pretty." And so young, Kate thought sadly. "Rory favors her quite a bit."

"Dad says she looks just like Mom," Shawna agreed. "He says I take after his side of the family, but personally, I don't think I look like anybody."

"Oh, heavens, even I can see that except for the blue eyes, you're the spitting image of your father. Or at least you will be when you're older, and your features lean out a bit."

The girl brightened. "You think so?"

"Absolutely." Kate's gaze returned to the photograph. An empathetic ache twisted inside her chest. "Such a lovely, gentle face," she murmured. "You and Rory must miss her terribly."

The comment was greeted by silence. When Kate glanced up, Shawna's eyes were misted by tears. "Rory was only four when Mama died, so she doesn't remember much about her. But I remember," Shawna finally whispered. "I remember that the kitchen always smelled like cinnamon when she was here, and the parlor smelled like fresh lemons. When I was real little, I used to sneak into Mom and Dad's bedroom to play with the pretty bottles on her vanity. They smelled good, too, like summer flowers. She caught me once, and I was afraid she'd be mad, but she wasn't. Instead, she picked up the prettiest bottle and said I could have it for my very own."

As Shawna turned away to dab at the insistent moisture gathering on her tawny lashes, Kate's feelings spiraled well beyond compassion. She actually experienced Shawna's pain as a throbbing, tangible knot deep in the pit of her own soul. Kate felt an uncanny connection with this motherless girl, an emotional bonding that cried out for completion.

Instinctively realizing that Shawna needed to articulate her loss, Kate gently replaced the portrait in its place of honor on the end table, then laid a comforting hand on the teenager's shoulder. "Your mother sounds like a wonderful woman. I'd like to hear more about her."

Sniffing, Shawna managed a jerky nod. It took a moment for her to gather enough composure to speak in a halting voice. "My mother loved being a mom, and said she'd rather stay home and take care of us than anything else in the world. And she was smart, too, real smart. No matter what needed doing, she always figured out a way to get it done quick, and without spending a whole bunch of money. Everything was always so clean, and she still had time to bake bread from scratch, and sew all our clothes, and make all kinds of pretty things for the house. She made those curtains."

After gesturing toward the softly draped lace that framed the front window just beyond the glittering tree, Shawna turned her attention to a ripple-weave afghan folded over the sofa arm. "I remember when Mama crocheted that. It took months and months, but she never got discouraged. She loved all kinds of needlework. Said it soothed the soul."

Something about the afghan intrigued Kate. Brushing her palm over the supple surface, she studied the rippled rows of delicately twisted yarns worked in hues ranging from muted teal to deep forest green. She unfolded one corner to inspect the end weaves, where the various shades of yarn had been seamlessly integrated, and the raw ends invisibly woven back into the work.

"Your mother was incredibly talented," Kate murmured. "A perfect texture, with stitch tension that doesn't vary a millimeter throughout the entire piece. It's really quite extraordinary."

"You know how to crochet?" Shawna asked, clearly surprised.

"Hmm?" Glancing up, Kate returned Shawna's incredulous stare with one of wary caution. An image flashed through her mind of a shiny fat hook diving into patterned yarn, retrieving a perfect loop through which a separate strand was pulled to complete the stitch. "Yes, apparently I do."

Shawna's eyes were huge. "Can you embroider, too?"

Pursing her lips, Kate massaged her eyelids, considering the question. After a moment, she looked up. "Cross-stitch, satin stitch, fish-bone, French-knot—"

"Oh, this is too perfect!" Shawna shrieked, clapping her hands. She spun around and dashed into her bedroom, returning a moment later with a stuffed tapestry tote, which she immediately emptied on the sofa. Pushing away the clutter of thread skeins, hoops and pouched needles, she located a crumpled piece of folded linen. "Mama was working on this while she was sick," Shawna said, spreading the partially completed wall hanging over the cushion. "When she got too weak to do it anymore, she gave it to me. I promised that I'd finish it, only I never learned how. Will you teach me?"

"Oh, I don't know, Shawna. This is a very complex design."

"Please?"

Chewing her lower lip, Kate studied the intricate details of the piece, which contained an exquisite floral border around the cross-stitched message Bless This Family. She could literally feel the love emanating from the partially embroidered linen, and the responsibility of helping complete something so very special weighed heavily on her shoulders.

"I don't think I'm as accomplished as your mother was," she said honestly. "But I do recognize most of the techniques she used, so if you're willing to take a chance—"

"I am!" Shawna dug what was left of her chewed fingernails into Kate's arm. "Please, it would mean so much to me... and to my mom."

Smiling, Kate unfurled the teenager's taloned grip, patting her hand. "All right. I'm willing if you are."

As Shawna glowed with excitement, Kate heard a soft sigh of contentment, and could have sworn the sound had come from the portrait.

Hours later, Kate sat in the darkened living room, alone except for the twinkling Christmas tree. Rory was in bed, presumably asleep, although a few suspicious thumps had filtered from behind her closed bedroom door. Shawna had retired early, barely suppressing a gleeful grin as she'd slipped away to work on the embroidered piece that would be a very special gift to her father.

It wouldn't be completed in time for Christmas, of course, but Shawna had whispered to Kate that she already had the perfect gift for her father, a replica of an old-fashioned bootjack. Shawna was also excited about her gift to Rory, a book on the history of Japanese samurai that she feared might be a bit grown-up for the eight-year-old. Still, she'd placed the bowed present under the tree with great flourish and a secretive grin that had driven her younger sister to the brink of frantic curiosity.

Later, when caught inspecting the wrapped present from her sister, Rory had sheepishly explained that Shawna's presents were always her very favorite.

Kate had thought that sweet. Despite constant squabbling and overt sibling rivalry that seemed to drive their poor father to the brink of distraction, the sisters obviously cared deeply for each other. Kate envied that, although she didn't know why. There was a sharing, an inner closeness between the girls that struck a yearning chord deep inside. In the tragic aftermath of their mother's loss, the girls could turn to each other for the kind of comfort that a surviving parent, no matter how loving or well intentioned, could never provide.

Frowning, Kate absently fingered a sparkling tree ornament, wondering about the poignant direction of her thoughts, and her emotional reaction to them. There was a fuzzy image in her mind, soft and fragrant, yet lingering just beyond reach. The harder she focused on it, the further it slipped away until nothing remained but a dark void and a coldness of spirit that saddened her deeply.

Standing there in the midst of holiday cheer and inviting homey warmth, Kate shivered inside. Lost, frightened and emotionally isolated, she found herself moving toward the kitchen, staring at the closed door leading into Reed's garage workshop.

He'd been in there all evening, working on some kind of secret project. Not surprising, considering that tomorrow was Christmas Eve. Kate knew that the girls weren't allowed in the workshop, but Reed had never said anything about houseguests.

And she felt so desperately alone.

Before she realized what was happening, her hand had encircled the doorknob and she was peeking into a din of manly clutter illuminated by an umbrella of flickering fluorescents. Pungent fumes stung her nostrils, perhaps from paint thinner or cleaning chemicals. Her eyes started to water, making it difficult to focus on the flannel-clad figure hunched over a workbench. "Ah, hello?"

Straightening quickly, Reed spun around, relaxing when he spotted Kate. "Hi," he said, obviously relieved that it wasn't one of his daughters. "I didn't hear the door open."

"I should have knocked."

"No, that's all right." He glanced past her shoulder, assuring himself that she was alone. "Come in, if you want. Just close the door behind you."

Kate complied, casting curious glances at the peculiar wreaths of wire and rope coiled in haphazard stacks and strewn across a concrete floor coated with sawdust and boot dirt. Piles of lumber were also scattered about, along with cardboard boxes jammed with jumbled plumbing fixtures, electrical stuff and other unrecognizable thingamajigs.

"So," Kate murmured, stepping around a sheath of rusty garden tools. "This is it."

Reed, who was using steel wool to polish a slender blade of shiny metal, glanced over his shoulder. "This is what?"

"Cave of the tool-bear, the last remaining male enclave in America." Wiping her eyes, Kate sidled around the shop centerpiece, a table saw doing double duty as temporary home for a well-used belt sander. "Are you aware that it's freezing in here?"

"I like fresh air."

"Then you should be positively ecstatic," she mumbled, rubbing the gooseflesh covering her upper arms.

He angled a sideways glance. "Is this a social visit, or is there something I can do for you?"

The question was posed in a friendly tone, although Kate was acutely aware of an underlying wariness that was understandable if somewhat unnerving. She licked her lips before stretching them into a nervous smile. "I just wanted to, well, apologize again for the mashed potatoes."

To her relief, a glow of genuine amusement lit his dark eyes. "Don't worry about it. Potato soup is quite nourishing, and besides, I knew we were in trouble when I saw you trying to scrape the spuds with the wrong side of the peeler."

"You mock a traumatized woman?"

"Sure, why not?" His grin broadened. "Come on now, you have to admit that the expression on your face was pretty funny."

"I wouldn't know. I couldn't see it." Feigning indignation, she made a production of straightening the hem of her borrowed T-shirt. "Besides, it's all your fault for not being more specific with your instructions. A 'dollop' of milk, for goodness' sake. What does that mean, anyway?"

"It doesn't mean a quart."

"Apparently not." She cleared her throat, avoiding his gaze. The truth was that her efforts to assist in the kitchen had been a total disaster, and she didn't have a clue as to why. When she'd volunteered to help, Reed had pointed to a stack of potatoes and asked her to prepare them for mashing. Her mind had gone absolutely blank, so she'd picked up one of the lumpy things, eyeing it as if seeking instructions. It had felt so odd in her hand. Even when Reed handed her a vicious-looking instrument that he'd referred to as a peeler, Kate still hadn't a clue as to how to use the darn thing.

Still, she'd been giving the process the old college try, and had one potato nicely shredded, when Reed had burst out laughing. He'd taken the peeler, turned it around and slapped it back into her palm.

Kate had to admit that it had worked better that way.

After that, things had gone fairly well. She'd watched closely as Reed had cut the peeled potatoes into chunks, then boiled them until tender. He'd let Kate drain them, which she had done quite well, thank you very much. In fact, she'd been feeling pretty confident in squishing the boiled spuds up with that flat-headed masher-thing when Reed had told her to add some butter and that disastrous 'dollop' of milk.

Fortunately, there'd been a package frozen French fries in the freezer, although they did look a bit odd under the gravy.

Sighing, Kate glanced around the shop, aware that her eyes were still stinging. She wrinkled her nose against the pungent aroma wafting from somewhere behind them. "What's that god-awful smell?"

Reed glanced up as if surprised to see her there. "Hmm? Oh, varnish. Even with the window open, the fumes have a tendency to build up. After a while, you get used to it."

"Probably because your brain cells have shut down in self-defense. This can't be good for you." She stifled a cough, focusing on the culprit, an open container of varnish sitting on a plywood plank that was propped between sawhorses to form a makeshift table. "Putting the lid back on the can might help."

"Did I leave the lid off?" Frowning, he glanced over his shoulder, then angled a sheepish smile. "That's the problem with being one of Santa's elves. Notoriously long hours, lousy working conditions, and improper training."

"You should file a grievance with the elves' union."

"No time," he said, laying down the odd-looking blade long enough to replace the varnish can's top. "A daddy's work is never done."

"So I see. What's that tent thing?"

He followed her gaze to the gauzy fabric draped over a frame beside the sticky can of varnish. "It's a dust cover to protect the floor slats until the varnish dries."

"Floor slats?"

"Uh-huh. For the sled."

"You're actually building a sled?"

"Well, no, not exactly." He returned his attention to the metal strips he'd been polishing, which Kate now recognized as the sled's skids. "Rory has been bugging me for a sled ever since she was old enough to roll a snowball. Last summer, I found a really neat one at one of the local flea markets. Some of the slats were warped, and the skids had started to rust, but it had a solid frame, so I figured it was worth refurbishing."

After blowing steel wool dust off the skid he was polishing, Reed held the sparkling strip up to the light, eyeing it critically. He glanced over at Kate, as if judging her reaction. "I could have bought her a new sled," he said quietly. "It's just that things with a history bring their own kind of richness, you know?"

"Yes," Kate whispered, touched by the sudden softness in his eyes. "And a gift created by loving hands is the most precious of all. The sled will be all the more special to Rory because you've put so much of yourself into it."

"I doubt that. If all goes well, Rory won't have a clue that I've so much as looked at the darn thing, let alone had my grubby hands on it."

"But why? I mean, surely you're entitled to have your hard work appreciated."

"A happy smile will be enough appreciation." Reed glanced over, obviously amused by Kate's puzzled expression. "The sled will be from Santa," he explained.

"Oh." A warm flush crept up her throat. "Of course. I forgot."

"You forgot about Santa?" Tsking sadly, Reed shook his head. "Don't let Rory hear you say that. She'll nail a clove of garlic over your bed. Could you hand me that axle?"

Kate glanced around the tool-ladened workbench, following Reed's gesture to an extruded bar with flattened ends. "Do you need any help? I mean, sanding or polishing or whatever." When he slid her an amused glance, she felt an embarrassed flush crawl up her throat. "If I'm given *precise* instructions, I'm quite capable of following them."

"In that case, I could use another pair of hands," Reed replied, seeming extraordinarily pleased by the offer. "Unless you have something better to do, that is."

"Like calling a broker to check on my portfolio of blue chips?"

He chuckled. "Point taken. Grab a hunk of wool out of that bag—oops, not so much. That's better. Now all you have to do is rub out the rough spots until the metal is bright and shiny.'' Taking a sideways step, he moved behind her, then reached around to guide her hands. ''Be sure to rub lengthwise, like this.''

Kate froze, befuddled by her tumultuous reaction. One minute, she'd been chatting amiably, enjoying the conversation and his company. Then, before she'd had a moment to contemplate what was happening, he was so close she could feel the warmth of his breath brushing her cheek, the vibration of his heartbeat against her shoulder blades. Every inch of his body radiated a dizzying amount of heat. His touch seared her skin; his voice, a soft murmur filtering into the deepest recesses of her mind, became a mesmerizing mantra of enticement.

She couldn't think, couldn't breathe, couldn't control the sudden pounding of her own heart as it exploded with a wild, pagan rhythm that scared her half to death. Her knees trembled first; then the quiver climbed her spine, jiggled her shoulders and finally, shuddered down her arms.

When the wad of steel wool slipped from her hands, Reed stiffened, stepping away so quickly that Kate had to steady herself against the workbench. ''I'm sorry,'' he whispered, looking stricken. ''I'm not usually so thoughtless.''

Before Kate could digest the implications of the ambiguous comment, Reed spun on his booted heel and disappeared behind a stack of, well, unidentifiable junk. A moment later, he returned shaking out a hunk of gray fleece that might once have been clothing. At the moment, however, it resembled a fat dust rag with arms.

Ignoring the fresh cloud of airborne particles encircling his head, Reed hurried back to the workbench and wrapped the fleecy fabric around Kate's shoulders. ''Better?'' he asked anxiously.

''Ah, yes. Thank you.'' She slipped her arms into the garment, which she now recognized as a zip-front sweatshirt, and allowed Reed to roll up the sleeves until her hands appeared. Wiggling her fingers, she gave him a grateful smile. "Very nice. Cozy."

He seemed pleased. They stood there a moment, smiling stupidly at each other. Finally Reed cleared his throat, rubbed his hands together and went back to work.

Taking the hint, Kate retrieved her steel wool and awkwardly rubbed at the corroded metal bar. By watching Reed carefully, she emulated his technique and soon got the hang of what promised to be a long and tedious process.

They worked for hours, alternately chatting and teasing each other, cracking jokes and occasionally broaching more serious subjects. Even after they'd spread the sled parts on the workshop floor and sat on the cold concrete to complete the process, their lively conversation continued.

Kate marveled at Reed's down-to-earth intelligence, his stunning ability to cut through pompous philosophical complexities right to the rational core of the matter. His views on life were wholesome but not naive, cautiously optimistic and intrinsically logical.

Two distinctly differing subjects, however, made his eyes light with particular pride—Fagan the baby bull, and his daughters, who were quite clearly the center of his universe.

"Shawna's one in a million," Reed murmured as he finished bolting the polished axle to the sled frame. "I don't know what I'd have done without her, but she's taken over so many household responsibilities that sometimes I think she's forgotten how to be a child. That worries me. Can you hold these pieces up while I bolt them together... great, thanks." He leaned over, inspecting the work. "I know I shouldn't let Shawna work so hard, but she's pretty obstinate when she sets her mind to something. And she's sexist, too."

Kate's hand slipped off the axle. "Sexist? What on earth do you mean by that?"

"She doesn't think a man has any business in the kitchen, or the laundry room, either, for that matter." Reed readjusted the metal pieces and waited for Kate to hold them in place.

"Little girls are nurturing by nature," Kate told him. "It's normal for them to want to take care of their daddies."

"True, but I let things go too far. By the time she'd chased off the fifth housekeeper, I should have realized there was a problem. Can you hold it just a bit tighter?"

Kate shifted positions to comply with his request. "I think you're being too hard on yourself. Single parents have a really tough job. Everyone in the family has to pitch in and do their share."

"Shawna does more than her share. Got it. Thanks." Laying down the socket wrench, Reed straightened, rolling his head. "I've encouraged her to be more social with kids her own age."

"That hasn't worked?"

"So far, no. Maybe next year when she gets to high school things will be different."

Kate hiked a brow. "Things will be different, all right. Boys will enter the picture."

"Ouch." Reed shook his head, mumbling. "I'm doomed."

"Hey, look at the bright side. You've got lots a good years left with Rory before she'll be ready to eyeball the opposite sex."

"Now there's a happy thought." He cocked his head, smiling. "Maybe by then she'll be a black belt. That'll really ease my mind."

"Black belt? Ah, karate." Pulling herself up on the workbench, Kate stood and brushed sawdust off the seat of her jeans. "Is that why you enrolled the poor girl in martial arts, to fight off future boyfriends?"

"That's an added benefit," he acknowledged, rising from his cross-legged position in a single, fluid motion. "But the real reason was that I'd hoped karate would teach her focus and self-discipline. You know, coordinate mind, body and spirit toward the path of inner harmony."

"That sounds like a quote from a marketing flyer."

"It is." Glancing around the workshop, he blinked tiredly. "The slats will be dry by tomorrow, then we can finish up."

Kate heaved a contented sigh. "This has been so much fun. In a sense, this will be my first Christmas. Thank you for letting me share it."

He regarded her thoughtfully, but made no comment as he followed her to the door. They spoke briefly in the kitchen, then said their good-nights. Reed went to his bedroom.

Kate went to hers.

But she couldn't sleep. Instead, she replayed the evening in her mind. Surely she'd never had a more enjoyable time in her life. True, she couldn't remember much of her life... all right, she couldn't remember any of it, but even if she could, she doubted anything could have topped the satisfaction she'd gotten out of working to create something wonderful, something that would bring squeals of joy on Christmas morning.

Christmas was, of course, all about giving. Kate wished that she had something to give.

Sighing, she sat heavily on the bed. There was nothing, of course. She had no money. The clothes on her back were borrowed. She didn't own a darn thing, except a pair of presumably *faux* pearl earrings, which were much too formal for the girls even if either of them had been willing to have their ears pierced to wear the darn things.

But as her gaze fell on the satin wedding gown, she realized that there was indeed one other thing she owned.

Kate smiled, rubbed her hands together and went looking for scissors.

Chapter Four

"E-e-e *ya!* Hai, hai, hai. *Ee-e—*"

"Oh, for crying out loud, toad, give it a rest!" Shawna spun away from the stove, waving a spatula like a sword. "In case you hadn't noticed, Dad's trying to get some sleep."

"Not anymore."

Shawna's head snapped around. "It's not my fault, Dad. I told her to be quiet."

Jamming her hands on her hips, Rory took a wide-footed stance and stubbornly lifted her chin. "*Sensei* says I hafta practice my *uchi*s."

"I'm going to *uchi* you, you obnoxious little—"

"What smells so good?" Reed asked, interrupting the argument a moment before he was overtaken by a jaw-cracking yawn.

After casting a final scowl at her sibling, Shawna presented her back to Rory and fixed her father with a proud grin. "It's a special Christmas Eve breakfast. Apple pancakes. I found the recipe in *Woman's Day.*"

"Sounds great." Rubbing his grainy eyes, Reed flopped into the nearest chair. He propped his elbows on the table, lowered his head and massaged the top of his scalp with his knuckles. Turning his head from side to side, he glanced around the room, blinking. "Is Kate still sleeping?"

"Oh, no, she's been up for hours," Shawna said without looking up from the griddle. "She grabbed a cup of coffee, asked to borrow Mamma's sewing basket, then disappeared back in her room."

"Sewing basket?" Reed straightened, mumbling a quick thank-you to Rory, who'd just set a steaming mug of black coffee in front of him. "Did she mention why she needed it?"

Shawna shrugged. "Uh-uh, but the jeans I gave her are a little big. Maybe she's taking them in."

"No, she's not," Rory insisted, with a smug smile. "*I* know what Kate's doing."

Reed looked up, waiting, but Shawna just rolled her eyes and went back to flipping pancakes.

After sticking her tongue out at Shawna, a fairly safe endeavor considering that her sister's back was turned, Rory flounced to the table, fairly bursting with pride at being able to share such juicy news. "Kate's learning karate."

That wasn't exactly what Reed had expected to hear. "How do you know?"

"'Cause she wanted to borrow my karate book," Rory announced, skewering her visibly annoyed sister with a slitty-eyed stare. "And then she asked all kinds of questions about what the funny symbols mean, and wanted to know absolutely everything about *obi*'s and *gi*'s, and stuff like that."

"Really?" Reed tugged his earlobe. Although not particularly well versed in the terminology of karate, he did know that an *obi* was the belt or sash of the traditional uniform, or *gi,* worn by devotees of the craft. That information did little to explain Kate's sudden interest in such matters.

In the midst of his curious contemplation, Reed heard the guest room door open. A moment later, Kate hurried into the kitchen, looking excited and beautifully radiant.

When she saw Reed, she jerked to a stop. A guilty flush crept up her throat. "Ah, good morning," she murmured, curling a supple strand of gleaming midnight hair around her index finger. "Did you sleep well?"

Reed leaned back in his chair, noting the nervous shift in her stance and the peculiar way her gaze darted around the room. "Not particularly," he drawled. "In fact, I barely slept a wink all night."

"That's good," she replied, obviously distracted. After chewing her lip for a moment, Kate flashed Reed a preoccupied smile and sidled over to whisper in Shawna's ear.

The teenager drew back in surprise, then shrugged and said, "Yeah, I think so."

For whatever reason, Kate looked massively relieved.

"Dad, could you watch the pancakes for a minute?"

"Hmm?" Reed glanced up, taking a moment to register the expectant look on his daughter's face. "Pancakes? Oh, sure." He pushed back the chair, poising on the edge of the seat as if preparing to spring, his gaze sliding from Kate's joyful grin to Shawna's perplexed frown. "Ah, what's going on?"

"Nothing," Kate replied quickly. Too quickly. She covered a nervous laugh with her hands, then snagged Shawna's arm and hustled her out of the room.

While Rory muttered soft karate commands across the table, Reed tapped his coffee mug, listening to various clicks and thunks of doors being opened and closed. Rushed footsteps echoed from the hallway, followed by a duet of feminine giggles. The first thing that hit Reed was how lovely the sound of a woman's laughter was; the second, was sadness at how long it had been since he'd heard it.

Another door squeaked open, then closed with a soft thump.

After a moment, Shawna returned, grinning madly. Without so much as a glance at her curious father, she went directly to the griddle and proceeded to shovel overcooked apple pancakes onto an already heaped serving platter.

Reed leaned forward. "Well . . . ?"

She glanced over her shoulder, batting her eyes with exaggerated innocence. "Well what?"

Narrowing his gaze, Reed offered his most effective I'm-your-father-so-don't-mess-with-me scowl. "What was that—" he gestured toward the hallway for emphasis "—all about?"

Shawna smiled sweetly. "I can't tell you."

"Huh?" Alerted by a draft on his tongue, Reed closed his mouth, while his oldest daughter, humming happily, slipped a fragrant plate of steaming pancakes in front of him.

Still sporting that infuriating secretive grin, she pushed a sticky syrup bottle across the table. *"Bon appétit."*

"Why can't you tell me?" Wincing at the uncharacteristic whine in his voice, he made a production of clearing his throat. "I mean, I'm certainly entitled to know what's going on in my own house." He shifted his eyes without moving his head. "Right?"

Puckering her brows, Shawna laid a parental hand on his shoulder. "Honestly, Dad, you really should talk to someone about this control fetish of yours."

"Fetish? Me?" Stunned, he pressed a hand to his chest. "I don't have any fetishes, control or otherwise."

"You're in denial," she replied knowingly. "A classic case. I saw it on Oprah."

Clucking sadly, she patted her father's head as if he were an untrainable puppy, then heaved yet another martyred sigh and swished dramatically out of the room.

"You see what I hafta put up with?" Rory muttered, plopping into a chair and spearing a forkful of fat pancakes. "Want me to *uchi* her?"

"No."

"Well, someone oughta *uchi* her. Shawna can be a real pain, you know?"

"So can you. Eat your breakfast."

The command was completely unnecessary. Having already drowned her pancakes in a gooey river of maple syrup, Rory proceeded to gobble up the entire plateful before her father had managed more than a few bites. Still, Reed found satisfaction in having established at least the illusion of parental control.

The moment was fleeting.

Rory leapt up from the table, snap-kicking her way to the back door with a jarring series of spins, thrusts and shouts. By the time Reed could swallow, she had the back door open.

"Hey!"

As his exuberant daughter turned expectantly, Reed took the opportunity to swallow the last bite down with a gulp of coffee, then pushed away from the table, dabbing his mouth with a napkin. "And just where do you think you're going, young lady?"

"Outside."

"Nice try." He flipped a thumb toward the living room. "Homework first."

Her jaw drooped. "But Dad, it's Christmas!"

"We've already had this discussion, Rory. If you'd kept up with your assignments in the first place, you wouldn't have to spend your Christmas vacation doing makeup work."

"I'll do it, honest I will. But it's *Christmas!*"

"Technically, it's only Christmas Eve. You can start with your spelling list."

"It's too hard, Daddy. Teacher gives us really big words."

"Then you'd better hop to it, because the bigger the words, the longer it'll take to learn them."

"Da-addy!"

Reed suffered a frisson of guilt as tears spurted into his daughter's desperate little eyes. Something in his chest cracked. He looked away, twisting the napkin into a sticky spear and feeling like the world's most sadistic father. After all, he was well aware that Rory's hyperactive personality made it extremely difficult for her to concentrate on quiet activities, let alone handle the mental focus required for solitary study.

For most children, homework was annoying; for Rory, it was nearly impossible. She fidgeted. She gazed into space. She was beset by stomach aches, unscratchable itches, and so many calls to nature that Reed was beginning to wonder if there was a biological link between textbooks and bladder function. Either that or Rory had a magic tutor secreted behind the shower curtain.

The sad truth was that Reed's youngest child would rather shovel horse apples with a teaspoon than spend sixty seconds staring at a spelling list. And her grades showed it.

Still he was unnerved by the child's tears, and the perfected quiver of her lower lip had an uncanny ability to replace parental reason with empathetic emotion.

Wasn't this supposed to be the season of joy and good cheer, of sugarplums and jolly elves and happy children anxiously scrutinizing a starry sky? What kind of parent would ruin all that by forcing a child to do schoolwork on Christmas Eve?

The kind of parent who doesn't want his kid to spend the rest of her life in third grade.

Reed swallowed hard. "We had a deal, Rory. I agreed to the karate classes because you promised to spend more time on your academic lessons."

The tears stopped instantly, as if an inner faucet had been suddenly shut off. "Aca-what?" she asked with a blank stare.

"I rest my case." Shifting, he rubbed the back of his neck, gazing out the window at the thickening clouds. "Look, punkin, I have to track down an electric short in the fence wire, but as soon as I'm finished, I'll help you with your spelling, okay? Then we'll do something fun."

Wiping her wet cheeks, Rory issued a pathetic sniffle. "L-like what?"

"Well, let's see. Maybe we can, uh—" his gaze fell on a row of worn cookbooks "—bake Christmas cookies, or something."

"The kind with sugar sprinkles?"

"Sure, why not?" Panic was setting in. Reed had never baked a cookie in his life.

Then again, the past four years had been filled with frightening firsts—first load of laundry, first pot roast, first sewed-on button. In that context, Reed wondered how hard it could possibly be to bake a stupid cookie.

If only he'd known.

Clutching the broken-framed portrait of the girls' mother, Kate poked her head into the hallway, listening. Except for the muffled strains of mangled guitar music filtering from behind Shawna's bedroom door, the house was quiet. She slipped stealthily toward the living room, only to be thwarted by an unexpected sight. Rory, looking sullen and bored, was sprawled on the sofa, folding a sheet of paper into some kind of winged object. A moment later, the paper plane floated over the coffee table and nose-dived into the floor.

Ducking back into the hallway, Kate considered her options. She'd managed to retrieve the portrait without being seen, and so far no one had noticed its disappearance. But she couldn't afford to push her luck. Somehow, she had to return the picture to its rightful place without getting caught. The sooner, the better.

She sagged against the wall, blinking her tired eyes. The last time she'd glanced in a mirror, they'd looked like a pair of squashed cherries, but staying up all night was a small price to pay for the enjoyment she hoped her efforts would reap.

Another peek into the living room revealed that Rory was now lying on her back trying to balance a pencil on her forehead. Odd, Kate thought, that such a hyperactive child wasn't outside burning off some of that abundant energy. Clearly there was a conspiracy afoot here, a clandestine plot to foil Kate's heartfelt attempt to spread a little Christmas cheer. Well, it wasn't going to work.

Ingenuity was the key, and over the past twenty-four hours, Kate had discovered that a blank mind can be surprisingly creative.

So she shoved the picture under her baggy T-shirt, crossed her arms to hold it in place and sauntered over as casually as her floppy bedroom slippers would allow. "Hi, Rory. What are you up to?"

The child leapt up so quickly that the balanced pencil did a somersault from her forehead and bounced off her bent knee. "Um, I'm doin' homework."

"My, how stoic of you." Kate perched carefully on the edge of the armchair, keeping her torso stiff so the sharp corners of the broken frame wouldn't poke holes in the underside of her breasts. "What are you working on—history, math, geography?"

"Spelling." She spit the word out like a bad taste, glaring down at the thin, soft-sided textbook as if wishing it dead. "I hate spelling. It's the most awfulest thing in the whole world. And it's really stupid, too. I mean, who cares how to spell, anyway? I'm gonna be a cattle rancher like my dad, so it's not like I'm ever gonna use it or anything."

"Of course you're going to use it. My goodness, how can you write letters to your friends if you don't know how to spell?"

"I don't hafta write letters to my friends," she said with a dismissive flick of her wrist. "I just call 'em on the phone."

"Oh." Kate slipped a sideways glance at the bare spot on the table beside her chair. "Well, I'm a pretty good speller. Maybe I can help you out."

Rory heaved a listless shrug. "The words are real hard."

"I'll bet they are," Kate murmured, spotting a wrinkled sheet on the coffee table. "Is that the list you're supposed to learn?" When the girl allowed that it was, Kate took the paper and scanned it quickly. "From what I recall—and we both know that my memory isn't the best right now—but it seems to me that my friends and I used to study by having one person read off the word while the other one spelled it out loud. Shall we try that?"

After a silent moment, Kate looked up and saw that Rory was bent in half. Although her bottom was still perched on the edge of the sofa cushion, her head was now dangling down between her ankles. "Rory?"

The child swung upright, her face flushed. "There's a lot of dust under the couch."

"Is there?"

"Uh-huh. Wanna see?"

"Ah, maybe later." Kate rubbed her eyes, then strained to focus on the list. "The first word is *daily*." She glanced over the top of the sheet. "*Daily*. Can you spell it for me?"

Rory, who was now twirling her pencil, looked up. "How come pencils have numbers?"

"Excuse me?"

"It says right here that this is a number two pencil. How come it can't be a number one pencil, or even a number five?"

Kate stared at her. "The word is *daily*. Spell it or die."

Rory dropped the pencil and stared at her knees. *"Daily,"* she droned, her eyes glazed. *"D-A-Y...um...L-E-E."*

"Not quite, but close. It's *D-A-I-L-Y.* Try it again."

Sucking in a massive breath, Rory held it a moment, then blew it out all at once. *"Daily. D-A-Y—"*

Kate interrupted. "No, sweetie. *Day* is a noun, but *daily* is an adjective. In this case, the *Y* becomes an *I,* and then—"

"I gotta go," Rory announced, then she leapt up and dashed into the bathroom.

For a moment, Kate was too stunned to move. Then she leaned forward to drop the spelling list back onto the coffee table. A painful poke issued a reminder of her original mission, so after a quick glance over her shoulder to assure herself that she was truly alone, she slipped the portrait from beneath her shirt. She'd just set it on the table when Reed walked in the front door.

Since her hand was still touching the frame, Kate jumped as if shot. "Ah...hi, there."

"Hi there, yourself." Sighing wearily, he shrugged out of the waist-length denim jacket that made his ample shoulders look even broader, and provided sexy contrast to slim hips that for some odd reason drew Kate's gaze like iron to a magnet.

Draping the jacket over a nearby coatrack, he tossed his hat onto an empty hook, then ambled toward the sofa, where he flopped down, moaning and rubbing his neck.

"You look tired," Kate said.

"I'm whipped," he admitted, propping his booted feet on the coffee table. "I just spent half the day crawling the perimeter of a twenty-acre pasture looking for a hot-wire break."

That meant nothing to Kate, although she made an effort to appear enlightened. "And did you find it?"

"Eventually." He stifled a yawn, then rubbed his eyes. "A droopy tree limb was shorting out the circuit. My chain saw and I were forced to perform an emergency amputation."

"Ouch."

"The patient is doing fine. The doctor could use some serious shut-eye." His gaze swept the coffee table, landing on the abandoned spelling list. "Where's Rory?"

"In the bathroom."

"Of course she is," Reed murmured, seeming sadly amused by news. He picked up the list. "I was supposed to help her with this."

Since no reply was required, Kate offered none. A moment later Rory emerged from the bathroom. Her face lit up when she saw her father. "Are we gonna bake cookies now?"

Kate could have sworn Reed flinched, but all he said was, "What about your spelling?"

"All done," she announced, twirling across the room to flop affectionately across her dad's lap. "Kate helped me."

Reed looked up, his eyes glowing with surprised pleasure. "You did?"

"Well, ah, the truth is—" Kate hesitated, not wanting to mislead Reed, yet touched by Rory's pleading eyes "—that I'm not much of a teacher."

Instantly Rory leapt up, massively relieved, and tugged on her father's hand. "Come on, Daddy, you promised."

Reed stood, groaning, and slipped Kate a questioning look. "Is there any chance you're better at cookie baking than you are at potato mashing?"

"There's always a chance, I suppose." Rising from the armchair, Kate rubbed her palms on her thighs and slid a nervous glance toward the kitchen. "But I honestly doubt it."

"Pity."

It was Reed's final utterance before his daughter dragged him away.

Kate stood there a moment, staring at the Christmas tree. She knew it wasn't the first such tree she'd ever seen, although she couldn't focus a specific memory of any others. There was something special about this tree, something deeply touching and poignant.

She moved closer, marveling at the unique ornaments, many of which had quite clearly been handmade. There was a miniature cradle constructed from ice-cream sticks; sequined balls with small school photos of Shawna and Rory secured by pinned pearls; tiny wrapped gift boxes; and an assortment of hand-crocheted snowflakes creating the ambience of a lovely winter wonderland.

Of all the Christmas trees Kate may have seen throughout her life, she knew without doubt that this one was by far the most beautiful. Soon she would place her own contributions beneath its sparkling boughs. And she would become a part of it.

The floor suddenly vibrated with rushing feet. Kate turned just as Rory sprinted from the kitchen into the hallway.

"Shawna!" the child hollered, pounding on her sister's door. "What's the name of those cookies Mommy used to make, the one with sugar sprinkles on top?"

Kate couldn't hear the teenager's reply, although she apparently gave one because Rory zipped back into the kitchen. The sounds of serious discussion filtered back, a high-pitched childish voice mingled with mellow male tones.

A moment later, Rory ran back to Shawna's door. "Dad wants to know where the recipe is."

This time Shawna emerged, frowning, and tromped into the kitchen with Gulliver the cat cradled in her arms.

Kate was sorely tempted to follow, but hesitated to interrupt what was clearly a family gathering. Besides, her own projects were spread across the guest room in organized chaos, waiting for the finishing touches. Since she had plenty of work ahead of her, there was no reason for Kate to intrude.

But she still found herself lurking outside the kitchen.

Shawna, who was standing beside her father, shifted the cat in her arms to point at something in the open cookbook her father was scrutinizing with an expression that could only be described as one of abject horror. He read aloud. "'Cream sugar and butter until fluffy...' What the devil does *that* mean?"

Shawna shrugged. "I guess it means to mix them together."

"Then why doesn't it just say so?" Pushing the open book to the side of the table, he stomped around the kitchen, muttering to himself.

While her father gathered the needed ingredients, Rory scampered to retrieve a large plastic bowl, into which two measuring cups of sugar were eventually poured over a rock-hard stick of butter. Reed poked at the mess with a wooden spoon. "It's not mixing."

Shawna peeked over his shoulder. "The butter's too hard."

"I can see that," Reed replied patiently. "The question is, now what?"

"I dunno," Shawna said. "I've never baked cookies by myself."

Kate cleared her throat. "Maybe that potato-squasher thing would help."

Reed looked up with a smile that took her breath away. "Great idea."

Encouraged, Kate sidled to the table while Rory retrieved the requested item. Taking the flat-headed masher firmly in hand, Reed sucked in a deep breath and plunged the utensil into the bowl. The butter stick shot out like a rocket, whizzed past Kate's head and splatted into the wall.

"Uh-oh," Rory mumbled.

Reed's shoulders slumped in defeat. "Actually, raw vegetables can be just as festive as Christmas cookies and they won't rot your teeth."

His woeful expression broke Kate's heart. "Surely, you're not going to give up that easily? I mean, anyone who can fry chicken that melts in your mouth can certainly figure out how to make a tiny little cookie."

Neither praise nor logic loosened his furrowed brow. "That's like saying anyone who can paint a house should be able to build one."

"Now, Dad, you know that Kate's right." Shawna set Gulliver on a chair, then grabbed a spatula and scraped the butter blob off delicate country wallpaper that now bore an indelible, oil-stained reminder of the incident. "Besides, who is it who's always saying stuff like 'if at first' and 'try, try again'?"

"No one I'd ever want to know," Reed grumbled, but to his credit, he retrieved another stick of butter from the fridge and set it reverently on the table beside the bowl of sugar.

Five figures—four human and one feline—hunched around the tiny wrapped block as if seeking mystical revelation. Kate tested the unyielding surface with her fingertip. "Maybe if we put it in the sun to soften?"

"There isn't any sun," Reed observed. "It's colder outside than in the refrigerator."

"Hmm. Well, I guess we'll just have to create our own sun." Kate looked up. "Got a really hot lamp?"

Reed smiled.

The next three hours were a happy blur of laughter and amused chagrin, of flour fights and giggling games of dough-ball tag, and in the end, the satisfaction of having created a sweet, fragrant platter of sparkling cookies that were surprisingly tasty.

Naturally the kitchen looked as if it had been bombed, but Kate volunteered to shovel the place out so Reed and the girls could dash out for some last-minute Christmas shopping.

By the time they returned, looking flushed, excited and extraordinarily pleased with themselves, the kitchen was sanitary if not exactly gleaming, and it was time to mess everything up all over again to prepare dinner. Since the entire family had viewed Kate's limited culinary skills up close and personal, so to speak, her cooking contribution was curtailed by popular vote; she was, however, allowed to set the table, which she did with great gusto and a persnickety perfection that surprised everyone, including herself.

As usual, the meal itself was marvelous. Reed outdid himself by proudly presenting a luscious baked ham with a gorgeous glaze, the secret of which he steadfastly refused to reveal even when presented with the incriminating evidence, an empty jar of apple jelly that a gloating Shawna retrieved from the trash. Reed pierced her with a narrowed stare, insisting that she couldn't prove a thing and he wasn't going to say another word without a lawyer.

After their Christmas Eve dinner, the girls rushed into Shawna's room with arms filled with wrappings and ribbons while Kate and Reed locked themselves in the shop to complete Santa's work.

By eleven, Kate and Reed were sipping spiked eggnog, unwinding from the raucous round of off-key Christmas carols that preceded Rory's solemn sock-hanging ceremony.

The house was quiet now, glowing with soft warmth from the blazing wood stove and glittering tree lights. Kate relaxed on the sofa, smiling at the withered little stocking tacked to the front door, a less than traditional location necessitated by the lack of a proper chimney. A glass of milk and plate of infamous sugar cookies had been lovingly placed on the coffee table, along with a note scrawled in Rory's less than perfect hand.

Deer Santa,
I have bin good but if you bring me sumthing nice, I will be even beter.

Thank you.

P.S. Pleeze reed my other letter so you will no what I wont.

"That's too adorable," Kate said, then cast a skeptical eye at the carefully laid-out treats. "But I'm not sure about this milk-and-cookie thing. Looks like a bribe to me."

Balancing the egg nog glass on his knee, Reed considered her observation. "*Bribe* is such an ugly word," he said finally. "Why don't we just consider it a tip for services rendered?"

"Tip, bribe, it's all the same."

"Obviously, you've never been a waitress."

Kate made a valiant effort to keep her wavering smile in place. She knew Reed hadn't meant to make her feel bad, but his comment had nonetheless served as an unintentional reminder that she didn't have a clue of who she was or what she might have been. A sip of eggnog provided time to compose herself, then she glanced away, acutely aware that Reed was watching her closely.

For a moment she feared he might steer the conversation back to her past, or lack thereof. Instead, he gave her an empathetic smile and set his glass on the table. "So, what do you want first, the milk or the cookies?"

"Excuse me?"

"We certainly can't leave this lovely repast unconsumed. Rory would be shattered."

That was a detail Kate hadn't considered. "Well then, you do it."

"Ah, but I can't." He spread his hands dramatically. "Children are clever little creatures, you see, and ever since Rory has been old enough to reason, she's made me promise that I would never, ever touch so much as a drop or morsel of Santa's goodies. Tomorrow morning, she'll quiz me relentlessly about whether or not I kept that vow. Naturally, I can't lie."

"Naturally."

"So you can see that you have to be the one to eat them."

"But what if she asks me?"

His tawny brows dove into a sexy frown. "Hmm. That could be dicey, I suppose."

"Well, what did you do last year?"

Chuckling, Reed nodded toward the snoozing cat. "Last year Gulliver helped me out. Unfortunately, the poor little guy barfed up the cookies and the milk gave him, ah, intestinal problems. I doubt he'd be willing to go through that again."

"Oh, poor baby," Kate murmured, petting the animal's furry side. "You've certainly done your share, haven't you, Gully?" The cat stretched, purring, and presented his soft belly for stroking. Kate complied. "Why can't we just bury the cookies in the backyard and water them with the milk?"

Reed considered the suggestion. "Wouldn't that fall under the heading of having thrown them away? Because I had to promise I wouldn't do that, either."

"My, Rory's a suspicious little thing, isn't she?"

"What can I say?" he said sadly. "She's my kid."

"Ah." Kate nodded as if that explained everything. "Well, in my humble opinion, burying something is definitely not the same as throwing it away."

"Are you sure? Because my nose twitches when I lie."

"Absolutely. Burying is burying, and throwing away is throwing away." She did a double take. "Your nose twitches? Are you serious?"

"Unfortunately, yes. It's a hangover from childhood guilt or something." He gave a sheepish shrug. "I suppose a shrink would have a field day with that, but the point is that both my girls know what it means when Daddy's nose quivers."

"A man who can't lie," Kate murmured, barely able to keep a straight face. "How wonderfully refreshing."

Sobering instantly, Reed regarded her thoughtfully. "Have you been lied to, Kate?"

"Hmm?" She clutched her stomach, strangely distressed by the question. "Most people have been lied to at one time or another, I suppose, but I can't remember anything specific, if that's what you're asking."

Apparently that was indeed the gist of his question, because he leaned back, sipping his eggnog with an expression Kate interpreted as one of disappointment. She swallowed hard, gazing toward the safety of the sparkling tree. As she did so, the glittering lights mesmerized her, taking her back to another time, another place, another tree.

It was a massive thing, thickly coated with white flocking and rising up to fill a cavernous room with ceilings high enough to brush the sky. Beside the formal tree, on which shimmering blue satin bows and balls were so perfectly coordinated as to appear professionally arranged, was an immense fireplace with a carved mantel of the kind one would expect to see in a palatial manor house. An extravagant mass of elegantly wrapped gifts was piled beneath the tree, but despite expensive decor and a huge fire crackling in the mammoth hearth, the room seemed strangely cold and foreboding.

"Kate?"

She looked up, blinking, and realized that Reed was watching her with obvious concern.

"Are you all right?" he asked.

"Yes, certainly. I'm fine. When, ah—" she covered a nervous cough "—is Santa going to do his thing, anyway?"

Reed's knowing gaze seemed to bore right through her, but all he said was, "Soon."

Kate dried her palms on her jeans. "Well, you know, if Santa isn't going to need any help stuffing stockings or whatever, there are a couple of things I have to finish up."

"Santa can manage," Reed said softly. "He's had plenty of practice."

"Yes, I imagine he has." Kate stood, then hesitated. She wanted to tell Reed how much this beautiful day had meant to her. She wanted to tell him how grateful she was that he'd allowed her to share this special holiday with his family. She wanted to tell him so many things that words failed completely.

In the end, she whispered simply, "Good night," then retired to her room, and picked up her needle and thread.

At 3:00 a.m., Kate crept back into the deserted living room. The silhouette of a bow-bedecked sled beckoned from beneath the darkened tree, and the sock pinned to the front door bulged with hidden treasures. A contented warmth seeped from body to soul. This was, she realized, a rare and special place, a house that was truly a home. There was love in the air, the unconditional love of a real family.

Kneeling beside the enchanted tree, Kate reverently laid three gifts beneath its fragrant boughs and was instantly transformed. She became a part of that love, a part of that magic. And suddenly, it didn't matter who she was or where she'd come from, because she was exactly where she was supposed to be, exactly where she belonged. She was home.

Chapter Five

Still hovering in a dream state, Reed heard a bloodcurdling shriek emanating from somewhere outside his body. A moan vibrated the cold mattress. That sound, he knew, had come from him. But the other noise, the frightening scream . . . had he dreamed it?

"Daa-a-ddy!"

Jolting upright, Reed spun his legs over the side of the bed and stumbled to his feet just as his bedroom door crashed open.

"Daddy!" Rory hollered, leaping in place like a frog on a hot griddle. "Come see what Santa brought me! You won't believe it, you just won't believe it!" The excited child emitted another joyful squeal, performed a stunning, midair pivot and propelled herself back into the dark hallway.

A moment later, a thunderous pounding vibrated the entire house. "Kate, Kate! Come see what Santa brought me!"

Reed groaned, wiping his palms across his face. Christmas had officially begun. And it was barely five o'clock.

Stumbling through the darkness, he felt around until he'd located the corner chair where he'd draped his clothes just a few hours ago. He stuck one leg into his pants, then hopped around trying to poke his limp foot into a pocket before realizing the error and correcting it. Grabbing a fresh T-shirt from the bureau drawer, he shrugged the garment on and shuffled out the door, yawning.

He would have killed for a cup of coffee.

Just as he emerged from his bedroom, Kate's door opened. She stood there rubbing her eyes, looking for all the world like a beautiful, rumple-haired child.

But only from the neck up. The rest of her lush body was stunningly displayed by a worn knit sleep shirt that Reed recognized as having once belonged to his daughter. When Shawna had worn it, however, the baggy garment had extended to her knees and looked like, well, a nightgown. On Kate, who was several inches taller, the shirt only reached mid-thigh and clung to her small but shapely breasts like a second skin.

Blinking and disoriented, she squinted toward a spray of light from the living room, which rang with childish shouts and trills of delight. "Wha's going on?" she asked, her voice slurred by sleep. "Is something wrong?"

Oh, yes, something was most definitely wrong, because Reed's gaze was riveted on the outline of taut nipples protruding beneath flimsy fabric, and he couldn't force himself to look away. Somewhere deep in his fogged mind, a voice whispered that he should answer her question. And he was going to answer it, too, the moment he remembered how to speak.

Fortunately, his mental lapse was effectively covered by Shawna, who stuck her head into the hallway, every bit as excited as her young sibling. "Hurry, Kate! Come see what Rory got for Christmas!"

"Christmas?" Kate repeated dully, as if having forgotten the meaning of the word. Then her eyes sprang open to absorb the sparse light and reflect it with breath-stopping intensity. "Ohmigosh, it's morning. It's Christmas, Reed, it's *Christmas!*"

Reed simply stood there with his mouth open.

He might have spent the entire day rooted in place had Kate not spun back into her room, breaking the visual stalemate. When she reappeared, rushing and breathless, she was tying the sash of a fat chenille robe that was as discreet as it was unflattering.

"Hurry," she said, her voice high-pitched and squeaky. "I don't want to miss a thing!"

With that, she scurried down the hall and disappeared into the living room, leaving a shaken Reed to sag against the wall, wiping sweat from his brow. His breath came sharply, with a guttural rasp that made him flinch.

What was wrong with him? he wondered, both awe-struck and horrified by the plethora of sensations coursing through his reawakened body. The fact that Kate was a lovely young woman was indisputable; but she was first and foremost a guest in his home. As such, she was entitled to privacy and courteous treatment, neither of which included lustful ogling of her feminine features.

Lust was the operative word here. Reed was disgusted with himself.

Not that he was a saint. Far from it, although the responsibilities of single parenthood had kept him too busy to fret about enforced celibacy. Still, he'd admit that over the past few years he'd occasionally eyed attractive women with a certain amount of sensual longing.

Grown women, not females barely out of their teens.

As for Kate, who couldn't be more than eleven or twelve years older than Shawna, she was clearly too young for the kind of thoughts that had rocketed through Reed's mind.

Or maybe she wasn't too young at all; maybe Reed was just too damn old.

At thirty-five, he'd never considered himself over the hill, although sometimes when the stress got to him and his body creaked like a used car, he'd confess to having felt positively ancient.

But his body wasn't creaking now. It was humming, tingling with a vitality and vigor that he hadn't experienced in a very long time.

Hell of a Christmas present.

"Uh-oh, caramels...they're my very best favorite." Straddling her shiny new sled, Rory dumped the contents of her stocking onto the freshly polished wooden slats to take a closer inventory of her haul. "Two candy canes, a whole bunch of raspberry chewies, an apple and the fattest orange I ever saw in my whole entire life! Wow, I can't believe Santa got so much stuff to fit in there."

"Santa's magic," Shawna said cheerfully. "And the fact that you used a stretchy tube sock didn't hurt, either."

Unwrapping a caramel, Rory popped the sticky square into her mouth, talking between chews. "How come you didn't hang up a sock, Shawna?"

"I'm too big now. If Santa doesn't save his stuff for little kids, there won't be enough to go around."

Reed shifted on the sofa, casually tossing an arm over the back cushions. "I don't think Santa would have minded filling an extra stocking," he said with a smile that Kate found strangely poignant. "In fact, I imagine he was pretty sad when he came and saw that yours was gone this year."

Since the teenager was clearly flustered, Kate interpreted her look of dismay as an indicator of embarrassment at having her father reveal that this was Shawna's first non-Santa Christmas, particularly when the now-mortified girl had gone to such lengths to impress Kate with the depth of her maturity.

It was an embarrassment that Kate, who was sitting crosslegged on the floor, could personally understand and sought to soften by leaning over to whisper in Shawna's ear. "If I'd known how generous Santa was going to be, I'd have hung up a pair of panty hose."

Although Shawna was visibly tickled by the joke, Rory was absolutely intrigued. "Wow," she murmured, her eyes huge. "I bet Santa could fit about a million caramels in there."

Kate sobered instantly. "Now, wait just a darn minute. I don't happen to have any panty hose, but if I did, I guarantee they wouldn't be *that* big. They wouldn't hold more than—" a smile quivered at the corner of her mouth "—a half million, tops."

Rory lit like neon, causing her beleaguered father to snap forward. "Don't get any ideas, punkin. Panty hose aren't allowed."

"How come?"

"Well, ah, because Santa is, um—" Reed coughed, angling a get-me-out-of-this glance at Kate, who responded with a chuckle.

"Don't look at me," she purred.

Heaving a defeated sigh, Reed answered his daughter's question while giving Kate a hard stare. "Because Santa is allergic to nylon, okay?"

"Oh." Rory, although visibly disappointed, accepted the explanation without further comment. Instead, she leapt off her refurbished new sled and rooted around under the tree until she'd located the gift she'd been searching for. She grabbed the tiny box, her face flushed with excitement, and offered it to Shawna. "It's from me," she announced with great pride. "I made it myself."

"Really? Then I know I'm going to love it." Shawna ripped the wrapping paper without ceremony, then emitted a cry of genuine pleasure. She held up the beaded rope on which a carved, wooden pendant was suspended. "It's beautiful, toad. It's the most beautiful thing I've ever seen."

"Do you really like it?" Rory asked, wringing her chubby hands. "'Cause I can make you another one, if you want different colors or something."

"I love the colors. Earth tones go with everything." Shawna hooked an arm around Rory's neck, hauling her over for a series of grateful kisses that left the smaller girl sputtering with feigned indignation.

Kate watched the loving scene, her heart swelling with emotion that was part joy, part envy. Despite the sisters' frequent squabbles, they plainly adored each other, and shared an emotional bond that made Kate ache with a longing she didn't understand and dared not examine too closely. Still she wondered what it must be like to share something so special, and to know that whatever happened, you would always be loved. You would always belong.

It must be the most exquisite feeling in the world. Perhaps someday, she'd experience that feeling for herself, but for now, she felt truly blessed to be able to share these precious moments and bask in the reflected glow of familial love.

Her introspection was interrupted by a joyful shriek when Rory opened her gift from Shawna, who promptly pointed out the richly detailed illustrations in the handsome volume and promised to help her sister with the more difficult words of text.

The girls' excitement was contagious, and for the next hour, Kate was swept into the thrilling world of a Morgan family Christmas. Each gift was inspected with unhurried admiration, complete with appropriate oohs and ahhs from recipients and spectators alike. The girls were delighted by presents from their father—a furry, muted mint sweater and matching skirt for Shawna, a western-style shirt and straw cowboy hat that sent Rory into an enthusiastic frenzy. In turn, Reed seemed genuinely pleased by his new bootjack, which was Shawna's gift to him, and a leather-stamped key ring that Rory had made with her own little hands.

During the flurry of ripping wrapping paper and hastily discarding bows, Kate had glanced up to see Reed watching her with unnerving intensity. There was a quizzical look in his eyes, along with a peculiar sense of surprise, as if he were actually seeing her for the very first time. Kate was as perplexed by his scrutiny as she was by her own reaction to it. Each time their eyes met, a frisson of charged energy skittered down her spine. Her skin warmed. Her mouth went dry. A tight ball of heat formed low in her belly.

Something had changed between her and Reed, something that was obliquely disturbing yet strangely wonderful. Kate couldn't identify what was happening; she knew only that it—whatever it was—had incredible power, a mesmerizing force with the uncanny ability to tantalize and frighten at the same time.

Kate, dizzied by the effort to conceal the mounting tension, was relieved when Shawna offered the perfect diversion.

The bewildered teenager held up a small, perfectly wrapped gift. "This is for you, Rory. It's from Kate."

Rory looked up, her cheeks bulging with caramels. Clearly surprised, she took the present, holding it gently until she'd managed to swallow the candy. "You didn't hafta get us anything," she murmured. "I mean, we know you don't have any money, or credit cards or stuff."

Reed frowned, and seemed ready to scold the girl for her impolite reference to finances when Kate interrupted.

"It's not much," she said, feeling suddenly anxious about the worthiness of her offering. "I hope you can, uh, use it."

Plucking at the bow, Rory took a deep breath, then tore off the paper so quickly that the process was a blur. The child gasped. "Oh!" She raised her stunned gaze toward Kate as if struck mute.

Kate felt as if she'd swallowed a brick. "It's okay if you don't like it. I understand."

"Let me see." Shawna impatiently yanked the crumpled wrapping paper out of her sister's lap, then sat back, stunned. "Why, it's an *obi*."

Rory held up the white satin sash on which Japanese symbols had been delicately embroidered in black and outlined with vivid crimson. "It's the prettiest *obi* in the whole world," Rory murmured. "I never saw one like it before."

"That's because Kate made it," Shawna said, tracing the embroidered symbols with her fingertips. "She made it out of her wedding gown."

Rory spun around as if she'd been shot. "You cut up your pretty dress?"

Decidedly uncomfortable, Kate tried for a casual shrug. "The truth is that I'm not sure if the dress even belonged to me, but considering its current condition, I doubt the owner would want it back. The outer layer of the skirt was fairly well thrashed, but the satin underlayer was in perfect condition. It seemed a shame to let it go to waste. Honestly, I do know that cotton *obi*'s are traditional, but I thought, well, you might have a special tournament or something that, uh…" Kate paused for a breath. "I guess it was a silly idea."

Tears spurted into Rory's eyes. "It's the bestest *obi* I ever had in my whole life," she whispered, wrapping her arms around Kate's neck in a wonderful strangling hug. "I love it, Kate. I really, really love it."

Feeling her own eyes mist up, Kate returned the child's fervent embrace, although acutely aware that Reed was watching with an expression that bordered both disbelief and wonder.

After a long moment, Rory sat back, admiring her gift.

"May I see that?" Reed asked.

Kate's heart nearly stopped as Rory gingerly draped the embroidered *obi* over her father's outstretched hand. Reed studied the satin sash with a precision that made Kate squirm. She wondered if he was annoyed that she hadn't consulted him about the gift. It hadn't occurred to her to do so, but perhaps that had been her failing. The last thing Kate wanted was for Reed to feel left out—

"This is exquisite," he said quietly. "It must have taken hours and hours. No wonder you've been so tired."

She licked her lips. "I guess I should have told you, in case you were planning to give something, ah, similar. I'm so sorry..."

A sudden softness in his eyes took her breath away. "Don't be. I love surprises, too, and this is a wonderful surprise." Returning the *obi* to Rory, Reed smiled with genuine pleasure, regarding Kate as if she were the most precious person on earth.

That peculiar throb started again, emanating from deep inside her belly. She felt dizzy, mesmerized. Reed's gaze enveloped her, entered her, touched her very soul.

Rory's cheery little voice broke into her trance. "What does the funny writing mean?"

When she'd managed to refill her aching lungs, Kate forced herself to focus on the embroidered design. "Those are Ichito symbols. Roughly translated, they mean 'the path of harmony.'"

"So that's why you wanted my karate book?" Rory asked. When Kate nodded, the child heaved a disappointed sigh. "I was hoping you were gonna learn karate so we could, you know, spar together and stuff."

"Spar?" Kate flinched as a vision of purple eyes and broken noses danced through her mind. "Perish the thought. There's no way on earth I would ever be able to, ah, *uchi* anyone."

"It's real easy," Rory assured her. "I could show you how."

"I'm sure you could, but right now—" Kate reached under the tree, retrieving two more packages. "Right now, there are more presents to open.'' She handed one gift to Shawna, whose lovely young face glowed with delight, and one to Reed, who simply stared at it, dumbfounded.

"You didn't have to do this," he said finally.

Despite the fact that her heart was trying to pound its way out of her rib cage, Kate managed a nonchalant shrug. "You didn't have to take a total stranger into your home, either. But you did what you did, so I did what I did and, well, I hope you like it."

Behind her, a series of loud ripping sounds was drowned out by Shawna's squeal. "Oh, Kate! Oh, it's gorgeous. Is it really for me?"

"Of course it is," Kate replied, smiling down at the huge satin hair bow, which was a complex series of fat, lace-trimmed loops studded with seed pearls from the gown's bodice. "I know it's a little dressy for school, but it would be perfect for parties, or even for church. Your hair is so pretty...if you gathered up the crown, like this—" she demonstrated by deftly twisting the girl's sleek blond hair atop her head "—then fastened the bow at the crown, the rest of your hair will cascade out of the satin like strands of polished gold. It would make you look five years older."

At that, Reed's head snapped up, but despite her father's obvious chagrin, the idea of appearing more mature made Shawna's eyes shine like polished lapis. "Five years? Really?"

"I guarantee it." Patting the girl's shoulder, Kate angled an amused grin at Reed, who'd paled three shades at the thought of his little girl growing up before her time. "Aren't you going to open your present?"

"Hmm?" Reed glanced down at the flat package on his lap. "Oh, sure."

Rory flounced to the sofa, dying of curiosity. "What is it, Daddy? What did Kate make for you?"

"I don't know yet," he murmured, slowing his deliberate pace as if enjoying his daughter's torment. "If you don't give me some elbow room, this might take hours, even days.''

Clearly horrified, Rory scooted to the far side of the sofa, then stretched forward, straining to see.

From her vantage point on the floor, Kate crossed her fingers and silently prayed that she hadn't made an error in judgment. In her haste and exuberance, she probably hadn't given enough thought to how her gifts would be received. So far she'd been lucky. The girls had been pleased. But this gift, Reed's gift, had been special to Kate. She'd worked the hardest on it; she'd spent the most time.

Now, as Kate held her breath, it took a small eternity for Reed to unwrap the package. He was one of those people who carefully peeled away each piece of tape and seemed to take great pleasure in removing the wrapping paper intact. Kate couldn't remember if she'd ever known anyone who spent so much time opening a gift; if she had known such people, she certainly must have considered them aggravating.

Eventually Reed accomplished his task by unfolding the entire undamaged sheet of wrapping paper. He stared silently at the contents while Kate clutched her stomach.

Rory knee-hopped across the cushions. "What is it, Daddy?"

"It's a picture frame, I think." When a covert glance at Kate garnered an acquiescent nod, he held up the padded satin frame that had been lovingly trimmed with lace and furled satin roses. "It's beautiful, Kate. Thank you."

Rory, who'd yet to develop the skill of polite evasion, was more direct. "But what's it *for?*"

"I know," Shawna whispered, her voice thready with emotion. "It's for Mama's picture."

Reed's eyes darkened. His gaze slipped from the satin frame to the photograph of his wife. "Is that right, Kate?"

Feeling sick, Kate was certain she'd made a terrible mistake. She'd realized how special the portrait was to Reed, how dear the memories represented there, but it hadn't occurred to her that he might consider her gift intrusive to those memories. She swallowed hard. "It's just a picture frame. You can use it for anything you want."

Shawna wiped her moist eyes. "I knew you were making a surprise for Dad, but I didn't know what it was. I never dreamed it would be a frame for Mama's picture, but it is, isn't it?"

Since a lie on Christmas would be heresy, Kate squared her shoulders and faced Reed's shattered expression. "Yes, it is, but that doesn't mean you can't use it somewhere else. I never meant to upset you. I just... I mean, the original frame is broken, and I thought because the portrait was so special—" With her voice breaking, she ended with a helpless shrug. "I'm sorry."

Reed wasn't looking at Kate. Still cradling the satin frame in hands that seemed too large, too work worn to be handling something so soft and delicate, he bent his head. When he looked up, Kate could have sworn his eyes were redder than they'd been a moment earlier.

"Bonnie loved pretty things," he said quietly. "Nothing would have pleased her more than being remembered by something so exquisite. It was the nicest thing you could have done for her, and for us. I'll cherish this, Kate. We all will."

Kate sat there, stunned. The air was charged, so thick with emotion that it was impossible to breathe. Her lungs ached. Her heart felt swollen and tender.

And just when Kate thought she'd faint from the unbearable tension, Shawna reached out and took the picture off the lamp table. "Can we put the frame on right now, Dad? I really want to see how it looks."

"Yeah!" Rory hollered, climbing down from the sofa. "It's gonna be great."

As Reed issued an affirmative nod, he touched a callused finger to a moistened corner of his eye.

Ten minutes later, the smiling portrait of Bonnie Morgan was nested in a cloud of white satin. After pronouncing the result "perfect," Shawna startled Kate by plopping an oblong gift box in her lap. "Here," she said, grinning smugly. "This is for you."

Astonished, Kate stroked at the metallic silver bow, glancing from Reed to Rory and back again. "For me?"

"Uh-huh." Folding his arms, Reed leaned back, propped his ankle on his knee and grinned like a coyote in a chicken coop. "Well, are you going to worry that bow to death, or are you going to pull it off sometime before New Year's?"

"I...ah..." Kate chewed her lip, completely confused as to what she should do. "It's just that I didn't expect this."

"It's Christmas, Kate," Rory explained in that patronizing tone children love to use on unenlightened adults. "Everybody gets presents on Christmas."

Shawna laid a concerned hand on Kate's shoulder. "You *do* remember how to open presents, don't you? You just gnaw the ribbon off with your teeth, then rip the wrapping paper into Christmas confetti."

Managing a nervous smile, Kate stroked the gift, loath to destroy the beautiful gift wrap. When Shawna issued a pained sigh, Kate finally turned the present over and gently scratched at the tape with her fingernail.

"Oh, no," Rory moaned. "She opens presents just like Dad."

"I don't!" Kate's indignance melted into a sheepish smile. "Then again, maybe I do. I can't really remember."

"Just grab the bow and yank," Shawna suggested.

"It's too pretty."

"For goodness' sake, it's only a five-cent stickum bow. We have tons of them—so many that Gully uses them for toys." Throwing up her hands, Shawna grumbled, "I might as well start breakfast. I could probably bake a half-dozen waffles before Kate makes her way through the dumb ribbon."

Reed merely grinned. "Impatient little devils, aren't they?"

"Should I torture them for a while?" Kate asked Reed, angling an amused glance at Rory's frustrated face.

"Sure, why not? Pain builds character."

"Oh, gracious, I certainly wouldn't want anyone to suffer on my account." Sucking in a deep breath, Kate wiggled her fingers under the taped ribbon and tugged it loose.

A moment later, surrounded by gift wrap that had been shredded in a sudden burst of excited anticipation, Kate was staring at a brand-new pair of white leather athletic shoes.

Shawna leaned anxiously over her shoulder. "Do you like them? Dad wanted to get some ugly clunkers."

"Hey, those were tanned cowhide with durable polyurethane soles. Very practical." Reed's protest was punctuated by an adorable sulk that did peculiar things to the inside of Kate's chest.

Shawna, however, just rolled her eyes. "Men," she whispered.

Suppressing a smile, Kate returned the teenager's just-between-us-womenfolk look with a sage nod, then returned her attention to the snazzy sneakers. "These are perfect. I love them." Her grateful gaze shifted between the girls, then lingered on their father. "Thank you."

His eyes were the color of sun-warmed brandy. "You're welcome, Kate. I just hope you're still thanking me this afternoon."

Rory looked up, her cheeks again bulging with caramels. "Thish affernoon?"

"Yep, this afternoon, when we drive up to Tahoe—" Reed slipped Kate a conspiratorial wink "—to play in the snow."

"*Snow?*" Swallowing so quickly she nearly choked, Rory leapt to her feet. "That means I can try out my new sled!"

Feigning surprise, Reed snapped his fingers. "Why, so it does. Quite a coincidence, hmm?"

Rory didn't bother to answer since she was too busy jumping in place, shrieking wildly and clapping her fat hands. Kate was barely aware of the childish din. Her attention was focused on her wonderful gift. She held the sneakers up, inhaling their pungent leather scent. These shoes weren't borrowed: they actually belonged to her. Not only did they represent the only thing in the world that Kate actually owned, they were in a very real sense the first gift she'd ever received.

Maybe that's why she was crying.

The moon was visible only for a moment, sneaking a luminescent peek before disappearing behind thickening clouds. It would rain tonight, Reed thought. That was okay. The orchard needed rain. Although the cherry trees were denuded and dormant now, it wouldn't be long before tiny swells at the bud joints would form, preparing for the blossoms of spring that would become a fruitful—and hopefully profitable—summer harvest. For that seasonal miracle to occur, the soil had to be damp several feet below the surface, where deep roots could soak up needed nourishment.

So rain was good. Besides providing the earth with sustenance, it made a warm house seem even cozier and more intimate. Behind Reed, the wood stove blazed and the Christmas tree twinkled. For the first time in many years, he felt at peace with his world and with himself. He was content.

Alerted by footsteps, he turned to see Kate emerge from the kitchen carrying two steaming mugs. She crossed the room hesitantly, as if worried about sloshing the hot liquid, then issued a relieved sigh as she handed Reed one of the mugs.

"Hot chocolate," she announced proudly. "I made it myself."

"From those little packets that say 'just add water'?"

She nodded, beaming. "How is it?"

"Well, let me cool it off a minute...." He blew gently into the cup, then took a cautious sip. "Hmm. Very nice. Good job."

Her grateful smile lit up the entire room. "Thanks." She sipped her chocolate, then looked up, surprised and delighted. "Say, it really *is* good!"

"Would I lie?"

"Wait a minute... let's check that nose." She narrowed her gaze, inspecting his face with eyes that twinkled. "Nope, nary a twitch."

"I never should have told you about that. Now every time I open my mouth, you're going to stare at my nose. It's embarrassing."

"I'll try to be discreet," she said, laughing. "It's just that I've never met a human lie detector before, and I'm dying to see just one little quiver. Lie to me."

"No."

"Aw, c'mon. I want to watch it wiggle."

"Oh, for—"

"Please?"

"I do have some pride, you know."

"Spoilsport." She tossed him a cheerful grin, then gazed out the window. "This has been the most wonderful day of my entire life."

"All five days of it?"

"No, I mean all twenty-four years of it."

"But you can only remember the past few days."

"That doesn't matter," she murmured, her eyes soft and wistful. "If I lived a thousand lifetimes, there'd never be a day as magnificent as this one. I don't know how I can ever thank you for making me feel so special."

A discomfiting lump settling behind Reed's larynx. He tried to cough it away. "You are special, Kate. The, ah, girls adore you."

She cocked her head, searching his eyes with a boldness that shocked and unnerved him. After a long moment, she smiled. "I adore them, too. They're such wonderful children. You must be so proud."

"I am." He turned away, strangely shaken by the intimacy he felt toward her. There was something about Kate that drew him in, made him want things. Not just physical things. Emotional things. Spiritual things.

That scared him, because he knew that Kate wasn't what she seemed.

His fear wasn't generated by anything he'd learned from the sheriff's department, which was very little at best. Deputy Matthews had called yesterday to report that Kate's fingerprints hadn't popped out of any computer, which only implied that she'd never been arrested or served in the military or held a security level job. It also meant that she hadn't been incarcerated in a mental institution, an unpleasant possibility that Reed had been relieved to discard.

He'd also learned that no missing person reports had been filed on anyone matching Kate's description. Reed thought that strange, but the deputy had posed several logical scenarios, including the possibility that Kate either had no family or had limited contact with them, and a suggestion that her disappearance might not have caused alarm if her absence had been scheduled—a business trip, perhaps, or a vacation.

Or even a job modeling wedding gowns.

In a nutshell, the emotional crux of Reed's dilemma was that Kate couldn't be what she seemed because for all intents and purposes, she simply didn't exist. At any moment this beautiful young woman who'd fallen from the sky to enhance and enrich their lives could suddenly remember who she was and where she belonged. When that happened, when Kate returned to her world, Reed knew that his own world and that of his children would be a little dimmer.

And that's what frightened him.

Chapter Six

Stepping up to the lower slat of the equine pasture fence, Kate held out a carrot, cooing softly to the chestnut mare. "Come on, Molly. I know you want it."

The animal snuffled softly, scraping the cropped grass with a hoof. Clearly the older horse was reluctant to take food from a stranger, but the young Appaloosa had no such problem. The muscles of his majestic neck rippled with enthusiasm as the blotchy black-and-white gelding, to whom Rory had given the unimaginative name Spot, eyed the juicy treat. Kate held the carrot up, giving it a tantalizing wiggle that proved too much temptation for a hungry horse to ignore.

With a here-I-come whinny, Spot galloped from his grazing place across the pasture and made a beeline for the carrot, snatching it from Kate's hand while still on the run. She laughed out loud, then pulled a second carrot from the pocket of the oversize denim jacket Reed had loaned her.

"Let that be a lesson to you," she told the recalcitrant mare. "She who hesitates misses all the fun."

This time, Molly took the caution seriously and trotted over, head high, ears perked. The mare slowed at the fence, her regal gaze moving from the coveted carrot to the untrustworthy soul who was holding it. "It's all right, Molly," Kate murmured when the animal's nostrils flared slightly. "I know you're not too sure about me right now, but I just want to be your friend. A girl can't have too many friends, right?"

Apparently not, because Molly gave the horsey equivalent of a shrug, then stretched out her neck and delicately removed the carrot from Kate's hand. The fact that the mare had deliberately maintained sufficient distance to avoid being stroked didn't escape Kate's attention.

Brushing her hands together to signal that the goodies were gone, Kate stepped down from the fence. "Don't worry, pretty lady. I won't touch until you say it's okay."

With an amiable snort, Molly backed away, bobbing her head. A moment later, after the mare had resumed her grazing duties, Kate wandered around the stable toward the cattle pasture, which was considerably larger than the area in which the horses were confined. Shading her eyes, she counted about two dozen head of cattle scattered throughout the larger pasture.

A few of them glanced in her direction, as if sizing up her intentions. Three of the animals, including the little red bull, apparently decided that she was standing close enough to the alfalfa bin to bear closer scrutiny. The two largest animals, a couple of blocky, coal black females, ambled over, eyeing her placidly. Fagan, however, pranced, danced, zigzagged, hopped and bounced in a bovine version of Rory's hyperactive exuberance.

As he skittered closer to the fence, Kate was amazed to note that the animal's red coat, which from a distance appeared sleek and close to its body, was actually a woolly swirl of thick, coarse hair. Tufts of the stuff tweaked around a face that was absolutely adorable, with a huge moist nose and massive brown eyes sparkling with mischievous intelligence.

Now Kate was hardly an authority on cows—she wasn't even sure if a heifer was male or female—but at that moment she was absolutely certain that this bright-eyed little fellow must be the cutest, most cuddly bull on the planet. No wonder Reed was nuts about him.

"You really are the sweetest thing," Kate told the curious animal as she reached into the alfalfa bin, which resembled a large trash Dumpster with a hinged cover. "Any woman on earth would kill for those eyelashes. But then, I bet you hear that all the time, don't you?"

Fagan didn't bother to reply. He did, however, quiver with excitement when she retrieved a flat chip of dried green alfalfa from the bin. He bounded to the fence and was immediately crowded out by the two larger animals, both of which had moved with surprising speed the moment Kate stuck her hand into the alfalfa.

"By the way, I love your ear tag," Kate commented genially to little Fagan. "Scarlet is definitely your color. And it's so practical, too. If identification tags were an acceptable human fashion, I wouldn't have had to draw my name out of a hat. Oh my, aren't we the hungry ones?"

Emulating what she'd seen Reed and Rory doing the day she'd watched them from the front window, Kate tossed torn hunks of alfalfa over the fence, laughing as three happy heads dipped down to dine. Her laughter died, however, when a din of excited moo's drew her attention, and she realized that the entire herd was now stampeding toward her.

She backed away, horrified as two dozen head of bellowing determination converged on the few remaining hay strands. Little Fagan was instantly surrounded by the larger animals and disappeared from view.

"Oh, Lord," she muttered, terrified that Reed's prized baby bull would be trampled. Spinning around, she shoved both hands into the alfalfa bin, yanked out as much as she could carry and ran down the fence line, flinging hay and hollering, "Here cows, here cows!"

It worked. The hungry cattle followed the baited fence line. Fagan, perky and oblivious, emerged unscathed to dart between his herdmates in search of a second helping.

Kate steadied herself on the bin, certain she was flirting with cardiac arrest. It took several minutes for her heart to resume a normal rhythm. By then the cattle had finished off the alfalfa and were ambling back across the pasture as if scaring weak-kneed humans into near-death experience were a daily occurrence.

Meanwhile, they'd offered a valuable lesson about acting on instinct without considering potential consequences. Kate had no knowledge of bovine behavior; therefore, she'd had no business interacting with the animals without Reed's permission. He'd be furious when he learned what she'd done. And she'd have to tell him. Her conscience would insist.

She hoped that a verbal description of the incident would be less upsetting than having actually witnessed it. Fortunately for her, Reed was working in the orchard on the other side of the ranch, and the girls were preoccupied in the house. Shawna was hard at work on her mother's sampler, and Rory was ostensibly working on her homework.

In fact, everyone was hard at work. Everyone except Kate.

That bothered her immensely. She simply couldn't go on living in the Morgans' home, eating their food, accepting their gifts without giving something in return. Certainly she'd done a few small chores, but nothing that could honestly be considered a meaningful contribution to the household.

She knew that the family needed money. Not that Reed had said anything, but there were subtle signs that the Morgans were not particularly wealthy. The furniture, for example. Although clean and well tended, the upholstered pieces were saggy and frayed with age, and the occasional tables could only be described as early yard sale. Other indicators included fading clapboards on the house and stable, both of which could use a fresh coat of paint, and the fact that the mechanical workhorse of the ranch, Reed's old pickup truck, had racked up enough miles to bridge the distance between earth and the moon.

If Kate could only get a job, she could pay for her room and board, which would doubtless be a tremendous help to Reed. The problem was that legitimate jobs required legal identification.

The key words, however, were *legitimate* and *legal*. The alternatives might be unpleasant, even distasteful. Considering her current circumstances, Kate knew that she might not have a choice.

After spending the rest of the morning studying a scant column of Help Wanted ads in the tiny local paper, Kate was feeling even more depressed and frustrated. Even if she managed to bluff her way past the identification dilemma, all of the listed jobs required experience.

She could lie, of course; it wasn't Kate who was cursed by a built-in truth-twitcher. She did, however, have a rational mind that repeatedly questioned how she or anyone else could possibly finesse a job requiring specific skills.

Then again, maybe she *did* have a skill and simply couldn't remember what it was. Perhaps if she sat down at a typewriter, her fingers would suddenly fly over the keys. Perhaps one glance at a blinking monitor would remind her that she was a crackerjack computer programmer.

And perhaps the odor of airplane exhaust would make her sprout wings and fly.

Disgusted, Kate roughly refolded the newspaper, tossing it onto the kitchen table as she headed out the back door. At the moment, she felt like a fish flopping on the edge of a pier. The water of life was all around her. She could feel it, she could smell it. But no matter how desperately she tried, she couldn't seem to reach it, and knew that she'd die trying.

An unpleasant thought. Kate pushed it away, deciding that there simply had to be something she could do, something that would make her believe that her actual existence mattered. Consuming the kindness of others without a reciprocal contribution made her feel like a societal parasite, shallow and useless.

Jamming her hands into the pockets of her jeans, she wandered across the damp ground, shivering. She'd forgotten to wear a jacket, but no matter. A few slaps of cold air might knock the fog out of her brain to make room for some helpful ideas. Assuming, of course, that she was even capable of original thought, which at times like this, she seriously doubted.

As Kate crossed the yard, she heard soft murmurings coming from behind the barn. Following the mumbled sounds, she stepped around an untidy stack of used lumber, avoided a couple of rusty farm implements and emerged into a cleared area that had been carpeted with thin, vinyl-covered gymnastic mats.

In the center of the workout area, Rory was performing what appeared to be a ballet of synchronized karate moves. The child's expression was fixed, her eyes focused, her physical movements surprisingly precise. The effect was startling, since Kate hadn't believed Rory capable of such rapt concentration.

She watched in utter fascination until Rory clasped her hands together and issued a reverent bow, murmuring, *"Sensei-ni-rei."*

Not wanting to distract the child, Kate waited until Rory's stocky little body had softened in a relaxed pose. Then she cleared her throat. "That was lovely."

The girl spun around, clearly surprised to have an audience but not seeming particularly displeased. "Hi, Kate! I'm learning *kata*s. They're lots of fun."

"*Kata*s?" Kate frowned. "Are those anything like *uchi*s?"

Rory giggled. "No, silly. *Uchi*s are, um, you know, kinda like whacking stuff, like *haishu-uchi*—" she demonstrated a backhand strike "—and *teisho-uchi*." The heel of her palm swished outward, then she straightened and shrugged. "There's a whole bunch of 'em."

"Ah, yes." Kate vaguely recalled a lengthy glossary of terms from having perused the child's karate book. "And if I remember correctly, there are also dozens of stances, blocking techniques, kicks, thrusts, and so on, right?"

Rory beamed. "Right!"

"But I don't recall what a *kata* is."

"Oh, it's lotsa moves all put together. *Sensei* says it means to unite focus, flow and harmony, but it's really just kind of a dance. You wanna see me do one?"

"I sure do."

Flashing a proud grin, Rory hopped to the center of the mat and was instantly transformed. Her expression mellowed into one of solemn contemplation as she shifted her weight to the balls of her feet. Filling her lungs, she closed her eyes and was motionless for several seconds before exhaling.

Then she raised her right arm, simultaneously stepping forward, knees bent, head high. She murmured something in Japanese, then spun left into a cat stance, crossing her forearms in front of her face. Emitting another soft whisper, the child pivoted on one foot, striking out with her left palm, then performing a series of lightning-fast air punches. Spinning again, she gracefully lifted a leg, holding the pose for several seconds before snapping a complex sequence of side thrusts and back kicks.

When the routine had been completed, Rory pressed her palms to her chest, ending with the traditional bow. She looked up anxiously. "Whadaya think?"

"Oh, sweetie." Kate moistened her lips, completely blown away by the extraordinary performance. "It was breathtaking, Rory, so elegant and graceful. Why, it must have taken weeks for you to memorize all those complicated moves."

"Nah, I just started this morning."

"This morning?" Kate waved that away as impossible. "I don't believe it."

"It's not hard," Rory insisted. "I already know all the moves and stuff, so it's real easy to just put a bunch of 'em together."

Kate considered that for a moment. "So, if I were to name, say, five or six karate moves, how long would it take you to memorize them for a *kata?*"

She shrugged. "Heck, I only hafta do it once. *Kata*s are easy to remember 'cause they're real fun to do." Rory turned toward the corner of the barn, listening to the drone of a truck engine. "Dad's back," she announced unnecessarily.

Those two little words sent a nervous shiver down Kate's spine and wiped every other thought out of her mind. She swallowed hard, realizing that the time had come to bite the bullet and confess what she'd almost done to poor little Fagan. The mere thought of how Reed would react to stupidity that could have turned his beloved baby bull into flattened flank steak made her blood run cold.

"Are you okay?" Rory asked. "You look kinda sick."

Kate forced a thin smile. "I'm fine, sweetie, but I do have to talk with your daddy. You keep practicing and I'll be back in a few minutes, okay?"

"Okay." With that, Rory pirouetted back to the center of the mat.

While the exuberant child launched into a renewed series of fluid kicks, thrusts and strikes, Kate trudged back to the house, mentally rehearsing what she would say. Tiptoeing through the back door, she still hadn't decided on a reasonable explanation for her thoughtless stupidity, although the sound of Reed's voice filtering from the living room promised at least a short reprieve.

A peek through the doorway confirmed what she'd suspected. He was on the telephone.

Sighing, she sat at the kitchen table, absently fondling a small plastic tote of cleaning supplies that was usually kept on top of the washing machine. A sloshing vibration from behind the laundry room's louvered doors indicated that said machine was in use, which was probably why the supplies had been unceremoniously moved to the table.

Searching for distraction, Kate eyed the unfamiliar cleanser cans and plastic spray bottles, wondering why any one house would need so many different products. She forced herself to focus on the labels, a blue one that said glass cleaner, a yellow one for furniture polish, a green one that apparently was to clean ovens, and a white one that claimed to be an all-purpose cleaner—so why would anyone need blue and yellow and green bottles when the white bottle was supposed to clean everything? Housework was hardly rocket science. It didn't take a genius to figure out that when you saw dirt, you wiped it up. Anyone could do it, for goodness' sake. Even Kate.

Which is why the snatches of conversation emanating from the living room suddenly caught her attention. She sidled across the room to lurk beside the open door.

"Morning is flexible," Reed was saying. "But the hours between two and six are firm. It's critical that someone be here when the girls get home from school." He shifted forward on the sofa, holding up a sheet of paper. "Yes, references are important. I'll check them myself...excuse me? Ah, well, that's an exaggeration. It's true that Rory's an enthusiastic child, but I don't believe she actually put a frog in the last housekeeper's purse."

The poor man looked like he'd rather have hot needles shoved under his toenails than continue the conversation. Kate leaned forward, straining to hear.

"No, I'm not calling the woman a liar," Reed mumbled. "It's just that there was, ah, a slight misunderstanding. From what I was told, the frog in question was actually in the silverware drawer when it took an unfortunate leap—I'm sorry?" He massaged his eyelids, nodding. "Of course, you're quite right. It won't happen again. You have my word. Uh-huh. Right. Just light housekeeping, washing dishes, dusting, that kind of thing."

Kate went rigid. Her gaze landed on the tote of cleaning supplies. Before she had a chance to think twice, she'd snatched it up and hustled into the living room.

Flashing Reed a cheery grin, she snatched a cloth out of the tote and proceeded to dust the coffee table with such lusty enthusiasm that a thin cloud of translucent particles rose up to dance in a shaft of sprayed sunlight.

The receiver slipped away from Reed's ear as he sat forward, staring, with his chin slightly ajar. "Hmm?" He forced his attention back to the anonymous voice on the telephone, which Kate presumed to be a representative of the domestic service agency. "Sorry, I was, ah, distracted. Yes, of course. Let's see now, some of the other duties would include laundry, sweeping up, and mopping occasionally."

Kate dropped the dust rag, shot into the kitchen and returned with a broom, which she swished back and forth without paying particular attention to the fact that the dirt was simply being shifted from one area of the hardwood floor to another. A covertly angled glance confirmed that

Reed was indeed watching, albeit with the morbid fascination displayed by onlookers at a car wreck.

Humming softly, Kate and the broom swayed around the room in a fervent imitation of happy housewives on the television commercials. It wasn't exactly subtle, but there was little time to be coy.

Reed needed a housekeeper. Kate needed a job.

She swirled around the living room, alternately sweeping and swaying, then shifted a measuring gaze toward Reed, whose eyes still held a baffled and somewhat blank expression. Clearly, more overt persuasion was required.

Frowning, Reed cleared his throat, turning away to eliminate Kate from his line of sight. "No," he said into the phone. "The position doesn't require preparing the evening meal, although I'll expect the girls to have a nutritious lunch."

Kate straightened, squeezing the broom handle so tightly that her knuckles went white.

"Nothing fancy," Reed was saying. "A ham sandwich would be fine."

Spinning around, Kate dashed to the kitchen. She tossed the broom into a corner, snatched the plate of leftover ham out of the fridge, grabbed a loaf of bread and in less than fifteen seconds, charged out with a raggedy sandwich propped on a paper plate.

She'd barely cleared the doorway when she heard Reed say, "...with a couple scoops of potato salad. Carbohydrates build muscle."

Hanging a U-turn, she headed back to the kitchen, spooned a huge helping of lumpy salad onto the plate, kicked the fridge door shut, then skidded back into the living room to plop the heaped plate on the coffee table.

Reed, whose back was turned, didn't even seem to notice. "Yeah," he said into the receiver, "that would be great. Oh, and the girls like cookies for dessert."

Stifling a sigh, Kate hustled away, returning a moment later to dump a handful of chocolate chip cookies on the plate.

"And a beer."

Kate spun back toward the kitchen, took two steps then went rigid. *A beer?*

She glanced over her shoulder. Although ostensibly still on the telephone, Reed had retrieved the sandwich and was wolfing it down. It was at that salient moment Kate realized that since the girls would be at school during the noon hour, there would certainly be no need for a housekeeper to prepare their lunch.

Eyes narrowed, Kate marched over, yanked the receiver out of Reed's hand and held it to her own ear. As expected, she heard nothing but a dial tone.

Reed offered an innocent smile. "Could you bring a fork back with the beer? I hate to eat potato salad with my fingers."

Forcefully cradling the receiver, Kate fixed him with a narrowed stare. "I hope you enjoyed watching me make a fool out of myself."

"As a matter of fact, I did." He shifted the sandwich to his left hand so he could reach for a cookie. "It was great fun. I never realized you were so versatile."

"Yes, well, I'm glad you were amused." Face flaming, Kate squared her shoulders. Hoping he wouldn't notice that she was humiliated to the core, she attempted a nonchalant yet hasty retreat.

"By the way," Reed murmured. "You've got the job."

Kate jerked to a stop, looking over her shoulder as she struggled to suppress a gleeful giggle. "You won't be sorry."

He heaved a sigh, frowning at the dry, half-eaten sandwich. "I think I already am."

Chapter Seven

Reed went to work the next day, which was Friday, and planned to work Saturday, as well. He needed the money. Last year's cherry crop had been a poor one. Unseasonably late rain had swollen the ripening fruit, splitting the fragile skins and causing nearly a quarter of the crop to rot before harvest. If the orchard didn't come through this year, Morgan Ranch would be in serious trouble.

But that was a concern for later. At the moment, Reed's main worry was his houseguest-turned-housekeeper.

Despite her comical effort to prove otherwise, Kate didn't seem to be particularly familiar with the basics of running a household. Reed had caught her eyeing the vacuum cleaner as if she'd never seen one before. Although he'd been amused by her excitement when he'd finally showed her how to switch the darn thing on, he still felt a bit queasy about turning her loose on his unsuspecting home.

On the other hand, school wouldn't start until Monday, so Shawna would still be close by if there were problems.

Next week, however, Kate would be on her own. Then what?

"Mister, I ain't got all day."

"Hmm?" Blinking, Reed focused on the annoyed customer, who immediately tossed a loading slip and a credit card onto the counter. "Oh. Sure." He managed a thin smile, then rang up the sale.

Throughout the day, however, Reed's mind continued to wander at the least appropriate times. While loading hay into a customer's pickup, he'd found himself daydreaming about Kate's vibrant laugh as they'd romped through the Tahoe snow on Christmas afternoon. Then while ringing up an order, he'd suddenly spaced out, staring into thin air to mentally replay the vision of Kate standing in the darkened hallway wearing a clingy sleep shirt that showed off every luscious curve of her lithe young body. He'd only snapped out of his reverie when the stunned customer, convinced that Reed was having a seizure, had started hollering for help.

Eventually, however, the interminable workday finally ended and Reed anxiously headed home to assess the damage. With his foot relentlessly pressed to the accelerator, he whizzed past the orchard without indulging his usual habit of slowing to scrutinize the proud rows of now-bare trees that were the lifeblood of his land. Instead, he sped straight to the house, leapt out of the truck before the engine had stopped vibrating and hurdled over the back porch rail as if seeking Olympic gold.

Bursting into the kitchen, Reed half expected to find charred walls or other such catastrophic remnants. Instead, he found a meat loaf cooling on the stove.

Soft voices from the living room caught his attention, primarily because he realized that sound was not coming from the television. A glance through the doorway confirmed that the TV wasn't even on. That alone was a startling development, but the remainder of the scene was downright astounding.

Rory, dressed in her usual denim overalls, was standing in the middle of the room while Shawna sat cross-legged on the floor in front of Kate, who was perched on the edge of the sofa fiddling with the teenager's hair. Kate, with her fingers still buried in Shawna's blond tresses, glanced down at what appeared to be a sheet of paper on her lap.

"Skill," she announced, for no apparent reason.

Amazingly enough, Rory sprang to life. *"S!"* she proclaimed loudly, and to Reed's utter astonishment, swung her leg out in a side-snap kick. *"K!"* Her stiffened palm swished downward in a knife-hand strike. *"I—"* inverted fist strike *"—L-L!"* She performed two quick leg sweeps, then pressed her palms together and bowed, looked flushed and proud. "Skill."

Shawna applauded. "Way to go, toad."

"Good job," Kate agreed. "The next word is *horse.*"

"H-O—" Assuming a half-moon stance, Rory's arm shot around in an outside block. *"R-S-E!"* A quick reverse punch was followed by a side-snap kick and an elbow strike. "Horse," she murmured, bowing.

As Rory looked up, grinning, she spotted Reed. "Daddy, Daddy, wanna see my spelling *katas*?"

Shawna and Kate turned simultaneously. "Hi, Dad. You're home early."

"Uh, yeah, a little, I guess." Scratching his chin, Reed ambled into the living room, inspecting the homey scene for clues to the hidden catastrophe he was certain to find. After all, every one of their housekeepers had been deluged by disaster, and although it was clear that the girls liked Kate as a guest, Reed assumed that once she'd become an authority figure, she too would be considered part of the enemy camp.

His practiced gaze swept over the room, which was relatively neat despite a peculiar cloudy film dulling the wood furniture and a series of gummy smears distorting the view out the front windows. It looked like some kind of harsh detergent had been used to wipe down the entire room, from wood surfaces to glass. Even the black metal wood stove was blotched by ugly gray smudges.

"So, what's going on?" Reed asked in a voice that came out sounding more suspicious than pleasant.

"Kate's fixing my hair," Shawna announced, laying a hand mirror down on the coffee table, then tilting her head to display that half of her hair had been combed back from her face and twisted into a braided coil affixed to the top of her scalp. "It looks really neat, huh?"

Reed managed an agreeable nod before Rory leapt forward to snag his arm. "Stand here, Daddy, so you can see better." With that, the child backed into the center of the room, took a deep, cleansing breath and assumed a ready stance.

Kate shifted uncomfortably, angling a quizzical glance at Reed, who realized that an acute case of parental paranoia probably made him look like he'd been sucking lemons. Before he could rearrange his features into a more casual expression, Kate had turned her attention to the list on her lap.

"The word is *daily*," she said.

"*D-A-I!*" Rory shouted, performing a downward block, augmented forearm block, inverted fist strike. "*L-Y!*" A perfectly executed leg lift was followed by a *yoko* thrust-kick, and traditional bow. "Daily." She peeked up from beneath stubby dark lashes, fairly beaming with pride. "I know how to spell every word on my list now. That's pretty good, huh, Daddy?"

"Better than that, punkin. It's wonderful." From the corner of his eye, Reed saw Kate relax visibly. He cocked his head, regarding her thoughtfully. "This was your idea?"

Her pink tongue darted out to moisten her lips. "Well, ah, actually, we simply assigned one letter of the alphabet to each karate move and, um—"

Rory interrupted. "Kate said making *kata*s out of my spelling words would help me concentrate, and it worked, Daddy, it really, really worked!"

"I can see that." The smile tugging at his mouth finally broke free. "A stroke of genius, I'd say, although I wonder what your teacher will think during your next spelling test."

Kate's face was as red as Fagan's. "Rory knows that she can't actually perform the *kata*s in class."

"Pity," Reed murmured, grinning broadly. "It would certainly liven things up."

Puffing her cheeks, Kate blew out a breath and patted Shawna's shoulder. "We'd better get dinner on the table. Your father's probably starving."

To Reed's surprise, the teenager responded with an affable "Okay," then hopped to her feet, flipping her sleek tresses with her hand. "I love my hair this way, Kate. Will you teach me how to do it myself?"

"Sure, it's easy. You just have to remember not to pull the crown too tight, or you'll look like you've been scalped." Kate tossed a slender arm around the teenager's shoulders, and they headed toward the kitchen, engrossed in the casual chatter of lifelong chums.

Rory followed, half skipping, half running. "Can I set the table? Please, Kate, please?"

A moment later, the kitchen was filled with happy conversation. In the living room, Reed sat heavily in his arm chair, baffled, bemused and completely bewildered. Somehow, Kate had managed to connect with both of his daughters in a way he hadn't seen since their mother had died. Besides taking Shawna under her wing to turn the sullen, depressed adolescent into a cheerful, happy young girl, Kate had brilliantly channeled Rory's hyperactivity into positive focus.

Reed was as amazed by the girls' transformation as he was by the changes deep in his own soul. Kate had brought an aura of freshness to the house, a sense of wonder that made

Reed see everyday events through new eyes. She made him laugh. She gave him hope.

And with that hope came fear. Kate had made a palpable difference in their lives, yet someday she would leave them. What would happen then? he wondered. Would his emotionally scarred children be able to cope with another painful abandonment?

Would he?

"Great meat loaf," Reed said, laying his fork aside. "And to think I was worried about being forced to survive on a diet of dry sandwiches and tap water."

Slipping a nervous glance at Shawna, Kate fidgeted with her napkin. "I wish I could take the credit, but all I did was wrap a few potatoes in aluminum foil and toss them into the oven. Shawna made the meat loaf."

"You helped," Shawna replied cheerfully. "Besides, I saw you studying Mama's old cookbooks. Why, you'll be whipping up gourmet meals in no time flat."

Chewing madly, Rory washed down her final bite with a gulp of milk, then wiped her mouth with the back of her hand. "Yeah, and besides, there's lotsa stuff Kate's really good at, like, um ..."

Kate issued a morose sigh. "Like turning plain white underwear into chic pastels."

A covert glance across the table confirmed that Reed, who'd been reaching for his own glass, was frozen in place with his hand in midair.

She averted her gaze. "I, ah, didn't realize that a purple cheerleading outfit should be washed by itself."

Cringing as Reed's eyes widened with disbelief, Kate was struggling to explain when Shawna, bless her, tried to soften the blow. "Now, Dad, it's not like anyone's ever going to see your shorts, is it? I mean, who'll ever know? And lavender T-shirts are really hot this year—"

"Lavender?" Reed pushed back from the table, looking as if he were about to choke. "You're kidding, right? Please tell me you're kidding."

"I'm so sorry," Kate said miserably. "First, I nearly get poor Fagan squashed and now this. Naturally, you can deduct the cost of replacements from my pay."

Clearing his throat, Reed made a production of laying his folded napkin on the table. "Don't worry about it, Kate. It's no big deal." A stunned expression indicated that he was not particularly thrilled by the thought of wearing lavender undergarments, but to his credit, he managed a thready smile. "As for the unfortunate incident with Fagan, I've already explained that a five-hundred pound youngster isn't likely to let himself be trampled, but it's always a good idea to spread the hay out a bit, and give everyone a little breathing room."

"Understood," Kate murmured, wincing at the subtle ache that was spreading across her forehead.

Beside her, Rory pointed to the teaspoon Kate had placed over each dinner plate, precisely horizontal with the table edge with the bowl portion of each utensil pointing to the right of every setting. "What's this for?"

"Hmm? Oh, it's a dessert spoon."

"Really? Wow, that's so cool. So, what are we having for dessert?"

"Having?" With a confused frown, Kate massaged her throbbing temples. She felt dizzy and oddly nauseous. "I, ah, I don't really know."

"We could make pudding," Shawna suggested.

Kate skimmed her a wary glance. "Does it come in a box?"

"Yep, with instructions and everything."

"In that case, I'll make pudding..." A sharp pain stabbed through the top of her skull. Gasping, Kate stared down at the table, astonished as she watched the Morgan's stainless flatware evolve into sterling silver while the serviceable stoneware suddenly metamorphosized into glistening, gold gilded china.

Completely disorientated, Kate vaguely realized that her mind had transported her to another time, another place. It was a richly detailed place, opulent, extravagant, yet Kate didn't like it. She was frightened by it, and by the unnerving sensation that she'd somehow shrunk, because her shoulders barely rose above the edge of the mammoth dining table at which she was sitting.

The table, sheathed by fine linen and adorned with a fancy porcelain centerpiece of fresh flowers, was elaborately set with exquisite china, gleaming silver and cut crystal. Everything was perfect, down to the measured placement of each salad fork, and the sparkling dessert spoon arranged horizontally above each gilded plate.

A voice emanated from the end of the table. It was a shrill voice. Angry. Critical.

"She eats like a peasant, George."

Kate stared down at the plate, on which a small portion of unidentifiably creamed seafood had been placed. A liqueur smell wafted up from the sauce. It made her ill, but she knew that she dared not look up, dared not allow her gaze to fall on the source of that frightening voice.

"Her manners are positively disgusting."

"Sylvia, please. She's just a child."

"She's old enough to learn proper etiquette," came the sharp reply. "You know how much next week's dinner party means to me. I won't be humiliated in front of my friends."

Kate desperately wanted the man to say something, to defend her from the faceless shrew at the end of the table. In the thick silence that followed, Kate realized that she'd been emotionally abandoned. Again.

"Now we'll try it once more," the woman said harshly. "Lift the napkin thusly, and place it delicately across your lap. No, no! Not like that. Didn't your mother teach you any manners? Honestly, George, she can't do anything right. She's hopeless, absolutely hopeless . . .''

Hopeless.

"Kate?"

Hopeless.

"Is something wrong?"

Kate blinked, still staring at the table where the fancy china had thankfully materialized back into sturdy stoneware. She glanced up, still confused by the residual throbbing in her head. "I'm sorry . . . were you speaking to me?"

Reed's eyes reflected his concern. "Are you all right?"

"Yes, of course," she lied. "I was just a bit distracted, that's all." Gritting her teeth against the abominable headache, she forced a smile. "Now, what were you saying?"

"The girls were just reminiscing a bit," he said cautiously.

Rory was less discreet. "Mommy used to make pudding all the time," she chirped. "Having you here is almost the same as having Mommy back again."

Kate's head felt as if it were going to explode. Before she could stop herself, she'd pushed away from the table and leapt to her feet. "No, it isn't. It can't be the same, because mothers are sacred. They can't be replaced, and they can never be forgotten. Never."

With three horrified faces staring up at her, Kate emitted a hoarse gasp, then spun around, dashed into her room and fell across her bed, sobbing.

There was a soft knock at her door. "Kate, may I come in?"

Since her breath still randomly ripped her lungs with uncontrollable bursts, all Kate managed to do was sit up and grab a tissue before the door crept open.

Reed peeked warily inside. "Are you all right?"

She blew her nose, then nodded. "Sorry . . . don't know what came . . . over me."

Struggling to inhale, she used a fresh tissue to wipe her eyes as Reed entered the room, closing the door behind him. He regarded her for a long moment before speaking. "You've remembered something, haven't you?"

"No." She looked away to hide the guilt in her eyes. "I mean, not really."

Reed hesitantly sat beside her. "Would you like to tell me about it?"

Chewing her lower lip, Kate tossed the tissues into a trash can. "I don't think I can, because I'm not sure I understand it myself."

Reed just sat there, strong, silent, comforting her with his presence.

She sighed. "It's all so strange. Suddenly, I felt like a child. It was so—" she hiccuped "—so real. I remember feeling sick inside, and so empty that it hurt. I wanted to cry, but knew that it wouldn't be acceptable. It's just that I was so lonely, you see. I missed her so much."

Reaching over, Reed pressed Kate's hand between his own warm palms. "Who was it that you missed, Kate?"

A fresh round of tears spurted into her eyes. "My mother," she whispered. "Oh, Reed, don't you see? That's why I feel such an emotional bond with Shawna and Rory, and why I instinctively understand everything that they've gone through. My mother died, too, Reed, when I was very, very young. And after that, I felt as if there was nobody left to love me."

"Oh, honey." Reed gathered her in his arms, tightening his embrace as she melted against him, absorbing his warmth, his strength. "We all love you," he whispered, his breath soft against her temple. "You're not alone anymore."

Kate pressed her cheek in the curve of his throat, slipping her arms around him until she felt his firm back muscles ripple beneath her palms. The empty chill in her belly was instantly filled by liquid warmth, a soothing sense of well-being that calmed her to the marrow. She felt safe, protected. And she felt loved.

Gratitude swelled into something more, something deep and profoundly compelling. Kate turned her head, moving slightly away so she could see his face, study the magnificent planes of jutting cheekbones, and the fathomless depth of his eyes, eyes that were dark as the earth and ringed by flecks of iridescent gold. To her surprise, a slender hand was pressed against his shadowed cheek; then she felt the rasp of whiskered skin against her palm and realized that the hand belonged to her.

A flush of warmth brushed her brow, where the roughened pad of his thumb was stroking her. She closed her eyes for a moment, thrilled by the gentleness of his touch, and by the swirling warmth it created within her. When she looked up again, something cracked inside her chest. He was so pure, so beautiful, a suntanned masterpiece with golden eyes and sun-streaked hair.

Her fingertips caressed his tawny brows, his strong cheekbones, then moved down to trace the square line of his jaw and test the softness of his sculpted mouth.

"Kate..." The hoarse whisper was cut off with a shudder as Reed gently grasped her wrist, moving her hand away. He closed his eyes, shivering again, then brushed his lips across her palm. "So soft," he murmured. "Your skin is so delicate, so sweet."

When he kissed the quivering pulse on her wrist, Kate whimpered. Reed instantly drew away, forcing her to stop him by framing his face with her hands. "No... please, don't leave me."

"I won't leave you, Kate. I won't ever leave you."

The kiss came suddenly, with an explosive power that shook Kate to the soles of her feet. His lips were moist and tender yet demanding, insistent. Erotic.

With his fingers tangled in her hair, Reed deepened the kiss with a fiery passion that was almost frightening. They

Hurry!

...This (
Play yo oo!
TODAY! on the
en and
GAME"
FALL!"
rcles to
AR...it's
!
Game,
hances
CK OF

FREE
e Moon
quares.
gift that

to buy
e book
pment.
rchases
eceiving
ward to
y arrive

ing any
ut why
tled to!

ZODIAC
CHART GAME

PLACE
YOUR
ZODIAC
SIGN
HERE

Before you continue ... be sure
that your Zodiac Sign is in
alignment with your potential
**"$1,000,000.00 ALL-CASH
WINDFALL!"** — and we'll
assign you three Unique
Sweepstakes numbers. These
numbers could be your
luckiest numbers ever!

NOW, cross your fingers...
grab a lucky coin and scratch off all
3 silver circles below!

Revealing all three dollar signs qualifies you for a
chance to win the $1,000,000.00 Grand Prize or
any one of our other big cash prizes!

**LUCKY
STAR GAME**
Win $50,000 in
EXTRA BONUS MONEY!

Scratch off and
reveal the cash
amount of $50,000
and you are
definitely in — you
qualify for a chance
to WIN the EXTRA
BONUS PRIZE!
GOOD LUCK!

S
return
approx-
receive
ou six
4 each
k and
". You
oments
ipment
me...or
oks a
rs-only

l to one
ect to

WHAT'S YOUR SIGN?

INSTRUCTIONS:

Locate **your** Zodiac Sign above. Carefully detach and stick it in the space provided on your "ZODIAC CHART GAME" in alignment with your **"1,000,000.00 ALL-CASH WINDFALL!"** Your sign could bring you **your** luckiest numbers ever!

GO FOR AN EXTRA $50 FAST CASH – NOW!

Can you find the other half of this $50 bill? This offer is time sensitive–So be sure to respond <u>NOW</u>–you could be one of 50 drawn who will AUTOMATICALLY receive $50– IN GOOD OLD AMERICAN CASH! To play, detach this half of the $50 bill, moisten it and stick it in the space provided beside the other half. SEE BACK OF BOOK FOR CONTEST DETAILS.

▼ CAREFULLY PRE-FOLD & TEAR ALONG DOTTED LINES, MOISTEN & FOLD OVER FLAP TO SEAL REPLY ▼

IMPORTANT BEFORE MAILING...

1. Did you play your Zodiac Chart Game and Lucky Star Game? Did you print your name and address on the Game?

2. Did you play the Reach For The Moon Game for free books and a free gift?

©1994 HARLEQUIN ENTERPRISES LTD.
PRINTED IN U.S.A.

Limit one 1st 50 award per household.

PERF OUT AND
PLACE HALF
OF $50 BILL
HERE

B 72996425 B
2

Good Luck!

clung to each other in a frenzy of touch and taste so intense that the world around them disappeared and there was nothing but the throbbing pulse of two bodies trembling with passion.

Kate wanted it to go on forever. But it didn't.

As suddenly as it had begun, it was over. Reed released her, turning away with a ragged gasp. He stood on legs that shook visibly, and raked his hair.

Kate couldn't move. She remained rooted on the edge of the mattress, still struggling for breath.

After a moment, he cleared his throat. "I... didn't mean for that to happen."

She desperately wanted to reassure him but simply couldn't find her voice.

Reed, standing with his back to her, jammed his fists on his hips and bowed his head. "I should go talk to the girls. They're upset."

Moistening her lips, Kate again tried to speak. This time, it worked, although the strained voice she heard sounded little like her own. "They're upset about what I said, aren't they?"

He was silent for a moment. "They don't understand. I'll explain what happened."

"No." Wiping her hands on her thighs, Kate rose from the bed, hoping her jellied knees would support her weight. "I'm the one who said it. I'm the one who should explain."

Reed didn't respond. The truth was that he couldn't. His gut was balled into a fiery knot and his throat was drier than a tanned hide. So he didn't move as Kate brushed by him on her way to the door. He didn't stop her when she turned the knob. And he didn't speak out as she stepped into the hall-way.

Instead, he just stood there like a fool, wondering if he could knock some sense into his hormone-pickled brain by bashing his head against the nearest wall. He was sick inside, sick that he'd taken advantage of Kate's vulnerability, sick that he'd exploited her youth.

That had been unforgivable.

The shovel seemed heavier now than it had an hour ago. Kate straightened, rubbing her aching back. She probably shouldn't have volunteered to clean the stable by herself, but at the time she hadn't realized that her body had deteriorated into such a helpless powder puff. She was determined to whip her pansy-pathetic muscles into shape or to die trying.

Rolling her head until her neck gave a satisfying crunch, Kate rotated her shoulders, then heaved a sigh of relief and propped the shovel against an exposed stud on one of the stable's unfinished walls. After hanging the tack in place on hooks arranged for the purpose, she swept the final traces of crushed hay out of the four cramped stalls.

The temperature had dipped below freezing last night, and the chill had lingered throughout the morning. Reed's old denim jacket, sleeves rolled up to expose her hands, did provide some protection, although her fingers were half-frozen.

Kate put the broom down and tucked her hands under the jacket. A soothing warmth tingled through the numbness, a comforting heat that reminded her of last night, when Reed had kissed her.

The memory made her shiver with excitement. She could still taste him, still feel the tousled texture of his hair and smell the soapy scent clinging to his skin. He'd touched her with such tenderness and passion that Kate had nearly fainted from sheer joy.

She briefly wondered if she deserved such happiness, then discarded the negative thought. She didn't care if she deserved it or not, she was going to take it and revel in it and spend the rest of her life thanking God for it.

Something magical had brought her here, something mystical and enchanted. She belonged here. And she was incredibly happy.

Smiling stupidly, she grabbed up the broom and went about her work, singing to herself. As she swept the final dirt piles outside, she cast a thoughtful glance at the gray sky. Reed had said it was going to rain this afternoon. If it stayed cold enough, it might even snow. The mere thought had sent Rory into a sled-polishing frenzy. Kate chuckled aloud at the memory, then turned back into the stable.

Her smile instantly slipped away.

Something was wrong. Sunshine was spraying through the doorway at the far side of a building that stretched on forever. The Morgan's tiny four-stall stable had suddenly become a huge horse mansion, with dozens of sparkling stalls lining an immense corridor. Photographs were hung beside each steel-gated stall, around which ribbons and rosettes dripped like triumphant banners.

Kate walked forward, gazing at the strange surroundings, only to realize that they weren't strange at all. She knew this stable. She knew that there was a tack room at the end of the corridor. She knew that beyond that open, sunlit door was a huge training ring surrounded by whitewashed split rails, and beyond that were massive green pastures that went on for miles. She knew every inch of those pastures; she knew every inch of that land.

And with familiarity came fear.

A shadow fell into the corridor. Someone was standing in the doorway. Someone large. Someone frightening.

The voice was deep, soft. Chilling. "I know you're there. You can't hide forever."

Kate tried to run, but her feet wouldn't move. She was terrified, desperate.

The voice took on a chiding tone, dry and sardonic. "Come out, come out wherever you are."

"No!" she heard herself scream and wondered if it was a dream or a memory. "Go away! I don't want to talk to you. I don't want to see you. Go away!"

"Ah, but what we want and what we get aren't always the same things, are they?"

"Please, leave me alone."

"Now, you know I can't do that. We have an agreement. You're not going back on your word, are you? Life can be very unpleasant for people who don't keep their promises."

Terror slammed into her belly like a fist. She felt faint; the world went black.

When Kate dared to open her eyes, she was back inside the tiny four-stall stable. Her legs gave out and she slithered to the floor. She sat there, holding her head in her hands, while her heart pounded frantically. Squeezing her eyes shut, Kate tried to shake the hated memories out of her mind. She wouldn't allow herself to remember where she came from, because then she'd have to go back. She'd have to leave Morgan Ranch. She'd have to leave Reed.

And that would break her heart.

Chapter Eight

"She's doing good, Donald." Shifting sideways on the sofa, Reed tucked the phone under his chin and absently plucked a few colorful chocolate buttons from a bowl on the table. "I think she's had a couple of memory flashes, but nothing that provides any real information."

"Have there been any physical problems?" the doctor asked. "Headaches, blurred vision, anything like that?"

"Not that she's mentioned." Reed tossed a couple of tiny candies into his mouth, absently glancing outside, where darkness had fallen and a frigid wind whipped tree limbs into a frenzy. "Even if she had, I'm not sure she'd tell me about it. Kate's not one to complain."

A knowing hum filtered over the line. "Actually, I am a bit surprised that she hasn't recalled anything more substantial. It's been almost three weeks, yet this type of amnesia rarely lasts more than a day or so."

"So the longer she goes without remembering anything, the more likely it is that her memory might be gone forever?"

"There aren't enough statistics on that for me to venture a scientific opinion."

"I'd settle for gut instinct."

After a short pause, Donald sighed. "My instinct tells me that each passing day significantly decreases the possibility of complete recovery."

Reed considered that, struggling to suppress mounting optimism that Kate might never remember her past. He knew it was selfish, perhaps even cruel, but the truth was that Reed simply didn't want to lose her. He swallowed hard. "Well, that's a shame, but if that's the way things turn out, I guess we'll find a way to deal with it."

An astute chuckle from the other end of the line made Reed flinch. "Pardon my skepticism," Donald said in a voice that quite clearly conveyed amusement. "But for some peculiar reason I have the distinct impression you wouldn't be distraught if Kate's memory never returned."

"Hey, that's a lousy thing to say."

"Then it's not true?"

"That's beside the point. It's still a lousy thing to say." Reed grabbed another handful of candy. A few splats of rain hit the window, harbinger of the storm that was heading their way. "So, what's the latest on Pastor Hargrove's condition? I spoke to Patty after New Year's. She's planning a combination open house and prayer vigil next weekend to celebrate her husband's progress."

"Progress?"

"She said the pastor was improving."

"Wishful thinking, I'm afraid." A melancholy sigh was followed by crinkling sounds, as if the doctor were shuffling papers. "There's been some stabilization of his vital signs, but in cases like these, patients emerging from deep coma usually do so with very little warning. And as with

Kate's situation, the longer Phil Hargrove's condition remains unchanged, the less likely he is to recover."

The grim prognosis, although not unexpected, was deeply depressing to Reed, who'd known the Hargroves since his own childhood. During a particularly troubling time in Reed's life, when his father had been out of work and his mother had suffered her third miscarriage in as many years, the pastor's compassionate counsel had been invaluable. Reed, who'd been in high school, was devastated and in a self-centered, adolescent way, had actually felt responsible, believing his family's misfortunes were tied to his own failure as the eldest son. It had been Pastor Hargrove who'd helped a troubled teen find the strength to face his fears and to eventually overcome them.

Through the ensuing years, Reed's family had scattered. His parents had retired to the southeast and his siblings had settled from coast to coast, but Reed had never left his hometown, nor had he forgotten the pastor's wise words. "We will not be judged on how well we understand our problems, but on how well we resolve them."

"What on earth is that supposed to mean?" Donald replied irritably.

"Hmm?" It took a moment for Reed to realize that he'd spoken aloud. "Oh, nothing really. It's just something that Phil Hargrove once told me. I guess I was thinking out loud—"

A terrified scream startled him. Reed jolted forward, listening. For a moment, he thought it might be the wind howling beneath the back porch roof, but the next shriek was identifiably human.

"Got to go," he muttered into the phone. "Something's wrong."

He hung up without awaiting a response and bolted toward the back door.

Shawna emerged from her bedroom, holding some kind of hoop-stretched fabric. "What's going on, Dad, who's screaming?"

"It's not me," Rory announced as she skidded down the hallway. Her eyes rounded with fear. "Must be Kate. She took the trash outside and—"

The child's words were cut off by another terrified shriek, louder this time, and much closer. Reed crossed the kitchen with two massive leaps. Just as he reached the back door, it crashed open, thwacking his forehead with enough force to knock him backward.

Kate burst inside, screaming wildly. "Ohmigod, ohmigod, it's horrible, Reed!" She spun around and grabbed the front of his shirt, shaking him violently. "Do something! Dear Lord, you've got to *do something!*"

At the moment, Reed was barely able to blink away stars. He clutched his head, moaning. "What exactly am I supposed to do?"

Kate stared at him as if he'd gone mad. "Kill it!"

"Are the coyotes back?" Shawna asked calmly.

With her fingers still tangled in Reed's shirt, Kate spun around, dragging him with her. "There are *coyotes* here?" The pitch of her voice could have cracked glass.

Shawna shrugged. "A few. Usually they don't show up unless there are newborns in the pasture. Dad just fires a few rounds over their heads to shoo them off."

Clearly horrified, Kate's head snapped back toward her stumbling captive. "Did you hear that?" she shouted an inch from his face. *"Coyotes!"*

Wincing, Reed massaged his ringing ear. "Yes, I heard," he said, struggling to untangle her grasping fingers from his shirt. "Is that what you saw?"

She blinked. "Well, no."

Rory stepped forward, clearly enthusiastic about a potentially exciting development. "Maybe it was a mountain lion!"

Kate did a double take, mouthing the words *mountain lion* as if her voice had failed completely, a thought that gave Reed momentary comfort.

"I know!" Rory chirped happily. "I'll bet it was a bear, huh, Kate? A big ol' woolly black bear."

Releasing her grip so quickly that Reed staggered backward, Kate clutched her chest, sagging against the wall as if she'd been shot. Her eyes were huge, like blue-yoked eggs. She opened her mouth as if to speak, but instead, she simply sucked in a ragged breath while every visible trace of color drained from her face.

"Oh, for crying out loud," Reed muttered, smoothing the wrinkled puckers from the front of his flannel shirt. "You know perfectly well that bears don't come this far down the hill."

"They could if they wanted to," Rory insisted.

Heaving a frustrated sigh, Reed turned to Kate. "Did you see a bear?"

She twisted her fingers together. "Well, no, not exactly."

When she didn't elaborate, Reed folded his arms and skewered her with a hard look. "Then what, pray tell, am I supposed to kill?"

Kate cleared her throat, avoiding his gaze. "It's a, um, well . . . a rat."

He stared at her. "A rat."

When Shawna and Rory both burst into gales of laughter, Kate's cheeks turned an iridescent pink. "Now, wait just a darn minute here. I'm not talking about an ordinary, run-of-the-mill field mouse. This thing is gigantic! It's . . . it's—" Her frantic gaze settled on the gray and white lump of fur snoozing on the counter. "It's bigger than Gulliver!"

"Oh, come on, Kate."

"I'm serious, Reed. It's massive, and it has *teeth!*" When he bent to sniff her breath, she pushed him away. "I have not been in the cooking sherry," she snapped, plainly agitated. "Go out and see for yourself, and when you come back with a groveling apology, I might even be magnanimous enough to accept it."

Reed tossed up his hands. "Can't this wait until morning? It's freezing out there."

"Oh, just give me a rifle," Kate growled, her eyes narrowed into angry slits. "I'll shoot the darn thing myself."

"Nobody is going to shoot anything," Reed mumbled, digging through a nearby drawer. "Where's the flashlight?"

"I had it with me." Kate's gaze darted toward the back door. "I guess I must have dropped it."

"Swell." Slamming the drawer, Reed marched into his shop to retrieve a spare, then slipped on a jacket and headed out into the storm. "You girls stay here," he said as Shawna and Rory crowded toward the porch.

Their disappointed groans melted into the howling wind. Muttering to himself, Reed gripped his jacket collar, ducked into the wind and headed toward the trash containers. When he abruptly stopped to get his bearings, something bumped into his back. He looked over his shoulder and saw that Kate was clinging to the hem of his jacket like a terrified tick. "Go back to the house," he told her. "I can handle this."

"Uh-uh, no way. I want to see your sorry face when you look into those beady rat eyes."

"Lord, but you're a stubborn woman."

"*I'm* stubborn? You're the one who practically called me a liar." Spitting out a wind-whipped strand of hair, she squinted toward the rear of the house. "It was behind the trash cans," she mumbled. "Leering at me."

Reed chuckled. "Smart rat."

"What?"

"Never mind. Keep hold of my jacket so you don't blow away."

Following the flashlight beam, they edged around the corner to where several covered trash containers with bungee-tied lids to protect against foraging raccoons had been stashed in a wind-proof lean-to. The discarded flashlight was on the ground casting a weak beam out toward the back pastures.

Reed retrieved the light, handing it back to Kate, then used the larger shop light to flash a beam around the base of the cans. "I don't see a thing."

"It was right there, between these two— Ugh! There it is, there it *is!*" she screamed, jumping up and down until she'd nearly torn the unzipped jacket off Reed's back.

"There *what* is?" Frantically sweeping the flashlight beam along the rocky ground, he suddenly spotted what appeared to be an eighteen-inch length of skinny pink rope protruding from behind one of the containers. He dragged the can away to reveal a white-faced creature with round black eyes, and a pointy snout tipped by a wriggly pink nose.

Behind him, Kate emitted a sick gurgle. "I told you, I told you, o-o-oh, God, it's so gross."

Reed tried desperately not to laugh. "Well, you were right about one thing. It is about the same size as your average house cat. Then again, most possums are."

"Possum?" Kate went rigid. "Is that a special kind of rat?"

"It's not a rat at all, Kate. It's a marsupial. Perfectly harmless. Unless, of course, you try to pick one up. They take a dim view of that."

"Pick it *up?* You mean, like to actually *touch it?*" She shivered in disgust, then emitted an adorable squeak, leaping aside as the placid creature emerged from its hidey-hole and lumbered away. Kate wiggled a frantic finger at the ropy pink tail disappearing into the darkness. "Are you just going to let it go?"

"Like I said, he's perfectly harmless. All the hungry little fellow wants is a meal. He probably just dropped by to see if we were careless enough to leave the lid off one of the trash cans.''

''What if it comes back?''

Reed shrugged his displaced jacket up over his shoulders. ''He probably will. I imagine he lives around here.''

''Well, how convenient. That way it can spend Saturday nights playing poker with the coyotes, mountain lions and bears.'' She pushed a handful of blowing hair out of her face, and held it firmly at the side of her head, casting a fishy eye at the concealing brush just beyond the house. ''So, what else is lurking out there—rattlesnakes?''

''Don't worry about them. They're asleep now. They won't be back until spring.''

Her eyes narrowed. ''Goodie.''

''You might want to watch out for skunks, though. They really do resent intrusion, and trust me, an irritated skunk can ruin your whole week.'' He turned to leave, but couldn't resist a final glance over his shoulder. ''Now, if you should ever see a skunk during daylight, run like hell, because it's most likely rabid.''

''Rabid,'' she muttered with a sickly sway. ''You mean the foaming-at-the-mouth, Old Yeller kind of rabid?''

He smiled, hiked up his collar and ducked back into the wind. In less than a heartbeat, Kate was right behind him, clutching the hem of his jacket like a confused pachyderm. Reed guided her to the back porch. ''You go inside,'' he told her. ''I'm going to check on Fagan.''

She squinted toward the pasture. ''Why, what's wrong with him?''

''Probably nothing, but he had a runny nose this morning and was a bit off his feed. Just a cold, I imagine.''

''You mean calves get head colds, the same as people do?''

''Yeah. They're just like fat, hairy kids.'' Reed blew into his palms to warm them. ''Fagan's a pretty tough little fellow, but the storm tonight is supposed to be a doozy. Since he didn't seem to be feeling too good, I decided to bed him down in the stable until the weather clears."

"Oh." Kate glanced toward the stables, imagining the brown-eyed baby bull all warm and comfy, tucked into a spare stall. "Can I go with you? To check on him, that is."

The request seemed to startle Reed. "Sure, if you don't mind freezing for a few more minutes."

"Frankly, it's a better option than facing the girls with the traumatic tale of my possum encounter." Kate turned her head, allowing the wind to blow the hair out of her face. "Unless, of course, you'd be willing to stretch the facts a wee bit ... ?"

"Sorry." He pointed to his nose. "I can't."

"Ah, yes, the curse of the old truth twitcher." She cocked her head, grinning, then fell into step beside him as he headed across the yard. "I'm surprised you haven't tried to sell me a bridge."

"What, you don't believe that I'm a perennially honest fellow?"

"Of course I do, just like I believe in the tooth fairy."

"Tsk-tsk. So young, yet so cynical." He swung open the stable door, struggling to hold it with his shoulder while she ducked inside. When he stepped in beside her, the wind slammed the door shut and the startled horses nickered nervously. Reed flipped the light switch, then reached out to comfort Molly, who was bobbing her head from the nearest stall. "There, girl," he whispered, stroking the white star on her forehead.

When the mare had calmed, he moved to Spot's stall to soothe the skittish Appaloosa. Kate watched, fascinated by Reed's instinctive ability to provide Molly with soft reassurance while comforting the exuberant Spot with a lighter voice and firmer touch.

The now-familiar warmth radiated deep inside her chest. Every time Kate looked at Reed, she felt that same tingling heat. He was so very special, a golden giant of a man with an aura of tender strength that made Kate's legs go all weak and wobbly.

It had been days since they'd shared the kiss that had changed Kate's life. Reed hadn't spoken of it again, but Kate had seen him watching her, his eyes glowing softly. As soon as he realized that Kate was looking back at him, he'd turn away, pretending to busy himself. Part of Kate wanted to shake him, force him to acknowledge what was happening between them.

The other, more rational part of her understood and even approved of his reticence. But sometimes at night, when the house was dark and silent, she'd lie awake thinking about him, wishing she had the courage to sneak into his bedroom just so she could watch him sleep.

So far, she'd resisted the urge, fearing he'd awaken and recognize the love in her eyes. The sad truth was that Kate didn't want Reed to know how she felt, because she had nothing to offer him. Without a past, she could have no future. Obviously Reed understood that. But what Reed didn't understand, and what Kate instinctively knew, was that if her past ever did catch up with her, she'd be lost forever.

That was the most frightening thing of all.

Now, however, she pushed those thoughts to the back of her mind and concentrated on Reed, who'd turned away from the quieted Appaloosa and was moving toward the far end of the stable. With a ragged breath, she followed him to the gate of Fagan's stall.

"Hey there, little guy," he murmured, leaning over the stall gate. "How're you feeling?"

Peering around Reed's shoulder, Kate saw the young bull lying in the corner, with his hoofed feet tucked under him. "Oh, the poor thing," Kate murmured, noting the animal's listless appearance and lusterless eyes. "He really does look ill."

Reed nodded toward a bucket of sweetened mash tied to the front of the stall. "He's eaten some. That's a good sign.

If he isn't better by morning, I'll have the vet come out and take a look."

"It's so cold in here. Maybe we could set up a space heater or something."

"Cattle are bred to withstand cold weather—that coat of his has more thermal power than a goose down sleeping bag. Besides, heaters in a barn or stable are lightning rods for disaster." He kicked at the loose hay strewn across the weathered plank floor. "It wouldn't take much of a spark to ignite this kind of fuel."

The thought of these beautiful animals being trapped in a stable fire made Kate shudder. A sudden pounding on the roof nearly stopped her heart. "What's that?"

"Sleet." Reed grabbed her elbow, hustling her back toward the front of the stable. Heaving the big door open, he held it with his shoulder and wrapped the right half of his open jacket around Kate, pressing her face against the warmth of his chest. "Keep your head under the jacket. At forty miles an hour, an ice pellet in the eye can do a hell of a lot of damage."

"But what about you—?"

The question was muffled against Reed's rib cage as he hauled her out into the storm, gripping her so tightly against him that she could barely breath. She felt the sting of wind-driven ice on the back of her legs, and realized that Reed was guiding her sideways toward the house. Stumbling blindly, Kate felt as if she were being pummeled by frigid fists. Had Reed not been holding her up, she would have been knocked to the ground by the first icy blast.

But he was holding her up, giving her the strength to fight her own surging panic and struggle forward for what seemed an eternity until finally she tripped over the porch steps.

They'd been outside for over half an hour before Kate finally found herself inside the warm kitchen, shivering as Reed stripped off her soaked jacket. He rubbed her hands, calling over his shoulder. "Shawna, draw a warm bath."

Although Kate was chilled to the bone, she certainly didn't expect Reed to kneel in front of her and massage her quivering legs. To her shock, he scooped her into his arms and carried her into the bathroom, where the faucet was still blasting, and steam wafted up from the partially filled tub. He lowered her into the water, clothes and all. For some odd reason, that made sense to her, although she didn't know why.

With contented sigh, Kate slid down until the delicious heat sloshed beneath her chin. She was safe, she was warm, she was home. And she was loved.

The thunderous crack was like a cannon shot outside the bedroom window. Kate jolted from the bed to dash across the room to look, but her view was obscured by a thick layer of ice coating the exterior of the glass. The howling wind was drowned out by the din of the pounding storm, yet Kate still heard another series of loud pops similar to the one that had awakened her, only more distant.

Concerned, she stepped into her slippers and grabbed her robe. The hallway was dark, as expected. She tiptoed down the corridor, emerging into the living room, which was a deserted collage of shadows and silhouettes. Her gaze was drawn to the bare corner where the Christmas tree had stood. They'd taken it down last week, repacking each ornament with extraordinary care. Even in the dark, the room now seemed naked and strangely sad.

An orange glow beckoned from the kitchen. She followed it, finding a flickering oil lamp on the table. Reed was leaning against the sink, watching the storm through one of the few windows on the southwestern side of the house that was protected from the wind-driven sleet.

When Kate flipped the light switch, Reed spoke without turning. "No electricity. The ice has probably ripped down half the lines between here and town."

"Oh." Rubbing her upper arms, she crossed the room, eyeing the propane stove, which thankfully required no electricity. "I could make you some coffee, if instant is all right."

"Instant is fine, thanks." He glanced down as she reached for the faucet to fill the kettle. "The electric well pump is out. You'll have to get water from the emergency bottles in the back of the pantry." Reed's gaze moved beyond Kate, and he managed a thin smile. "Hi, honey. Did the storm wake you up?"

Kate turned to see Shawna, disheveled and sleepy, standing in the doorway. "Something hit the wall outside my room," she said, yawning. "I think the barn door blew off again."

"It did," Reed said sadly. "Flew into the pasture about an hour ago. What you heard was probably a tree limb. The buildup of ice is cracking branches right and left."

Shawna shuffled to the table, rubbing her eyes. "What about the cows, Dad? Are they going to be all right?"

"They'll find shelter," he said, although Kate thought Reed's voice held more conviction than his eyes. Taking a deep breath, he turned away from the window. "How about some hot chocolate? Kate was about to put the kettle on."

"Sure," Shawna murmured nervously. "Sounds good."

"Can I have some, too?" asked Rory, who'd suddenly appeared in the doorway looking scared and shaky.

Kate hurried over to slip a reassuring arm around the child's chubby shoulders. "Of course you can, sweetie. And how about a couple of cookies to go with it?"

With a jerky nod, Rory allowed Kate to guide her toward the kitchen table. Just as the girl started to sit down, another sharp crash shook the rafters. "We're gonna die!" she shrieked, whirling to grab Kate around the waist. "We're all gonna—!"

"Now, you know perfectly well that your daddy wouldn't let anything bad happen to us." Kate hugged the trembling child, pressing a kiss to the top of her ruffled head. "We're all going to be just fine, aren't we, Reed? Reed?" She looked from the vacant spot where Reed had just been standing, to Shawna, who pointed toward the hallway.

"Dad probably went to check the attic in case something came through the roof," Shawna said, displaying admirable composure. "We have some plywood stored up there for emergency repairs."

Peeling her lips away from her teeth, Kate managed a thin croak. "So this happens a lot?"

"Not really."

Kate stroked Rory's hair until the child was calm enough to sit at the table beside her sister, then she filled the kettle and put it on to boil. "I'm going to see if your father needs help," she told the girls. "Keep an eye on the kettle for me, okay?"

Without waiting for an answer, Kate hurried into the hallway and nearly ran into a ladder that had been set up beneath a square opening in the hall ceiling. An acoustic tile the same size as the attic entrance had been removed and propped against the wall.

Kate tested the ladder, then climbed up and poked her head into the dusty opening. A flashlight beam flickered between exposed beams at the far end of the attic. "Reed, is everything okay?"

"There aren't any holes in the roof." His reply was muffled.

"Well, that's good, isn't it?"

"Yeah, it's just dandy."

Taken aback by the uncharacteristically bitter edge on his voice, Kate pulled herself farther into the opening. "Can I help?"

"No. I'm coming out." The light beam swung around, illuminating a maze of heating ducts and mounds of pink insulation.

Kate waited, watching the jerky light beam moving closer until Reed finally emerged from behind a huge taped tube that had been strapped to the rafters. His face was grim, too grim for a man who'd apparently not found the problem he'd been fearing. "What's wrong, Reed?"

"Nothing." He swung his leg over the duct, pausing as Kate descended the ladder.

She stepped off the final rung, then handed Reed the attic cover and steadied the ladder while he snapped it back into place. "Are you sure there wasn't any damage to the roof?"

"None that I saw." He moved the ladder into the hall closet, avoiding her gaze. "Most of the shingles have probably blown halfway to town, but it's nothing that can't be fixed."

"Then why are you wearing that shell-shocked-soldier expression?"

A subtle quiver running down his shoulders was the sole indication that he'd heard her. When he turned around, only his lips were smiling. "Do you remember how to play Monopoly?"

Kate blinked. "Ah, yes, I think so."

"Good. I get to be the banker."

With that, Reed brushed past her and joined his daughters in the kitchen.

For the next three hours, the family hunched around the kitchen table, throwing dice, moving markers and basically pretending that the outside world wasn't going through cataclysmic change.

To Kate the experience was awesome, not so much because of the laughter, which was forced at first yet became strangely natural as time plodded on, but because each member of the family displayed such stoic concern for the others. Even little Rory, who was clearly terrified by the storm, put on a stiff upper lip and pretended that there was nothing unusual about playing Monopoly at three in the morning in a house that sounded as if it were being battered by a bulldozer.

Throughout the long night, Kate watched Reed closely. He was jovial, laughing easily and often; yet his eyes held a secret fear, a quiet terror that was blinked away each time he noticed Kate looking in his direction. She knew he was deeply worried about something. The cause of his concern didn't seem to be that their home was being beaten to a splintered pulp. Reed simply reminded the family that the house was insured, and that was that.

Nor did he seem particularly apprehensive about the cattle, and had calmed Rory, who was truly upset about the fate of her beloved cows, by explaining how herds of Angus in the Montana highlands survive the bitterest of winters as long as their water supply was routinely de-iced and supplemental hay rations were provided.

His reasoning was so heartfelt and believable—nary a nose twitch in sight—that Rory was visibly relieved, and Kate mentally eliminated cattle as a potential source for Reed's furtive fears.

By dawn, the storm had blown itself out, and the brittle morning revealed a translucent wonderland. Sheets of blue ice coated the ground, dripping from eaves and tree limbs in shimmering stalactite prisms.

Yet despite its gift of breathtaking beauty, the storm had left carnage in its wake. The yard was littered by torn foliage, branches and building debris. It would take days to repair the damage, perhaps even weeks.

The shadow of night had barely lifted before Reed suited up in winter gear and ventured out to assess the damage. Kate watched him through the window as he picked his way across the treacherous ice, heading straight to the stable to check on Fagan and the horses.

She held her breath until he emerged with eyes that were somber but not totally bleak. Exhaling in slight relief, she clutched the kitchen curtains, straining to watch as he entered the pasture. She knew it would take time to search out and individually inspect each animal, but she stayed at her post, watching and waiting until he'd reappeared.

Reed glanced toward the house, spotting Kate's anxious face pressed against the window. He nodded, lifting a gloved hand, forming a circle with his thumb and index finger to indicate that the herd was okay. Kate smothered a happy giggle with her palms, so relieved that she could have fainted with sheer joy. Reed's cattle were his pride and joy. If anything had happened—

Kate shook away the thought, reminding herself that nothing *had* happened. The cattle were fine. Nothing else mattered.

Puffing her cheeks, Kate blew out a breath and stepped away, expecting Reed to head back toward the house. She rushed to flip a flame on under the kettle, then leaned over for another glance out the window to check on his progress. To her surprise, Reed wasn't moving toward the house. Instead, he was chaining up the truck tires.

Five minutes later, he climbed into the cab and the pickup rolled cautiously down the road.

Kate watched the vehicle disappear, and was still staring at the vacant driveway when the kettle whistled. A cold chill slid down her spine. Swallowing hard, she turned off the flame and went back to her watching post.

It was thirty minutes before the truck returned. When Reed emerged, his shoulders were bent, his expression shattered.

And Kate knew that the orchard was gone.

Chapter Nine

"Where are the girls?" Reed asked, hanging his hat on a coat peg.

Blinking back tears, Kate turned away to fuss with the still-warm kettle. "Rory went to bed. Shawna fell asleep on the sofa."

She took a deep breath, hating the cowardly quiver of her voice. Behind her, she heard Reed's booted feet drag toward the table. Chair legs scratched across the floor, followed by the muffled thud of a large body dropping heavily onto the seat. It took a moment to steady her trembling hands, then she poured two mugs of water, stirring a spoon of coffee crystals into each before carrying them to the table.

Reed nodded an acknowledgment as she set his mug in front of him. Then he simply sat there with his head bowed, immobile except for the movement of the steaming mug he twirled between flattened palms.

Kate yearned to embrace him, to press his cheek against her breast, comforting him with reassuring words and loving warmth. But she dared not, fearing he'd believe that acknowledging a need for comfort would be akin to admitting weakness, a mortal sin in the rugged, rural world where survival of the fittest was more than a colorful cliché: it was the eleventh commandment.

So Kate pasted on the mirror image of Reed's stoic expression, seated herself across from him in a manner that allowed her to toss a casual arm over the back of her chair. Still feigning nonchalance, she took a healthy sip of black coffee and nearly choked on the acrid stuff, which she'd forgotten to sweeten and mellow with cream.

She pushed the coffee away, crossed her arms and spoke quietly. "So, how bad is it?"

Reed stopped twirling the mug. "I haven't tasted it yet."

"I wasn't talking about the coffee."

"I know." Leaning back, Reed raked his hair. He looked drawn and pale, with the corners of his mouth pinched tight. "The mature trees lost thirty-five to forty percent of their fruit-bearing branches. Most will survive, but it'll take years before they come close to matching prior production, if ever. The young trees didn't fare as well."

"Young trees?"

"About five acres of them," Reed said quietly. "A while back, I put them in as yearlings. They would have fruited this spring. I didn't expect much for their first season, but I'd hoped it would be enough to increase the overall crop yield by five percent or so. Now..." His gaze wandered toward the window, then went blank.

Kate reached out, pressing her palm over one of his cold hands. "But don't you have some kind of crop insurance, just like the coverage you have on the house?"

"Hmm?" He blinked, forcing his attention across the table as Kate repeated her question. "Full crop insurance is too expensive for most farmers, but the bank insisted on enough coverage to pay off the loan I took out to plant the yearlings.''

''Well, that's something, I suppose.''

''I suppose.''

''Can you take out another loan to replant the same acreage?''

''I used projected production of the matured trees as collateral for the original loan.''

Kate sighed, shaking her head in frustration. ''So if this year's harvest is down thirty to forty percent, there won't be enough collateral for a loan, but without a loan, there won't be enough money to plant the new trees necessary to increase the harvest.''

''That's the system.''

''Well, the system stinks.''

''Yep.'' Pushing his mug aside, Reed stood and headed for the back door.

He'd just retrieved his hat when Kate leapt up from the table. ''Where are you going?''

''First I'm going to hunt up the barn door. After that...'' He shrugged, offering a brave smile that broke her heart. ''After that, I guess I'll just find what needs finding and fix what needs fixing.''

''I'll help,'' Kate said quickly. ''Just let me get a jacket—''

''The truth is that I'd rather have you stay here with the girls. They've had a tough night. I'd just feel better knowing you were with them.''

''Oh.'' Kate combed her hair with her fingers, wanting to argue the point yet instinctively knowing that Reed needed time alone. ''All right, then.''

Reed opened the door, casting a melancholy glance over his shoulder. ''Would you mind letting me know when the phones are back on line? I have a few calls to make.''

Kate assured him that she would.

* * *

The telephones were restored by midmorning, the electricity a few hours later. Local schools had been closed when school buses were grounded by impassable roads, but by afternoon most road ice had melted into a navigable slush. Except for a couple of brief house trips to make telephone calls, Reed had been working outside all day, splitting his time between storm repairs and clearing debris.

Every hour or so he'd head for the stable to check on Fagan. Kate knew that, because she'd been keeping track of his movements by interrupting her household chores every few minutes to stare out the windows.

By late afternoon, Kate had run out of busywork, so she grabbed her trusty cleaner and a roll of paper towels, reasoning that as long as she was spending so much time at the windows, she might as well clean the darn things.

Starting in the living room, Kate spritzed the glass with all-purpose cleaner—cleaner was cleaner, after all—then she scoured it with a sponge, and set about wiping the thick mess off with paper towels. Behind her, Rory was stretched on the sofa watching television, an old cowboy movie from the sound of it. Kate didn't pay much attention. She was more interested in Reed, who'd made a beeline for the stable after his last telephone call and had been in there for nearly an hour.

"Kate?"

She glanced over her shoulder just as Shawna entered the room carrying her ever-present hoop of stretched fabric. "Hi, sweetie. Problems?"

The girl sighed. "The violet petals look funny. They're all squinched up. I must have done something wrong."

"Oh?" Kate set the plastic spray bottle on the windowsill and added another wad of dirty wet paper to the growing pile on the floor. "Let's take a look."

Shawna handed over the hoop, then stood there skimming dejected glances from Kate to the work in question and back again. "The instructions said it was supposed to be a padded satin stitch, so I did everything just like you told me. Pretty awful, huh?"

"Well, it *is* a little puckered." Kate flipped the hoop over, inspecting the backside of the stitches. "Since a padded satin stitch is basically two layers of satin stitch in opposite directions over the same shape, the secret is to make certain that stitch tension on the finish layer is left slightly looser than the foundation layer. And if you use the same needle holes for both layers, your edges won't have that jaggedy look . . . like right here, see?"

With her tongue peeking from the corner of her mouth, Shawna furrowed her brow and studied the area Kate was pointing out. "Oh, yeah, I get it." She glanced up apprehensively. "Do I have to rip everything out?"

"No. Fortunately, you haven't knotted it yet, so all you have to do is unthread the needle, pull the finish layer and try it again."

"But looser, right?"

"Right." Smiling, Kate handed the hoop back and gave the teenager's shoulder a reassuring squeeze. "You really are doing a wonderful job, Shawna. Obviously, you've inherited your mother's talent."

Shawna beamed at the praise. "You think so?"

"I know so," Kate said, retrieving the spray bottle. "At the rate you're going, the piece should be finished in a few weeks and you're going to be chomping at the bit for another project."

"There's a neat little yarn shop in Grass Valley. Will you go with me, Kate, and help pick something out?"

"I'd love to."

The girl's delighted grin faded as her gaze settled on the bottle in Kate's hand. "You're not using that on the windows, are you?"

Kate glanced down at the bottle. "Sure, why not? It's supposed to clean everything. Look, it says right here that it 'cuts greasy dirt on most washable surfaces.' Well, windows are washable surfaces.''

"That stuff isn't made for glass, Kate, it's made for walls and floors and painted woodwork, and when the stove top gets all gunky, I use it there, too.'' Pursing her lips, Shawna eyed the smeared windows. "Yuck, what a mess.''

"I'm not done yet,'' Kate muttered, feeling a bit defensive. "I have to, ah, put on a second coat.''

Shawna flinched. "Jeez, Kate, that's just going to make it worse. Wait here.'' She dashed off, returning moments later with the plastic tote of cleaning supplies. "This,'' she said, retrieving a bottle of translucent blue liquid, "is for windows. Watch.'' Spritzing madly, Shawna misted one of the panes, then grabbed a fistful of paper towels and rubbed until the glass squeaked. "There. Better, no?''

Squinting at the sparkling glass, Kate suppressed the urge to shade her eyes. "Yes, much better, although it pains me to admit it.'' She slid Shawna a smug grin. "Get it? It *pains* me? Like in windowpane?''

Shawna moaned. "Oh, brother. And I thought Dad was corny.''

"Teenagers have no sense of humor,'' Kate muttered, grabbing a lemon-scented can out of the tote. "So, what's this for?''

"Furniture,'' Shawna said brightly. "But only the wood stuff. This—'' she grabbed a bright red spray bottle ''—is for upholstery. And the fat yellow bottle is for kitchen floors, but not the hardwood floors in the living room and hallway. For those, you have to use the green squeeze bottle. And only a *damp* mop.''

"Damp,'' she repeated numbly, wiping her moist palms on her jeans.

"If hardwood floors get too wet, they'll warp.''

Kate clutched her stomach. "Warp?''

"Uh-huh. Oh, and the foamy white stuff is for bathrooms, but not for bathroom floors, of course.''

"Of course," Kate mumbled, her head spinning.

"Kitchen cleanser is for sinks and tubs, except if they're made of fiberglass, in which case you have to use the white can."

"I thought that was for bathrooms."

"It is, but it's real good for fiberglass, too."

Kate's mouth felt as if it were lined with cotton. "What do we have that's fiberglass?"

"Well, nothing, but if we did, you'd have to use the white can. Got it?"

"Uh—"

"And you can use that all-purpose stuff for everything else . . . except for baked-on glop inside the oven, or anything made out of unfinished metal, like the wood stove, and oh! you should test it first, on account of it's pretty strong and sometimes it kind of eats up the paint."

"Eats paint?" Horrified, she leapt away from the benign white bottle as if it contained sulfuric acid. "Good Lord, what's in it, anyway?"

Shawna shrugged cheerfully. "I don't analyze 'em, I just use 'em."

Kate sagged against the wall, staring at the bulging tote with a whole new attitude. Maybe cleaner wasn't just cleaner. Maybe you really had to know what you were doing. If so, she was in real trouble. "It's like a chemistry lab in there. How on earth did you ever figure out which did what and why?"

"I don't know. Just from watching Dad, I guess." Shawna patted her shoulder. "Don't worry. You'll get the hang of it."

With that, she scooped up her precious hooped fabric and scuttled into her room.

Kate stood there feeling spent, broken and incredibly stupid that a thirteen-year-old girl had to explain something as simple as cleaning a house. It was humiliating, even frightening.

Since Kate could clearly remember details about needle-work and equine conformation among other things, her amnesia was apparently quite selective. That baffled her. Why, for example, couldn't she recall even the most mundane details of daily life, like how to wash a window or cook a meal? Everyone cooks, for heaven's sake, and anyone with the IQ of cabbage knows how to clean a house.

Everyone, it seemed, except Kate, who'd been utterly stymied by the intricacy of operating a vacuum cleaner and had spent thirty minutes studying the washing machine's instruction manual before she could figure out how to turn the dumb thing on.

And then there was the matter of the wedding dress, which still bothered Kate immensely. Why had she been wearing it? Was it possible that she'd been preparing to marry someone?

The thought made her cringe inside. No, that wasn't possible, it wasn't possible at all. Two weeks ago, Kate might have considered that prospect, but no more. Things were different now. Kate was different. She didn't need a flawless memory to realize that she never could have agreed to marry anyone, because she hadn't been in love with anyone.

Of all the things she'd learned since her arrival at Morgan Ranch, the most compelling had been a mystic, magical understanding of that profound emotion called love. True love was etched in the soul. It was an all-consuming emotion, a physical and spiritual completion that could never be dismissed, never be forgotten.

Kate knew that with absolute certainty, because she was deeply, irrevocably in love with Reed Morgan; and no power on earth could ever erase his memory from her mind or her heart.

After using her newly discovered window-washing talent, Kate removed the all-purpose cleaner scum, then stood back to admire the sparking glass panes. She glanced over her shoulder, feeling immensely pleased with herself and hoping for at least a small round of applause from Rory. Instead, she received an indifferent snore.

Rory was sound asleep.

Smiling, Kate covered the child with her mother's afghan, unable to suppress an urge to stroke her silky sweet cheek. Rory squinched her eyes, yanked the afghan under her chin and flipped over. Kate took the hint.

As she tiptoed to retrieve the cleaning tote, the sound of an engine caught her attention. A glance out the gleaming windows confirmed that a white van had just pulled up.

When a slender, middle-aged man emerged, Reed hustled out of the stable to meet him. They spoke briefly, then the man hauled a bulging valise out of the van and followed Reed into the stable. Since an insurance adjuster wouldn't be particularly concerned with the condition of animal housing, Kate realized that the stone-faced visitor must be the veterinarian.

A nervous sensation settled in the pit of her stomach. She'd been so upset about the storm damage, she'd forgotten to ask how Fagan was doing. Judging by Reed's bleak expression and the fact that he'd felt it necessary to call the vet, Kate assumed the little red calf must still be pretty sick.

As if Reed didn't have enough problems.

Snatching a jacket off the coatrack, Kate went out to the porch. Although her heart urged her toward the stable, her head reasoned that Reed was obviously busy at the moment, and he might resent the intrusion. So she sat on the porch steps, waiting.

About twenty minutes later, the vet emerged alone. He spotted Kate, nodding a curt acknowledgment before climbing into the van and driving away. The doctor's professional frown had not been encouraging. Kate felt ill.

It took a few moments to gather her courage, then she trudged through the blustery wind and fought the stable door open. As she slipped inside, she was greeted by an odd medicinal smell, a camphor odor similar to the goop mothers use to clear stuffy little noses. There was also a peculiar hissing sound. Kate was trying to identify the weird noise when Reed poked his head out of the calf's stall.

"Is everything all right in the house?" he asked.

"Everything's fine. I just came out to see how Fagan is."

Stress lines around Reed's eyes deepened. "He has pneumonia."

"Oh, my God. That's serious, isn't it?"

"Yeah, it's serious." Reed ducked out of sight for a moment, then the stall gate swung open. He emerged, looking gaunt and hollow. "Could you do me a favor and have someone bring me a sleeping bag from that tall cabinet in the shop? I'm not comfortable leaving him alone tonight."

"No, of course you wouldn't be." Licking her lips, Kate eased her way past the horse stalls, which were vacant now since the animals had been turned out this morning to graze. "Is there anything else I can do? Besides the sleeping bag, that is."

"A thermos of coffee would be nice."

"Of course." Kate watched him sag against the wall, then slide down to sit on the floor with his knees bent. "We can take turns watching him. You take the first shift and I'll come relieve you. That way, you'll at least get a few hours' sleep."

"I'll get enough sleep," he murmured, closing his eyes and propping his head back against the splintered plank wall. "But thanks anyway."

Kate had moved halfway down the short corridor, but had deliberately stopped short of being able to see into Fagan's stall. Now she sucked a deep breath and walked briskly forward, forcing herself to look inside. What she saw was absolutely heartbreaking. She pressed her hands to her mouth, to keep from gasping aloud.

The poor little bull was still curled in the corner of the stall, but his back was now oddly hunched. Despite a hissing vaporizer that filled the stall with medicated steam, the animal's breathing was labored. His head was thrust forward, his tongue lolled from his open mouth, and every breath was plainly a struggle.

"Oh..." Tears sprang to her eyes. "Isn't there anything we can do to help him?"

"Not much," Reed replied wearily. "Doc gave him a shot, but if the pneumonia is viral, antibiotics won't do much good. Nothing left now but to wait."

Panic set in, a frustrating fury that swelled from the very pit of her soul. "This isn't right," Kate muttered, raking her hair and pacing madly. "First the orchard, and now this. What are you supposed to do? How much is one man supposed to take without cracking?" She tossed up her hands, fighting tears, fighting the insane anger directed at a faceless cosmos that, after having stolen Reed's beloved wife, now seemed determined to rob him of everything else. "Aren't good and decent people supposed to be rewarded? Isn't it written somewhere that we reap what we sow, or some such garbage? You're the finest man in the entire world, Reed. You give so much of yourself, so much kindness and love, why would you reap such misery? I don't understand why this is happening to you."

In less than a heartbeat, Reed was on his feet, gathering the trembling woman in his arms. "Shh, Kate," he murmured, stroking her hair as her tears flowed openly down her cheeks. "It's all right. We're going to get through this."

"It-it shouldn't be happening. It's wrong, Reed, and it's not fair."

He cupped her face with his palm, sending a soothing warmth coursing through her entire body. His smile was sad, yet there was a mesmerizing softness in his eyes. "So young," he whispered. "So very young."

For some reason, Kate took umbrage at the observation. She stiffened, wiping her eyes. "I'm hardly a child, Reed. Unless my math is considerably off, you were a husband and father at my age. At the time, I doubt you thought of yourself as a child, either."

His gaze clouded. "I've never considered you a child, Kate. Trust me on that one. But you are young, and although you can't remember much of your life experience, I suspect that it's somewhat limited."

"Why do you say that?"

"Because if it wasn't, you'd understand that none of us comes into this world with a guarantee of happiness taped to our belly button. All we bring is our wits, and our hearts, and if we're fortunate, a stalwart determination to make the best of whatever we have to work with. Bad things happen to good people, Kate. It's not pleasant, it's not fair, but it's the way life is. We deal with it because we have no choice."

Feeling foolish and incredibly naive, she laid her cheek against his chest. Reed was right. In so many ways, Kate was little more than a child, untutored and ignorant of the ugly side of life. Perhaps her mind had shut out past incidents that would have provided more emotional depth, and made her seem less shallow to him.

But there was nothing she could do about her memory, there was nothing she could do about her lack of experience, and worst of all, there was nothing she could do to alleviate Reed's pain.

And here she was, crying like a baby while *he* comforted *her.*

Stiffening her spine, Kate sniffed, stepped away from the solace of strong arms and the reassurance of his heart beating beneath her ear. She clasped her hands together to keep from reaching out again. "I just wish there was something I could do to help you. I feel so . . . useless."

"Useless?" He shook his head, clamping his lips for a moment, then loosening them to inhale a shuddering breath.

When he opened his eyes, Kate felt as if she'd been completely absorbed by their intense glow. "You've given us so much that in a very real sense, you've made our lives whole again. The girls are happier than they've been in years. Shawna smiles all the time now and Rory, well, her teachers tell me that she's been so cooperative and cheerful, it's almost like she's evolved into a completely different child. You did that, Kate. You've helped Rory, you've helped Shawna, and only God knows how much you've helped me."

Kate was deeply touched by his sincerity, and humbled by his kindness. Not for a moment did she believe that anything she'd ever done or tried to do could possibly repay the debt she owed to the family that had accepted her and lavished her with love. The family had shared the good times and fond memories. Now that misfortune had struck, Kate was determined to carry her share of the load.

That afternoon, Kate fixed a simple but thankfully edible supper for the girls and carried a plate out to the stable for Reed. Later, when the potbellied stove's fire dimmed, she gathered wood to fuel it. As night fell, she stabled the horses and used a rusty pickax to smash the icy crust on the cattle's watering trough.

Throughout the long evening, Kate shuttled between the house and the stable, where she tried to buoy Reed's spirits with cheery chatter and tons of hot coffee. Reed, concerned that his daughters would be upset by the sick calf's appearance, had asked Kate to keep them in the house, so she'd kept the worried girls occupied with a board game spiced by her own forced optimism.

After the girls went to bed, Kate returned to the stable and discovered the poor man propped upright in the corner, sound asleep. She covered him with a blanket, returned to the house, then fell into her own exhausted slumber.

The next morning, Kate found Reed slumped over the kitchen table, staring into a mug of cold coffee. He said nothing.

He didn't have to.

Chapter Ten

Toying with her breakfast cereal, Rory moved soggy flakes from one side of the bowl to another. "Do cows go to heaven, Daddy?"

Reed braced his forearms against the table edge. "I like to think so, punkin."

"Good," Rory murmured, her lip quivering. "That means that Fagan is gonna be okay, because Mommy will be there to take care of him."

To his credit, Reed never allowed his impassive expression to crack, although from her vantage point across the table, Kate noted a subtle tremor ripple along his jaw.

Laying a napkin across his own untouched plate of scrambled eggs, he turned to Shawna, whose stoic features mirrored those of her father except that she was clutching Gulliver so tightly it was a wonder the poor cat's eyes didn't bulge. "Finish your breakfast," he told her quietly. "You don't want to miss the school bus."

"I'm not very hungry," she said, rubbing her cheek on the animal's furry forehead. "Can I be excused?"

Reed nodded without comment and made no attempt to stop Rory, who pushed away from the table at the same time as her sister.

After the girls left the kitchen, Kate chose her words carefully. "Is there something I can do to help with, you know, the arrangements?"

"No, thanks. I'll take care of it." Reed stood, reaching toward the counter for his hat. "I'm going to drive the kids to the bus stop, then I have some things to take care of. I'll be back in a couple of hours."

"Reed?" Kate waited until he turned expectantly, then rose slowly from her chair, clasping her hands together. "Are you going to be all right?"

His expression didn't change. "I've been raising animals since I was old enough to tote a feed bucket. One thing my daddy taught me was never to get attached because sooner or later, you always have to say goodbye."

"But I know Fagan was special to you."

"He was a cow, that's all. Just a cow." With that, Reed pulled his hat down to his eyebrows, snatched his jacket off the peg and went out the back door.

Kate spent the next few hours with busywork, polishing spotless counters, sweeping dust-free floors, rearranging magazines from one corner of the coffee table to another, then moving them back to their original position. Every few minutes, she'd gaze out the window, waiting for Reed.

After driving the girls to the bus stop earlier this morning, he'd returned with a little orange front-loader hitched to his pickup. With the aid of the rented tractor, Fagan had been laid to rest in the pasture beneath a gnarled oak that Reed considered a fitting memorial.

While Kate struggled to fight off her own tears, Reed, dry-eyed and stoic, had climbed back onto the tractor and rumbled away, ostensibly to clear debris from the ruined orchard. Apparently he was planning to sort salvageable branches to sell for lumber or firewood. The effort would bring only a fraction of their productive value; still, money was money and at the moment, Reed needed every penny.

Kate couldn't help but believe that there must be something she could do to help. There was a little money left from her first paycheck, since Reed had refused to accept more than a mere pittance for her room and board. Actually, they'd had a rather lively discussion about that. Reed had seemed quite stung by Kate's attempt to give the money back; she, on the other hand, had been deeply embarrassed by his reluctance to allow her to pay her own way.

In the end, he'd grudgingly agreed to accept a very small portion of her wages as rent. The token gesture had made Kate feel somewhat better, but even after a shopping spree for underwear, personal grooming items and a few pieces of inexpensive clothing, Kate still had about fifty dollars left. She wondered how many cherry trees that would buy. Perhaps four or five, maybe more.

Reed hadn't mentioned how many yearling trees he'd lost. All he'd said was about five acres of them. Unfortunately, Kate didn't know exactly how big an acre was, or how many trees it would hold, but twenty-five seemed like a nice round number. Nursery trees cost between $5 and $8, according to ads in a local paper.

Grabbing a scratch pad, she scribbled out some estimates, and figured that it would take at least two thousand dollars to replant Reed's lost acreage. Her wages didn't count, because that was money that came out of Reed's pocket in the first place. Besides, he was a proud man. Judging by the battle they'd had over rent, he'd rather eat dirt than take another dime from her.

Unless, of course, they could work out a business arrangement.

Excited, Kate dropped the scrawled sheet of paper onto the table and snapped her fingers. That was it! Crop futures, just like the commodities market. All she had to do was convince Reed that she was a legitimate investor.

And then come up with more money than she'd most likely ever seen in her life.

Her excitement died as quickly as it had erupted. At most, Kate could only come up with about a hundred a week from her wages, and that's if she didn't even buy her own toothpaste. Even so, it would take months to save up enough—assuming Reed could afford to continue paying her—and besides, she'd overheard him comment that if replacement trees weren't in the ground within a few weeks, he'd have to wait until the following spring. The one thing Reed didn't need at this point was another wasted year.

There was no doubt about it, Kate thought morosely. Despite a mountain of obstacles, not the least of which was a conspicuous lack of skill, she simply had to find a second job. Too bad her only talents were grooming horses and sewing.

Sewing.

Her gaze fell on the telephone book stored on a nearby shelf. Hadn't Shawna said something about a yarn and needlecraft shop in Grass Valley?

She thumbed through the pages until she'd found what she wanted. There it was, listed big as life. Kate swallowed hard, realizing that she'd have to lie on the application form by falsifying a last name and making up a social security number. It was risky, of course, but she had to try. Kate would have thrown herself off a mountain to save Reed; she would have emptied the ocean with a bucket, or tunneled through stone with her bare hands. There was nothing Kate wouldn't have done for Reed Morgan. She loved him that much.

Shawna and Rory returned from school to find their father pacing the yard, clutching the note Kate had written.

Gone to town, it said. *Back soon.*

Reed was beside himself. If Kate had needed something in town, why hadn't she asked him to drive her? Why had she felt the need to take off without a word, leaving a scrawled hunk of paper taped to the back door?

Shawna suggested that she might have wanted to pick up something special for supper, perhaps as a surprise, but Reed was inconsolable. This was his fault, he told himself, kicking a rock across the driveway. He wasn't sure how it was his fault, but still had no doubt that Kate's unexplained disappearance must have been caused by something he'd done. Or perhaps something he hadn't done.

All Reed knew for certain was that Kate was gone and he had to find her. He was about to jump into his pickup when he spotted a yellow cab cruising up the driveway. As Kate emerged, flushed and smiling, a wave of massive relief nearly knocked him over.

Before he'd managed to coerce his feet into gear, the cab was humming back down the driveway. Kate fluffed her hair with her fingers, then waved happily, as if everything was hunky-dory and she didn't have a care in the world.

She sidled toward him with a smug grin. "I hope you're hungry. I found a recipe for leftover roast that sounds so easy, even I'd have trouble screwing it up. It'll only take a few minutes to whip up—"

"I've been scared out of my mind," Reed blurted. "Where have you been?"

Her smile faded. "Didn't you get my note?"

"I got it," he muttered, holding up a fistful of wadded paper. "But the details were a little sketchy."

Pursing her lips, she studied her shoes for a moment, then shrugged. "Well, I was going to save the surprise until after dinner, but I suppose we can discuss it now. I have a business proposition for you."

"A what?"

Kate took a deep breath, then launched into a plan so ludicrous yet so thoroughly considered that Reed was quite astounded.

Speaking so quickly that she was nearly out of breath, Kate finished her spiel with a flourish. "The owners of the yarn shop want me to start next week, and since I'll only be working four hours a day, I'll be back long before the kids get home from school, but the best part is that you'll be able to replant this spring, and everything will be back the way it was. Isn't that wonderful?"

Reed stood there, feeling numb. "I don't know what to say."

"Don't say anything," she said, obviously thrilled. "Just run down to the nursery and buy trees."

He cleared his throat, wishing there was some way he could soften the blow. "Kate, honey, what you're suggesting is quite, ah, clever. I can't tell you how it makes me feel that you've gone to so much trouble."

Still beaming, she waved that away as irrelevant. "You're back in business. That's what matters."

"Well, not quite." He glanced away. "I know that you did quite a bit of research, and I'm very impressed with your ingenuity, but the thing is that commercial trees cost considerably more than the ones you priced at the local nursery."

She frowned. "Why?"

"Because they're hand-grafted stock, specially bred for disease resistance and high productivity. An order for 250 yearling whips would have to be placed months in advance—"

"*How* many?"

"Anywhere from forty-eight to fifty per acre. Why?"

"It, ah, works out to a few more than I thought, that's all." She licked her lips, slanting a wary glance upward. "So, exactly how much money would it take to replant the entire five acres with these special grafted trees?"

"Including labor, equipment rental, soil amendments and such, I could do it for eighteen to twenty thousand."

"Twenty thousand—?" She grabbed her throat as if choking. "Oh, good Lord, that's ten times more than— ohmigosh." Turning away, she steadied herself on the porch rail, her face ashen. For a moment, Reed feared she might faint, but just as he reached out, she straightened and glanced over her shoulder. "It may take a little longer than I thought to come up with my, ah, investment capital."

Reed stifled a smile. "I understand."

Wrinkling her nose, she slanted a peek in his direction. "But when I do get the money, we have a deal, right?"

Since there was about as much chance of Kate coming up with that kind of cash as there was for Reed to sprout antlers, he saw no reason to argue the point. Besides, he'd have rather gnawed his arm off at the elbow than hurt her feelings, so he shrugged and stuck out his hand. "Sure, why not?"

As they shook on it, an odd gleam in her eye gave Reed pause. He already suspected that it would be a big mistake to underestimate Kate; he just didn't know how big.

The girls fell asleep early that night, exhausted and emotionally drained. By nine o'clock, the house was still and dark, except for the kitchen where Kate was hunched over the table, studying some of Bonnie Morgan's old cookbooks.

Over the past weeks, her efforts had paid off. She'd managed to unlock at least a few mysteries surrounding the magical transformation of a raw potato and a few cubes of meat into a hearty meal. Kate certainly didn't consider herself a real cook, but at least she'd figured out the difference between a *tsp* and a *tbsp,* and actually understood what the word *sauté* meant.

Understanding, however, was not the same as performing. She still ran into problems with certain culinary descriptions, and had difficulty comprehending why chopped onions swished in hot butter were supposed to turn translucent when hers simply turned black. Vague instructions like "season to taste" eluded her, too, but no matter. If Rory could learn to spell, Kate could learn to cook. It was just a matter of concentration, effort, and saintly patience from those subjected to her epicurean experiments.

Sighing, Kate closed the book and rubbed her stinging eyes. It had been a long, grueling day. She was ready for some serious shut-eye but hesitated to retire while Reed was still up, particularly when she was so deeply concerned about him.

Since he'd been up most of last night caring for poor little Fagan, Reed desperately needed rest, but he'd been working nonstop throughout the entire day. After dinner, he'd retired to his shop, supposedly to repair one of the pasture gates damaged by the storm. Up until a few minutes ago, Kate had been comforted by the sound of his movements behind the closed shop door as he'd hammered and drilled and shuffled through organized piles of clutter.

Now an eerie silence piqued her curiosity.

Pushing away from the table, she went to the door and tapped lightly. "Reed?"

When he didn't answer, she peeked inside. The hanging fluorescent fixtures were alight and the finished gate was propped by the workbench, but Reed was nowhere in sight. Kate did notice, however, that the door leading from the shop to the side yard was ajar, and when she went outside, she saw that a light was on in the stable. A sick feeling settled in her stomach.

There was no reason for Reed to be in the stable tonight. In fact, Kate had made a point of bedding down Molly and Spot herself, then retrieving the sleeping bag, vaporizer and anything else that would serve as a sad reminder of last night's ordeal. She'd been trying to protect Reed's feelings, although he'd admittedly handled the heartbreaking incident with considerably more strength than Kate could have mustered under the circumstances.

Perhaps she'd overestimated his emotional attachment to the little red bull. After all, he'd been quite adamant that losing the occasional animal was an unfortunate byproduct of ranch life. That philosophy seemed a bit crass to Kate, who got a massive lump in her throat just thinking about Fagan's frisky bright eyes and playful disposition. Nonetheless, Reed had doubtless suffered many similar losses and had learned to deal with them by maintaining an emotional distance that Kate had yet to master.

Deep down, she wasn't sure it was even possible for her to master such a philosophical attitude about death. But she'd tried to be strong to garner Reed's approval, and because she wanted to demonstrate an ability to slip comfortably, and permanently, into his life.

There was no doubt in Kate's mind that her destiny was with Reed Morgan.

As she considered that, a frigid breeze suddenly slid through the clear, cold night, chilling Kate to the bone. She rubbed her bare arms, shivering, then forced her feet forward and went into the stable.

The horses nickered a soft welcome, but the corridor running along the stalls was empty. Kate hesitated, then moved softly over the weathered plank floor toward the far end of the stable where Fagan had been. A quiet sob, deep and ragged, floated from the last stall.

Then she saw Reed kneeling beside a bed of hay, his bowed head propped on clenched fists, his body racked by grief. So intense was his sorrow that Kate felt as if the breath had been punched out of her lungs. She was momentarily paralyzed, unable to speak, unable to breathe, unable to move so much as a single toe.

Reed Morgan was crying.

And as he wept with inconsolable sorrow, Kate was shattered, her heart cracking beneath the immovable weight of such intense anguish and utter despair.

For what seemed an eternity, Kate stood frozen, with hot tears coursing down her face until the numbness dissipated, allowing her legs to move so she could quietly enter the stall.

The flimsy gate creaked, alerting Reed to her presence. He stood instantly, spinning around only for a moment, then turning quickly away. "Kate." It was the only word he managed before his voice gave out. He ducked his head, wiping his face. A tremor vibrated the crest of his shoulders as he coughed to cover a muffled sob. "I, ah—"

When his voice cracked again, he gave up, slumping forward as Kate came up behind him. She slipped her arms around his waist, pressing her cheek against his strong back. "I understand," she whispered, her own voice thick with emotion. "I know how much you loved him."

Reed raked his hair, shuddering. "He was...just a cow."

"We both know Fagan was much more than that. He was very special to all of us." Kate tightened her embrace, taking comfort in the masculine warmth seeping through the thin denim of his jacket. "Every time I looked into those huge, puppy brown eyes, I saw an impish child in a cow suit. I imagine you did, too."

"Yeah, I guess." Reed's head was still bent forward, as if he were staring at the slender palms pressed over his chest. He stroked her knuckles with his fingertips. "The thing is that I never could figure out why I liked that silly little bull. He could be a real pain in the butt."

Closing her eyes, Kate rubbed her cheek against Reed's back, inhaling his special scent. "Tell me," she murmured.

Reed shuddered, but his voice held a wistful quality. "When Fagan was a baby, he had to be stabled every night. Only he wanted to stay out in the pasture like a big cow, so whenever he saw me coming to put him inside, he'd run off and hide behind a tree.''

Kate chuckled softly. ''That sounds like Fagan.''

''Yeah. Guess he figured that if he couldn't see me, then I couldn't see him, either, so he only worried about hiding his head and left his rump sticking out.'' Reed glanced over his shoulder with a sad smile. ''Poor little guy always looked real surprised when I found him.''

Kate wanted to respond, but the lump had reformed in her throat. A renewed surge of moisture in Reed's eyes revealed how deeply the fond reminiscence had affected him. A moment later, she found herself staring at the back of his head. She felt him loosen her hands, gently lifting them from his body. He would have moved away from her physically and emotionally, but Kate wouldn't allow it.

She pivoted quickly, moving around to confront him. ''You don't always have to be the strong one,'' she whispered. ''You're not alone. It's okay to feel sad, and it's okay to share those feelings with people who care for you.''

He shook his head, covering his eyes with his hand as if ashamed of his tears. As she touched his wrist, his body trembled violently. He spun away, dropping to his knees. In less than a heartbeat, Kate was beside him, stroking him, murmuring words of comfort, hugging his dear face to her breast, kissing his hair, his forehead, his eyelids. She was frantic to soothe him, to ease his pain, to touch that secret part of his heart that he kept walled off from the world.

Then something happened, something startling. Something wonderful.

Reed embraced her, accepting the solace she offered, returning her kisses with an urgency that took her breath away. Every inch of her face and throat was covered with warm kisses while his fingers tangled in her hair, his body pressing hers with an intensity that both thrilled and unnerved her. His strength was awesome, his need so fiercely acute that Kate suddenly felt powerless and vulnerable.

Apparently Reed sensed her uneasiness, because he instantly withdrew. Raking his hair and breathing hard, he turned away. "This isn't right."

A cold draft swirled around her, dissipating his comforting warmth. At that moment, Kate realized that her fearful reaction had been caused by inexperience. This was the man she loved, the man she cherished above all others. He needed her now, and she needed him. Nothing on earth could possibly be more right than expressing that love.

She reached out, cupping his face with her hands. "I want to be with you, Reed. Please don't push me away."

With a quiet shiver, he lifted her hands, pressing a sweet kiss in the center of each palm. "You're so beautiful," he murmured, "And so very, very sweet. You're everything a man could ever want, and then some. You deserve the best."

"You *are* the best."

He closed his eyes, sadly shaking his head. "I'm a common working stiff who just happens to be teetering on the brink of financial ruin. I'm not the kind of man you need."

"You're the man I want, Reed."

"That's because at the moment, I'm all you know."

"No." Shaking off his grasp, she cupped his face again and turned his head, forcing him to look at her. "I want you because you're kind and decent and loving, and because my heart swells like a balloon every time you come into a room. I want you because my pulse leaps when you look at me, and my knees wobble at the sound of your voice. I want you because I love you, Reed, and no matter what happens tomorrow or the next day or the next, I will always love you."

Reed's eyes clouded with conflict. "Kate, honey, you don't know what you're saying."

"I know what I'm feeling." Gazing straight into his eyes, Kate took his hand and pressed it against her breast. "Can you feel my heart? It's beating for you, Reed. Only for you."

His eyes darkened in surrender a moment before his mouth found her lips in a kiss so achingly sweet that Kate feared she might faint from sheer joy. She felt weightless, as if her body had levitated and was being swished through the air. When a frigid breeze ruffled her, she realized that Reed had gathered her in his arms and carried her out of the stable.

Closing her eyes, she nestled her face in the curve of his throat, clinging to him with a desperation that would have frightened her had she allowed herself to consider what was happening. All she knew was that Reed wanted her as much as she wanted him. To Kate, wanting and loving were the same; therefore, Reed must love her. And with that realization came a joy so exquisitely intense that it could only be visualized as an enveloping canopy of pure white light.

With her eyes tightly shut, she relied on other senses to orient herself—the scent of sawdust as she was carried through the shop, the feel of heated air on her cheek as they entered the house. Reed's booted steps were strangely muffled on the hardwood floor of the hallway, as if he were making an effort to be silent. A new scent stirred Kate's senses, the lingering aroma of after-shave and freshly laundered sheets.

A moment later, she was gently laid on a bed. But not her bed.

Trembling, Kate opened her eyes and saw the vaguely familiar shadows of Reed's bedroom. Moonlight sprayed through the undraped window, silhouetting his movements as he shrugged out of his jacket, tossing the garment aside. He unbuttoned his shirt, letting it hang open until he'd pulled off his boots and set them carefully at the foot of the bed. The rest of his clothing was discarded quickly.

There wasn't enough light to scrutinize the details of his body, although when Reed finally joined her on the bed, Kate was acutely aware of his nudity. She kept her gaze riv-

eted on the ceiling while every trace of moisture evaporated
from the roof of her mouth.

He stroked the sensitive flesh of her inner arm, regarding
her thoughtfully. "Shall I help?" he whispered, running his
fingertip up the sleeve of her T-shirt.

Kate blinked, suddenly realizing that she was expected to
do more than simply lie there like a terrified lump of coal.
"Uh...no, I'll do it." Bolting upright, she bent forward and
yanked off one sneaker without bothering to untie it. It hit
the floor with a thud. She winced, removing the other shoe
with more care.

There. Her feet were bare. She wiggled her toes to confirm it. Yes, she definitely had naked feet.

Now what?

Swallowing hard, she let her fingers dance on the hem of
her shirt, then took a deep breath and pulled the garment
over her head. She sat there, hugging the wadded fabric to
her breast while nervous perspiration beaded in cleavage
exposed by the flimsy cotton bra that had cost her $4.98 at
the local discount store.

Reed gently unscrewed the twisted T-shirt from her taloned grip. He kissed the side of her throat, distracting her
while her rigid torso was gently lowered to the mattress.
"This," he murmured between nibbles on her earlobe, "is
my favorite part."

With that, he skimmed his flat palm down her belly. Before Kate had a clue what was happening, he'd tweaked
open the button at the waistband of her jeans. A trail of intense heat followed his progress as he slipped beneath the
denim to trace the elastic band of her low-cut panties. During his leisurely exploration, Kate couldn't breathe. Every
touch sent a plethora of unexpected sensations coursing
through her body. It was the most incredible experience.

"Kate," Reed murmured, his breath warm against her
skin. "My sweet, sweet Kate. So soft, so beautiful..." He

paused to taste the pounding pulse at the base of her throat. "Mmm, so incredibly delicious."

It occurred to her that perhaps, just perhaps, she was supposed to touch him, too. She laid a hesitant hand on his shoulder, then mustered enough courage to direct her fingertips to the rippling muscles of his chest. To her delight, his skin was smooth and strong, with only the slightest smattering of tickly hair. But when Reed suddenly caught her hand, urging it lower, Kate froze. "I, uh— I mean, maybe I shouldn't—"

He instantly released her, whispering against her ear. "It's okay. I only want you to do what makes you feel good."

"But I want you to feel good, too."

A low chuckle rumbled from deep inside his chest. "Honey, if I was feeling any better, you'd be real disappointed in me."

That didn't make any sense at all, but not wanting to draw attention to her inexperience, Kate remained silent. Well, mostly silent, except for the soft moans that she couldn't seem to control, and the startled gasps that flew off her tongue without permission. This was all new to her, but beyond that, Kate was absolutely astonished by what was happening to her body, which seemed to know what it was doing even if Kate herself was completely clueless.

As her hips began a provocative, circular movement that seemed as natural as breathing, Reed continued to trace her body with his lips, spreading a moist trail of kisses around her covered breasts and down her quivering belly until every inch of her flesh seemed ready to explode in flames.

She was vaguely aware that fabric was sliding down her legs. Air brushed her thighs. Her jeans had magically disappeared, but she didn't care. Nor did she care that her breasts had been inexplicably released from their confinement, and her wispy panties had also been surreptitiously slipped away.

None of it mattered, because Kate was melting inside. The heat in her belly was building into an inferno, and she was crazed with a passion far beyond her experience. Reed was cherishing her swollen breasts with his mouth, teasing her into a frenzy while his fingers stroked her inner thighs with caresses that grew increasingly sensual and thrilling.

The strokes became deeper, more intimate, until Kate's fingers convulsively gripped the edges of her pillow and she was crying out for a fulfillment she didn't yet understand.

Then, just as Reed's caresses seemed on the very brink of providing that release, Kate stiffened at a sharp, tearing sensation that was as startling as it was painful.

Reed went rigid. He instantly withdrew, rearing up and staring at her in gaping amazement. "Why didn't you tell me?"

Panting and fuzzy minded, Kate pushed a tangled mass of hair out of her face. "Tell you what?"

To her horror, Reed pulled completely away, dropping his feet to the floor as he slumped at the edge of the mattress. He took a shuddering breath, then looked over his shoulder. "You're a virgin."

The statement was delivered like an accusation. Cringing, Kate plucked at the bedclothes, pulling the sheet up to cover her bare body. "You say that as if it's something awful."

"No, honey, it's something wonderful, only—" He sighed and shook his head. "You should have told me."

"I didn't think it would matter, and besides, I didn't want you to think I was, you know, a dweeb."

"A dweeb?" A restrained quiver touched the edge of his mouth. "Trust me, Kate. I would never think that." Turning away again, he heaved a regretful sigh and wiped his face with his palms. "But it does matter."

"Why?" Kate bolted upright, then scrambled to recapture the slipping bedclothes. "I mean, it's not like virginity is contagious or something. Everyone has a first time. This just happens to be mine." At least she fervently hoped that it would be, although that possibility seemed to be fading fast.

Reed was quite clearly distressed. Shifting to face her, he took her hand, holding it gently between the callused palms that moments earlier had caressed her with such aching sweetness. "The first time should be very special, Kate. You've been saving this moment as a gift to your husband. I can't take that away from you, or—" his voice hardened "—or from him."

Suddenly Kate was completely calm. She lifted Reed's hand, brushing her lips over his knuckles, then gazed straight at him and hoped that he'd recognize the love in her eyes. "I've been saving this moment for the man I love, Reed. You are that man. Please, don't send me away."

"Kate—"

"If this virginity thing is such a big problem," Kate blurted, "I'll, ah, I'll just go out and get rid of it."

"You'll *what?*" Reed's expression would have been comical if Kate hadn't been so panic-stricken.

"I'll get rid of it. I mean, surely there's someone out there who wouldn't mind relieving me of it—"

"This is a joke, right?"

"And then maybe you'll want me again."

Reed's expression crumpled before her eyes. "I want you, Kate. You'll never know how much."

"Then show me," she whispered. "Please, Reed, I need you to show me."

In the silence that followed, Kate was terrified that he'd simply get up and walk out of the room. But he didn't. Instead, he smiled softly and reached to stroke her cheek. "I think," he murmured, "that we should start all over again."

So with fair warning issued, he gathered her in his arms and a night of pure wonder began slowly, sensually, with a power and a passion so excruciatingly intense that Kate feared she would die of it. Reed loved her with incredible patience, bringing her to the brink time and time again, until she was crazed with desire. And finally, when every trace of shyness had dissipated into a sensual frenzy, Kate turned to her lover, doing everything for him that he'd done for her, and then some.

His groans of pleasure sent delicious chills down her spine, increasing her boldness. And while his manhood quivered beneath her brazen touch, her womanhood blossomed in reply, an uncontrollable burst of pleasure that shocked her to the core.

When they finally joined, Kate came to Reed with passion and with purpose. She came to him as a woman, not as a girl. And for the first time in her life, she understood the difference.

Reed lay there for hours, watching Kate sleep. Her breath was sweet and warm against his chest; her cheek was like silk against his bare skin. He stroked her raven hair, marveling at how moonlight enhanced its lustrous sheen.

The first time Reed had laid eyes on Kate, he'd thought her the most beautiful woman in the world. And she was, but her beauty went so much deeper than he could ever have imagined. Kate was loving and compassionate, quirky and cute, sizzling and sensual . . . she was everything wonderful rolled up into a perfect human being.

Kate was God's gift to Reed, and to his children.

And yet he was troubled.

Moving slowly, Reed slipped his arm from beneath Kate's sleeping form. After brushing a soft kiss across her cheek, he tiptoed over to retrieve his shorts, then crept quietly down the hall.

Except for a spray of moonlight from the bay windows and smattering of small embers glowing in the wood stove's belly, the living room was dark. Reed went directly to the sofa. He sat there a moment, staring into space. Something pulled his gaze downward, to the photograph on the table.

His heart twisted as he studied the smiling image, nested in the lovely satin cloud.

Reed laid the picture in his lap and spoke to it. "I miss you, Bonnie. So do the girls."

Bonnie smiled up in silence.

"Right before you left us, you told me something. Do you remember?" He waited a moment, as he always did when discussing matters of importance with the woman who'd once been the cornerstone of his life. "You said that you didn't want me to be alone, that I should look for someone else to love. I told you that wasn't ever going to happen, that I didn't want anyone else. And I didn't, Bonnie, I swear."

He stared at the photo, tracing the outline of her dear face with his fingertip. "I remember you telling me that the right person would come along when I was ready. I didn't believe you. But you knew, didn't you?" He could have sworn the image nodded. "You'd have liked Kate. She made this frame for your picture. It's pretty, isn't it?"

Reed looked away, ravaged by emotions he couldn't identify and didn't know how to control. "I've been thinking that maybe, you were right, that maybe it is time to, well, you know. Kate's a very special person. The girls are nuts about her. I am, too. I guess that scares me a little."

Closing his eyes, he took a deep breath. "The truth is that it scares me a lot. Losing you was like having a piece of my heart ripped out. I don't want to go through that again, but I love her, Bonnie, and I need to know if that's okay with you."

At the moment, an odd crackling caught Reed's attention. He glanced up, then turned toward the wood stove, where dying embers had inexplicably erupted into a roaring flame, dissipating the darkness with golden warmth.

Reed had his answer.

Chapter Eleven

"Rory, turn off the television. Breakfast is ready." Reed scooped a pile of scrambled eggs onto a waiting plate, glancing over his shoulder to see if his youngest had appeared. She hadn't, and slapstick cartoon music still blared from the living room TV. He set the egg platter on the table, and would have reiterated his request except that a movement out in the yard caught his attention.

He wandered toward the window to watch Kate de-icing the cattle's water trough with a pickax. Normally that was Reed's chore, although Kate had taken over, insisting that swinging a pick was therapeutic. Her enthusiasm for even the most mundane aspects of ranching was a refreshing reminder of what made this life-style unique. For all its tragedy and hardship, ranching was in Reed's blood. He wondered if it would someday be as much a part of Kate's life as it was his.

Leaning against the kitchen counter, Reed gazed out the window like a love-struck puppy, allowing delicious images to float through his mind, sweet memories of their love-making. Just before dawn, he'd become aware of his own arousal and had awakened to Kate's sensual strokes and mischievous smile. He'd reached for her and they'd made love again, giggling like teenagers as they'd tried to muffle the sounds of passion so they wouldn't wake the girls before Kate had a chance for a covert retreat back to her own room.

All that secrecy had been strangely erotic, reminding Reed of adolescent trysts in his daddy's old pickup truck. In those days, sexual exhilaration had been enhanced by the danger of discovery; any residual guilt had been drowned by a torrent of raging hormones.

But Reed wasn't a kid anymore. He was a grown man who accepted responsibility for his behavior, and although he cherished what he and Kate had shared last night, he was nonetheless chagrined by his startling lack of control.

It was just that when Kate confessed that she loved him, all doubt had simply flown out the window and Reed had been completely, utterly hers. Now in the harsh light of day, he feared she might regret what they'd done.

Especially if she regained her memory and realized that she was actually in love with someone else.

The mere thought clenched his stomach. It wasn't true. It couldn't be. If Reed allowed himself to consider the possibility that Kate would ever want to leave—

The kitchen door burst open with a blast of frigid air. Kate hustled inside. "Whew! It's so darn cold out there that even the trees are shivering." Shutting the door with a smart hip check, she shrugged out of her jacket, chattering madly. "I turned out the horses, but neither of them seemed too thrilled about being forced out of a nice warm stall. I can't say that I blame them. The pasture is frozen solid, and what self-respecting horse wants a grass-flavored slushie for breakfast? Yuck." Draping the jacket on a peg, she spun around, sniffing. "Mmm, what smells so good?" When she spotted the heaped platter, her eyes widened. "Scrambled eggs! Ooh, yummy. I am absolutely starved."

Reed just stood there, struck mute by her radiance. The icy wind had buffed her cheeks until they glowed like polished cherries and her eyes, although partially covered by a shiny tangle of windblown hair, were sparkling with unabashed joy. Kate had never looked so beautiful. And Reed had never been so tongue-tied.

Fortunately, Kate was talkative enough for both of them. "You know, I think Molly is beginning to like me. This morning, she actually nuzzled my pocket looking for carrots and let me pet her neck. Goes to show you, the smart ones always come around." An elfin twinkle in her eye suggested a double entendre for her last comment. Rounding the table, she angled a covert peek into the living room where Rory was still glued to the tube. "Alone at last," she murmured, shyly running a fingertip along the base of Reed's knuckles. "It seems a shame to waste all this wonderful privacy."

Reed's response was an unintelligible gurgle. He swallowed hard, coughed and tried again. "I, ah, just called Rory to breakfast."

Kate heaved an exaggerated sigh of disappointment. "So I'm reduced to worshiping you from afar. How sad."

Because he couldn't help himself, Reed cupped her sweet face with his hand. "She probably won't come in until the next commercial."

"A tantalizing thought," she whispered, mesmerizing him with her fathomless gaze. "What shall we do to pass the time?"

"Eat?"

"Not what I had in mind—" Kate leapt away as Rory rushed into the kitchen.

"Teacher gave out next week's spelling list," she chirped happily, sliding into her chair. "I've been practicing my new *kata*s. Will you test me later, Kate?"

"Sure. How about after lunch?"

Reed set a plate of toast on the table. "It'll have to be closer to dinnertime. The prayer vigil for Pastor Hargrove is this afternoon."

Rory slumped forward. "Do I hafta go?"

"The pastor's wife would be very disappointed if you didn't. Besides, we've been invited to the house afterward. All of your friends will be there."

The child considered that for a moment. "Is there gonna be anything good to eat?" she asked, grabbing her fork to scrape a massive portion of eggs onto her plate.

Reed frowned. "Knowing Patty Hargrove, I imagine she'll serve refreshments, but the purpose of our visit is to offer our friendship and support, not to eat the poor lady out of house and home."

The mild rebuke fell on deaf ears, however, as Rory's attention was diverted by the serious business of devouring breakfast.

"I could make a casserole," Kate suggested. "So you won't feel like you're arriving empty-handed." When Reed hesitated, she hiked a brow. "I promise it will be edible."

"In that case, I'm sure Patty would appreciate the gesture."

"I'll start as soon as I get the kitchen cleaned up." She glanced at the wall clock. "What time will you be leaving?"

"About one." Reed spoke again as Kate headed toward the pantry. "Actually, I was hoping that we'd all go."

Kate spun around, clutching a bag of noodles. "You mean, me too?"

"Sure, why not? You'll like Patty Hargrove. She's a lovely woman."

"Oh, I'm sure she is, it's just that ... I mean, I assumed that the gathering was just for friends and family."

Rory, having just taken a rather large bite of toast, wiped a greasy dribble of butter from her chin. "But you're family, aren't you, Kate?"

Kate's eyes brightened with sudden moisture. She looked from Rory to Reed and back again. "Yes," she finally whispered. "I guess I am."

With those poignant words, all of Reed's doubts evaporated like so much steam. Over the past weeks, Kate had touched and transformed each member of the Morgan clan, becoming not only part of the family, but the symbolic heart of the family. She loved them as much as they loved her. Now Reed saw that love shining in her moist eyes and knew that he had nothing to fear. Kate would never leave Morgan Ranch. She belonged here. And she knew it.

When the front door of the Hargrove home opened, a fuzzy-haired dumpling of a woman reached out to grasp Reed's hands. "Thank you for coming," she said as Reed bent to kiss her plump cheek. "Philip will be thrilled when I tell him how many of his friends have come to show their support."

A flicker of pain darkened Reed's eyes, but the moment was fleeting and Kate doubted that anyone besides herself had noticed. According to Reed, the pastor's wife had refused to accept the prognosis of doctors who expressed pessimism regarding her husband's odds of recovery. Despite a conspicuous lack of medical evidence, the woman continued to insist that the poor man was improving. Reed had confided to Kate that he was deeply concerned about Patty Hargrove's emotional health if, God forbid, the worst should happen.

Personally Kate couldn't think of anything worse than being condemned to a limbo existence, lost and alone in a bleak netherworld somewhere between this world and the next. If Kate had been in Patty Hargrove's shoes, she didn't know what she would do. She doubted, however, that she'd be able to set aside a role as grieving wife for one of gracious hostess, as Mrs. Hargrove was doing now.

Apparently Reed's fears were warranted. When it came to her husband's condition, the poor woman was clearly in denial.

To his credit, Reed composed himself quickly, squeezing Patty's hands. "The prayer vigil was lovely. I know the pastor would be pleased."

The woman's smile broadened. She slipped a quick glance over her shoulder, as if assuring herself that she wouldn't be overheard by the milling crowd in the parlor, then tugged Reed's shoulder until he'd bent down to her level. "Philip spoke to me last night."

Reed's smile froze into a grimace. "Spoke?"

"Not in words, of course, but I asked him to squeeze my hand if he could understand me, and let me tell you, that man mashed my fingers so hard I just about fainted." Flushed and radiant, Patty beamed at the startled family. "Philip is going to be all right, you know. It's just a matter of time."

As Reed and Kate exchanged a telling glance, Patty turned her attention to the girls, hugging each and directing them out to the rear yard, where other young people apparently were gathered.

"So," she said, eyeing Kate, "you must be the young lady I've been hearing so much about."

"You've heard about me?" Juggling the warm casserole dish, Kate shifted a nervous glance to Reed, who merely shrugged a brow.

"It's a small town," he said casually, then turned to the pastor's wife to complete the perfunctory introductions.

"I'm pleased to meet you," Kate murmured, thrusting out the steaming bowl. "I, ah, that is, we thought you might, um, enjoy this. It's nothing fancy, just chicken and noodles—"

"Oh, my stars, aren't you just the sweetest thing?" She tilted her head abruptly enough to vibrate her frizzy curls. "Would you be an angel and set that on the stove for me? Then you just make yourself at home, dear. There are goodies on the dining table. Do help yourself. And you," she said, tucking her hand through the crook of Reed's arm. "I need to borrow you for a few minutes. There's a burntout bulb in the chandelier, and I can't for the life of me figure how to get the doggone thing out of the socket."

With that, the peppy woman hauled Reed into the milling crowd, leaving Kate and her chicken casserole alone in the foyer. There was something unsettling about a house full of socializing strangers, an eerie déjà vu from a shadowy past on which Kate preferred not to focus.

Despite her reluctance, images nonetheless flashed through her mind, vague memories of swishing crepe and glittering jewels, of clinking cocktail glasses, and the throbbing buzz of soft conversation punctuated by the occasional forced laugh.

A tightness settled in Kate's chest as she shook off the strained memories, then moistened her lips, searching the unfamiliar surroundings until she spotted the corner of a kitchen cupboard through an open doorway.

Relieved, she wound her way past a chatting group, slipped through the door and emerged in a cheery kitchen decorated with wooden cow cutouts and dozens of perky houseplants in hand-painted clay pots. An old porcelain stove beckoned from the corner. Kate placed the casserole dish on an unlit burner, then turned her attention to a windowed door leading outside.

Crossing the room, she peeked through the sparkling glass at a compact, fenced yard where a dozen children of various ages scampered about. Rory was roughhousing with a gaggle of exuberant youngsters while Shawna huddled with a couple of giggling girls closer to her own age.

A surge of pure love brought a smile to her lips. Shawna and Rory were so very special; Kate adored them. And since she was reluctant to join the claustrophobic group of strangers lurking beyond the quiet kitchen, she settled in for a few minutes to watch the girls play and to admire the classic architecture of nineteenth-century Victorian homes dotting the lush hills behind the Hargrove house.

Twenty minutes later, Reed found her and coaxed her out into the frightening crowd. Keeping a firm but comforting grip on her elbow, he guided her through the house, proudly introducing her to anyone who so much as cast a quizzical glance in their direction. After an hour of smiling and nodding, Kate's cheeks felt like tanned leather and her neck wobbled like a bedspring.

Eventually she found herself backed into a corner of the parlor behind Reed, who was discussing cattle prices with an interested neighbor. Even a brief respite from forced conversation was a relief, so Kate nudged along the wall until her hip pressed a small round table on which framed family portraits were displayed.

She idly scanned the pictures, recognizing a snapshot of the Hargroves' daughter, whom Kate had met a few moments earlier. In the photo, Julia Hargrove was kneeling beside her own two children, a little boy who appeared to be about five, and a girl who'd been a toddler when the picture was taken. The kids were cute, Kate thought. Since Julia was about Kate's age now, she must have been barely out of her teens when her children were born. Kate looked for but didn't find a photograph of the children's father.

She did, however, find the picture of another man. It was a formal portrait of Patty Hargrove and an older gentleman, presumably her husband, whose lean, lined face was flanked by pendulous, protruding ears and topped by a shiny film of slicked-back, charcoal hair. But the man's most prominent feature was his eyes, piercing blue orbs that seemed to leap from the portrait and burrow into Kate's very soul.

She knew this man.

An icy fear skittered down her spine. The day Reed had first brought Kate to the house, she'd promptly fallen into an exhausted sleep. She'd had an eerie dream, part of which had been frightening, and part of which had been soothing and warm. She recalled dreaming about a weathered face with kind blue eyes, a man toward whom she'd felt deep gratitude.

The face in this portrait was the face in her dream.

But it couldn't have been. There was no way Kate could have ever met Pastor Hargrove because the poor man had been hospitalized before her own arrival.

Still the dream had been so real, the image so vivid. Bewildered, Kate studied the photograph. To her shock, the image winked at her, then seemed to slide out of the frame and reemerge in her mind.

A voice called from her memory. "Gracious, child, where are you off to in such a hurry?"

Squeezing her eyes shut, Kate saw only blackness, yet the voice in her head was clear, calm. Comforting.

"You climb on in here before you catch your death. The missus will give me what-for if I don't keep you warm and healthy."

A blur of light appeared, unfocused and fuzzy. Kate concentrated until the image became clearer, then clearer still. And she saw him sitting behind a steering wheel, smiling kindly.

Suddenly the images whirred backward, as though a filmstrip had been reversed. Before she'd met the man with kind eyes, she'd been running barefoot through a stone hallway with high ceilings. Shoes. She hadn't been able to find her shoes. Kate remembered her satin skirt rustling as she dashed through the halls carrying a pair of nylons and searching frantically for the white satin pumps that had been custom-ordered to match her gown. She hadn't found the shoes, but she recalled hearing voices. Whispered. Agitated.

Angry.

Now she mentally tried to follow the sound, but events were jumbled in her mind. She recalled seeing an older woman wearing a beige tea gown, and there were faceless men in tuxedos from whom she felt an odd sense of betrayal.

The next thing Kate remembered was the squeal of brakes as she'd run into the street. Pastor Hargrove had rolled down his car window. "Gracious, child, where are you off to in such a hurry?"

Kate couldn't remember what happened then, but the pastor's kind eyes and gentle voice were vividly etched in her mind. She vaguely recalled the thrum of a car engine, the blur of passing scenery and the strains of *Madam Butterfly* floating from the car radio. Perhaps she'd dozed off, she really couldn't remember. But she did remember that for the first time in a very long while, she'd felt safe and cared for.

Opening her eyes, Kate stared down at the photograph. Another memory flashed through her mind—the horrifying image of Pastor Hargrove's body slumped over the steering wheel. She remembered a scream—her own, she thought—and then she'd been falling, tumbling through air, rolling through brush.

Falling, tumbling, rolling.

Screaming.

Screaming in pain, screaming in fear, screaming because a good man would die. And she would be the one who killed him.

The portrait crashed to the floor.

"Is Kate all right, Daddy?" Rory was hovering in the hall outside the guest room, her dark eyes round with worry.

Reed clicked the bedroom door shut. "She's fine, punkin. She's asleep."

Slipping an arm around his daughter's shoulders, he guided her into the living room where Shawna waited with crossed arms and a tight frown. "What happened to her, Dad? Does she have the flu or something?"

"The doctor doesn't think so," Reed replied, grateful that Donald Stivers had been one of the Hargroves' guests. "It was probably a combination of having skipped lunch and being crushed into a room that was too warm for comfort."

"No one else fainted," Shawna observed.

Reed couldn't dispute that. "Kate's going to be fine, just fine. I'll start dinner."

With that, he headed toward the kitchen, hoping the girls wouldn't follow. What Reed really needed was a few minutes alone to think. Despite his optimistic words, he was deeply concerned about Kate. In the few seconds it had taken for Donald to rush to her side, Kate had revived. She'd been groggy, of course, and surprisingly uncooperative, refusing to permit more than a cursory examination. Insisting that she was perfectly all right, Kate had immediately asked to leave, a request that Reed had been more than willing to grant.

In retrospect, he realized that the moment they'd entered the Hargrove home, Kate's behavior had been, well, odd. Her normally sparkling, spontaneous personality had been dampened by a unique, almost bashful demeanor that was uncharacteristically rigid and formal.

At first, he'd suspected that she might simply feel shy with strangers, but as the afternoon progressed, he'd realized that although she hadn't appeared to be particularly enjoying herself, she certainly hadn't given any indication that she was bewildered by the situation. To the contrary, everything she'd done had been socially correct, from her consistently poised expression to the softly issued responses that flowed from her tongue with fluid and practiced grace.

But her eyes had been blank. It was as if Kate herself had simply disappeared, allowing someone else to borrow her body. That had concerned Reed, and it had frightened him.

Kate curled into a ball, buried her face in the pillow and feigned sleep until she heard Reed leave the room. The moment she heard the door close, tears seeped from beneath her quivering lids. Her limbs started to tremble. She was terrified.

The memories were a jumble of frightening flashes that made no sense. She couldn't remember why she'd run into the street, or why she'd climbed into a stranger's car. She knew that she'd been crying, but she didn't know why.

And she didn't want to know why.

Most of all, she didn't want Reed to learn what she'd remembered. If he ever found out what she'd done, he'd despise her. He'd send her away.

She wouldn't be able to bear that.

The jangling telephone jarred Reed out of a restless sleep. He rolled over, and fell face first onto the floor. It took a moment for him to realize that he'd fallen asleep on the sofa last night.

The telephone rang again. It seemed louder this time.

A glance at his watch confirmed that it was barely 6:00 a.m. He stumbled to his feet, reached for the phone and mumbled an unintelligible greeting.

Deputy Dale Matthews responded. "Sorry to get you up so early on a Sunday, Reed, but I figured you'd want to know."

Yawning, Reed rubbed the sleep from his eyes and tried to focus on the deputy's voice. "Know what?"

"Pastor Hargrove is out of the coma."

Reed's eyes popped open as if they'd been spring loaded. "When?"

"Last night."

"How is he?"

"Right as rain, according to Doc Stivers. Just suddenly sat up and asked for his wife."

Reed collapsed on the edge of the sofa, bending forward to prop his elbows on his knees. "Thank God," he murmured. "It looks like Patty's faith paid off."

"Yeah, looks like."

Along with relief came a feeling of sudden uneasiness. "I'm surprised that Don didn't call me himself," Reed said. "It seems kind of strange to be hearing medical news from the sheriff's department."

A strained silence filtered over the line, then the deputy cleared his throat. "This isn't exactly a social call, Reed. The pastor had quite a few questions last night, questions that were directed toward the sheriff's department for inquiry."

Something in the young man's voice made Reed uneasy. "What kind of questions?"

"The pastor was concerned about his passenger," Dale said quietly. "The hitchhiker he'd picked up in Southern California."

"I don't remember hearing that anyone else was involved in the accident."

"That's because the pastor was alone in the vehicle when we found him. Apparently, the hitchhiker had already left the scene."

"So he left. So what?"

"The hitchhiker was a woman, Reed. A young woman. Phil picked her up in Santa Barbara. And Reed...?" The deputy paused. "She was wearing a wedding gown."

With those words, Reed's entire world collapsed.

Chapter Twelve

"That's where it hit," Deputy Matthews said, pointing to a deep, indented vee in the metal guardrail. "Judging by the angle of impact and lack of skid marks, we figured Phil Hargrove's car crossed two traffic lanes and crashed into the rail going at least fifty miles per hour, then spun around and ended up over there." He nodded toward the far end of the railing, which was also badly twisted. "The passenger door latch was severed by the collision, which explains why the door was open after the accident. It also explains what happened to the pastor's passenger. Apparently, she wasn't wearing a seat belt. It's a miracle that she wasn't killed."

Reed stood at the edge of the embankment, stone faced and stoic. A steep, brushy ravine dropped fifty feet below him, ending at the intersection of the very road on which Kate had been wandering weeks earlier. It all made sense now, but desperation pushed logic aside. "There's still no proof that it was Kate who was in that car."

The deputy slid Reed an empathetic glance, then hooked his thumbs in his holster belt. "Under the circumstances, I think we can make some fairly accurate assumptions."

Rubbing his eyelids, Reed turned away from the edge of the ravine. "I want to talk to Phil."

"I'm sorry, Reed. Other than family, the doctors aren't allowing any visitors. I only got about ten minutes with him, and that was just because he'd been raising such a fuss worrying about the young woman that they were afraid he'd have a stroke."

Reed folded his arms, gazing at the speeding traffic along the interstate. "Tell me exactly what he told you."

"We've already gone over this twice." The deputy sighed as Reed speared him with a look. "All right, all right. Phil said that he was on his way home from a convention in L.A. when he stopped for lunch in Santa Barbara. Shortly after he'd pulled out of the restaurant parking lot, a woman wearing what looked like a wedding gown dashed across the street and nearly ran into his car. She was out of breath, as if she'd been running hard, and she seemed to be frightened."

"Exactly what did she say to him?"

"I already told you—" Dale held up his palms as Reed took a step forward. "Look, she asked for help, but didn't explain why. As she got into the car, Phil noticed that she wasn't wearing shoes. He asked where she wanted to go and she indicated that she didn't care, that she just had to get away before they found her. And no, she didn't say who 'they' were."

Reed shook his head, feeling sick. "So Phil just decided to bring her home like she was a stray pet?"

Dale shrugged. "You know Phil and Patty have always had a soft spot for young people in trouble. He thought they might be able to help."

Reed knew that his anger had nothing to do with Phil Hargrove's decision. It was his fear of losing Kate that was making him crazy, and on some level he understood that. Still he continued to grill Dale Matthews as if the deputy were personally responsible for a situation that was becoming more frightening by the moment. "It's a six-hour drive from Santa Barbara to Grass Valley. Do you expect me to believe that she didn't say another word during the entire trip?"

"I don't expect you to believe anything, Reed. You wanted me to tell what the pastor said, and I did."

Closing his eyes, Reed refilled his lungs, then emptied them with cleansing force. "I know, Dale, I know." He looked at the deputy, feeling drained. "And Phil is certain about the name she gave him?"

"He sure seemed to be. According to him, she was pretty spaced-out, but when he prodded her a bit, she said her name was Belinda MacGregor."

"She could have made that up."

"Could have, but didn't."

"How do you know that? I mean, the woman obviously didn't want to be found, so why would she give her name to a complete stranger?"

"Hell, I don't know, Reed. Why would she get into a stranger's car, and let him drive her halfway to Oregon? There are a darn sight more questions in this case than there are answers—" Dale's response was cut off by a crackling radio message from his cruiser, which was parked at the shoulder of the highway.

As the deputy headed toward the squad car, Reed returned his attention to the embankment. Despite his reluctance to accept that Kate had been Pastor Hargrove's passenger, his rational mind knew that it simply had to be true. There were too many coincidences to continue disputing the obvious, and despite Reed's desperation, the idea that more than one barefoot bride could have disappeared on the same day was too preposterous to merit serious consideration.

Besides, every aspect of what Reed had learned made unassailable sense. For example, if Kate had indeed been in the car when the pastor collided with the guardrail, she could easily have been thrown into the ravine, where darkness and thick brush would have concealed her location from rescuers up on the highway. Most likely, she'd been unconscious for a period of time, a theory that took on more credence when considering that the rescuers hadn't heard any cries for help.

Assuming her amnesia had been caused by the accident, she'd have awakened feeling lost and completely disoriented. To get back to the highway, she'd have had to crawl up an impossibly steep embankment, but if she'd taken the route of least resistance, she'd have walked downhill and run directly into the gravel road leading to Reed's ranch—the same road on which Reed had found her.

So there was no denying it. Kate and Belinda MacGregor were one and the same. Reed had to accept that, but it didn't mean he had to let her go.

The crunch of boots on loose gravel drew Reed's attention. He knew without looking up that Dale had returned. "I don't want Kate to know about this yet," he told the deputy. "Not until I find out why she ran off in the first place." When Dale didn't answer, Reed glanced over and was unnerved by his somber expression.

"You'll have the chance to ask someone who knows," he said finally. "I called the MacGregors last night to verify their daughter's description and vitals. The dispatcher just radioed to say that they flew up first thing this morning. They're waiting for us at the station."

Sometimes a memory-deprived mind creates fantasies. Fantasies.

Kate stood at her bedroom window watching oak limbs sway in the wind. Throughout a long, sleepless night, Dr. Stivers's words had circled a groove in her brain until she'd finally convinced herself that yesterday's experience at the Hargrove home had been nothing more than a fantasy, the creative illusion of a memory-deprived mind.

The man in the photograph had been a part of that illusion. He existed, but her memories of him were false. Kate had never met Phil Hargrove; she'd never been in his car. Her mind had simply merged information she'd learned about his accident with the image in the photograph to fabricate bogus recollections of an event that never happened.

It had never happened. Never.

And when Kate finally believed that, she felt safe again.

Back at the sheriff's station, Dale spoke with the Mac-Gregors while Reed stepped quietly aside to observe. Any lingering doubts he'd harbored about Kate's true identity were immediately dashed when he'd recognized her essence reflected in George MacGregor's shiny black hair and clear blue eyes.

The resemblance was startling, although Kate's fragile features were a stark contrast to those of her portly, mustached father. There was an aristocratic aura about the stocky man, who carried himself with quiet confidence despite a physical appearance that reminded Reed of the tuxedo-clad, monocled cartoon character on a Monopoly board.

Sylvia MacGregor was another matter. It didn't take a fashion expert to recognize that she was wearing some pretty pricey designer duds, not to mention that a rock the size of Montana glittered on her ring finger. Since everything about the MacGregors reeked of old money and elitist aristocracy, Reed figured the woman's diamonds were probably real, although that moussed-up platinum coiffure of hers looked as phony as a palomino mane on a coal black mustang.

All in all, the woman's outward appearance was harsh, unyielding. Whereas her husband was clearly concerned about his daughter's odyssey, Sylvia MacGregor seemed plainly annoyed by it. Still there was a childlike apprehension in her eyes that made her seem vulnerable, almost sympathetic. She was, Reed realized, a complicated woman. Had he not been so riveted by his own fears, he might have been curious about the cause of hers.

At the moment, however, he was concerned only what the discovery of her identity would mean to Kate. And selfishly, to him.

"This is Reed Morgan," Dale said, interrupting Reed's thoughts. "Your daughter has been staying with his family."

George MacGregor spun around, gaping at Reed as if seeing him for the first time. He rushed over to clasp Reed's hand. "Thank you," he said, his eyes shining with grateful tears. "Words can't express our appreciation."

Decidedly uncomfortable, Reed extricated himself from the man's viselike grip while tossing a pleading glance at the deputy, who thankfully took the hint.

"I do have a few more questions," Dale said. "Just to complete the paperwork."

"Yes, yes, of course." Brushing his lapel, MacGregor squared his shoulders and, Reed thought, appeared to be struggling with his emotions. "Perhaps we could hurry this along. I'm sure you can understand how anxious I am to see my daughter."

Issuing a noncommittal nod, Dale retrieved a file folder from the lobby desk, flipped it open and read silently for a moment.

"Is this really necessary?" Sylvia MacGregor asked, clearly irritated by the delay.

"I'm afraid so," Dale muttered, hiking a brow. "You are aware, Mrs. MacGregor, that your daughter has suffered a rather severe trauma?"

"Belinda is my stepdaughter, and yes, we understand that her memory has been somewhat impaired. Clearly, that explains why it's taken so long for us to locate her."

"Not entirely." Raising his eyes from the folder, the deputy focused a hard look on the stiff-spined woman. "Frankly, I'm curious as to why no missing person report was issued."

The apprehension in the woman's eyes deepened, as did the taut lines bracketing her mouth. "Our family is a cornerstone of Santa Barbara society. As such, we are vulnerable to tawdry speculation by the press and hurtful gossip by those who, shall we say, are less visible in the community. Tabloids make a living distorting small misunderstandings into front-page scandal."

Reed's ears perked. "What kind of misunderstanding?" he asked the woman, and was rewarded by a chilly stare.

"Actually, there was none," George said quickly. "At first, we didn't know what to think, but now that we've learned about this amnesia business, everything makes perfect sense." His attention was distracted as a well-dressed young man with broad shoulders, immaculately scissored hair and perfect teeth strode into the lobby as if he owned it. George hurried over to shake his hand. "Ah, Steven. We were afraid you wouldn't make it."

"The Learjet was grounded in San Francisco," the man said, casting a casual glance around the lobby. "We had to wait for the fog to lift. Where's Belinda?"

"She's, ah...?" Frowning, George angled a questioning look at the deputy, who in turn nodded toward Reed.

Although Reed would have preferred to keep Kate's whereabouts a mystery, at least for the moment, he settled on a vague reply. "She's at the ranch."

The man called Steven regarded Reed with polite disinterest. "I'm sorry, I don't believe we've met."

"This is Reed Mörgan," George said quickly. "Belinda has been staying with his family."

"Indeed?" A perfect smile warmed eyes so thickly lashed that any woman on earth would have killed to possess them. "Well, I certainly am pleased to meet you, Mr. Morgan. Your kindness will be generously rewarded."

Reed reluctantly accepted the man's proffered hand. "And you are...?"

"Steven Sebring," he replied smoothly. "Belinda's fiancé."

Reed felt the blood drain from his face. For a moment, he feared he'd be ill. This was the man Kate loved, the man she'd been planning to marry and the man for whom she'd been saving herself, until Reed had stolen her innocence.

Reed stood frozen, unwilling to look at the man he'd unwittingly betrayed yet unable to tear his gaze away. He couldn't speak, couldn't breathe, couldn't release his spasmed grip despite the grimace marring the young man's startled face.

Across the room, Dale Matthews tapped the file folder on the counter. "Sebring," he murmured absently. "Not *the* Steven Sebring of Sebring Farms?"

With an excuse-me smile, the man extracted his hand from Reed's grasp. "Yes, actually."

For some reason, the affirmative response elicited such surprised excitement from the deputy that one would think he'd just spotted the pope standing in line at the local burger barn.

Dale crossed the room fast enough to create a draft, and didn't stop until he was so close to Sebring that the poor man found himself pinned against the lobby door.

"So what's the scoop on the Triple Crown?" the deputy asked, his eyes glittering. "I hear the big money is riding on Not Of This Earth to take one of three, but those in the know are betting on Sebring's Serendipity in Blue for a clean sweep. Got any tips?"

Sebring favored the gushing deputy with a tolerant smile. "I may be rather biased, but my trainers are confident that if Blue holds peak form until spring, he'll be extremely difficult to beat.''

"All right!" Beaming, Dale slapped Reed's shoulder. "What do you say, Reed, want to dust off the old racing form and put up a small wager?"

The deputy turned his attention back to Sebring without awaiting Reed's response, which was fortunate since Reed couldn't have uttered a word if his life depended on it.

Not only was Kate's fiancé several years younger and light-years better looking than Reed, he also happened to be one of the wealthiest and most powerful men in Thoroughbred racing. Over three generations of Sebrings, the family stables had produced dozens of champions, including some of the top money-winners of all time. Reed had once read that the bloodlines of Sebring stock were so highly prized among Thoroughbred breeders that six-figure stud fees were considered routine.

There was no way a debt-ridden, middle-aged rancher could compete with that kind of success.

Sebring suddenly laid a hand on Reed's shoulder, startling him. "Thank you for taking such good care of Belinda. When she disappeared from the chapel—" He looked away, his voice breaking.

Sylvia hurried forward to solicitously tuck a perfectly manicured hand through the crook of Sebring's arm. "It was horrid," she said to no one in particular. "When we went to the bride's chambers to check on Belinda's progress, she was gone. There was a vase broken on the floor, and at first, we feared something terrible had happened. Later we learned from one of the chapel yardmen that she'd been seen rushing across the grounds toward town. Well, you can imagine our chagrin."

"Belinda had been nervous about the wedding," George explained.

"All brides are nervous," Sylvia snapped, annoyed by the interruption. "Belinda has always been high-strung and spoiled, George. It would have been just like her to have planned the entire charade simply to embarrass us in front of our friends."

Clearly stung by his wife's remark, George issued a mild rebuke. "That's unfair, Sylvia. You know as well as I do that Belinda's shyness makes socializing extremely painful for her. The truth is," he added, turning his attention to Reed and Dale Matthews, "I never involved the authorities in searching for my daughter because I honestly believed that she was having second thoughts about the marriage and had left of her own volition."

"George!" Sylvia tightened her protective grasp on Sebring's arm. "Have you no consideration for Steven's feelings?"

"It's all right," Steven murmured, patting the woman's clutching hand. "Under the circumstances, George's beliefs were quite logical. In fact, I must confess that I, too, wondered if Belinda had changed her mind about marrying me."

"Why, that's absurd," Sylvia murmured, gazing at the younger man with the gushing flattery of a syncophant groupie. "Any woman would be thrilled by the attention of a man of your stature."

Sebring smiled, seeming not to notice that the obsequious statement was delivered with an odd lack of conviction and a nervous eye-shift that caught Reed's attention, piquing his curiosity.

"You're too kind," Sebring murmured, squeezing the older woman's hand. "But since we now understand what really happened to poor Belinda, we can dismiss such unpleasant speculation and concentrate on nursing her back to health."

It was Dale who verbalized the question stuck on Reed's tongue. "What, exactly, is it that you believe really happened?"

"I think that's rather obvious," Sebring replied without rancor. "Unfortunately, during the turmoil at the chapel, we completely ignored the significance of the shattered vase."

Dale frowned. "The vase?"

"It was quite a large vase," George explained. "And apparently too heavy for the pedestal, one of those simulated Roman archetypes constructed of a lightweight material that resembles concrete but is much less stable."

After considering that for a moment, Reed didn't get the connection and said so.

Dale, however, did get it. "So you believe that Kate's... er, Belinda's amnesia wasn't caused by the traffic accident at all, but rather by an injury received in the chapel?"

"It would appear so," George said sadly. "Those who saw her outside of the church said that she appeared frightened and disoriented, which certainly makes sense if she'd been struck unconscious by a falling vase and upon awakening, had no memory of who she was or why she was there."

"Whoa." Puffing his cheeks, Dale folded his arms and rocked back on his heels. "That puts everything in a whole new light, doesn't it, Reed? Reed... are you all right? You look kind of funny."

Reed didn't answer the deputy's question, because he barely heard it. His last vestige of hope had just crumbled into irretrievable pieces.

Even after having met the MacGregors and Steven Sebring, Reed had clung to the belief that maybe, just maybe, Kate really had run away because she hadn't wanted to marry the man. It had never occurred to Reed that Kate's injury could have occurred before she'd left the church. If that was the case, then Kate had been happily preparing to wed when tragedy had struck.

Happily.

Preparing to wed.

That meant that Kate had been in love with Steven Sebring before she'd lost her memory; when her memory returned, she'd be in love with him again. And she'd despise Reed for destroying the purity that she'd been saving for him.

Shawna glanced up from her homework as Kate bounced into the kitchen, humming happily. "You're sure in a good mood this morning."

"Of course I am," Kate replied, pouring a cup of steaming coffee. "The sun is shining, the cows are mooing and the world is a beautiful place. Everyone on earth should be happy today."

"Yeah, well everyone on earth doesn't have old man Graviston for history," the girl grumbled. "He gave us three chapters to read by Monday, and we have to do the quiz questions, too."

"Hmm, that is a problem. Do you need any help?"

"Not unless you can read the darn stuff, then download it directly into my brain."

"I would if I could, sweetie." Kate slid into a chair, then leaned forward, sipping her coffee. Her gaze wandered toward the window. "Where's your dad?"

Stretching, Shawna ruffled her hair and rolled her head as if trying to ease tight neck muscles. "All I know is that he woke me up early this morning saying he had to go out for a while."

"Did he tell you where he was going?"

"Nope, only that I should let you sleep and that he'd be back later." Issuing a pained sigh, Shawna stared glumly at the open book. "This really stinks. Maybe I can get Rory to teach me a *kata* for history finals."

"Maybe," Kate murmured, distracted by the swirling black liquid in her cup.

"Kate?" Shawna hesitated a moment, then swallowed hard. "Are you okay? I mean, you really scared us yesterday."

Smiling, Kate reached across to squeeze the girl's hand. "Fantasies."

Shawna blinked. "Excuse me?"

"Fantasies," Kate repeated, stifling a giggle. "Did you know that the mind can actually create fantasies that are every bit as real as actual memories? Isn't that fascinating?"

Rearing back, Shawna regarded Kate with blatant skepticism and more than a trace of worry. "Yeah, fascinating. Are you sure you're okay?"

"I'm absolutely positive."

Heaving a resigned shrug, the teenager would have returned her attention to the hated history book had she not been distracted by a droning truck engine. She glanced toward the window. "Sounds like Dad's back."

The announcement was unnecessary, since Kate had heard it, too, and was halfway to the kitchen door. She couldn't wait to see Reed, to throw her arms around him and tell him how much she loved him, and that she wanted to be with him for the rest of her life.

Giddy with excitement, Kate dashed onto the porch with such momentum that she was carried forward even as her mind skidded to a stop.

Reed wasn't alone.

An expensive, silvery sedan was following Reed's truck up the driveway. Kate shaded her eyes, curious at first, but as she saw silhouettes moving inside the vehicle, a chill of apprehension skittered down her spine.

Two men emerged from the car simultaneously. Kate's frightened gaze slid past the driver, who was the taller and younger of the two, and she stared at the portly, mustached passenger who was striding directly toward her.

A steady hum circled her brain, growing louder, more terrifying as the mustached man grew closer. Images flashed through her mind, mental pictures of a wood-paneled library scented by pipe tobacco, and of a dining table set with fine gold-rimmed china. She heard voices from the past, saw a filmstrip of her own life rushing before her eyes. She remembered.

Dear God, she remembered.

Chapter Thirteen

Throughout his life, Reed had suffered more than his share of loss. No matter how deep the emotional anguish, he'd always understood that somehow he'd survive and find the strength to go on.

Today that strength finally failed him.

Stepping out of the truck, he saw Kate rush to greet him, only to hesitate, visibly bewildered as the MacGregors' rental car pulled up. Her gaze was now riveted on George MacGregor, who'd just emerged from the vehicle.

"Belinda," he murmured, rushing across the damp ground to sweep his daughter into a poignant embrace. "Oh, my sweet girl."

After accepting but not returning her father's hug, Kate took a step back and to Reed's horror, she seemed to shrink before his very eyes, metamorphosing into a woman he didn't recognize.

As her proud carriage shriveled in on itself, her shoulders rounded, her head angled into a submissive tilt, and her

normally direct gaze shifted downward to mimic the de-
mure demeanor of an obedient child.

His beloved Kate had vanished; Belinda MacGregor had
taken her place.

Reed felt as if his heart had been ripped out.

"Lord, child, we've been so worried." Stepping away,
MacGregor pinched the bridge of his nose and took a shuddering breath. "You look wonderful. You've been well?"

"Very well, thank you. I'm sorry you were concerned."
Kate's attention was diverted by the tall man striding up the
porch steps.

"Belinda. Thank God." Steven Sebring took her hands
and placed a chaste kiss on her cheek, which Kate had presented in a gesture that seemed more automatic than eva-
sive. Sebring smiled, still holding her hands loosely. "You
gave us quite a scare."

"I know, I'm sorry," she murmured to the top button of
his shirt. "You must all be very upset with me."

He waved that aside. "Nonsense. Now that we've learned
what happened, everyone understands that it wasn't your
fault."

Kate's eyes clouded. "Everyone understands?"

"Yes, we realize what happened at the church." Sebring
and MacGregor exchanged a questioning glance, then the
younger man slipped his index finger beneath Kate's chin,
raising her face in a gesture that Reed found uncomfortably intimate. "You do remember, don't you?"

"I, ah..." Licking her lips, Kate scanned the group, her
gaze settling on Sylvia MacGregor, who stood at the base of
the steps, clutching her designer handbag and wearing a
properly blank expression. "I'm afraid that part still eludes
me," Kate said finally, then added a thin smile. "Hello,
Sylvia. It's nice to see you."

The older woman's rigid countenance instantly softened
and, Reed thought, she seemed oddly relieved. "You gave
your father quite a scare."

"I'm sorry."

It occurred to Reed that although Kate had apologized three times in as many minutes, there was a monotonic quality to her voice that indicated the words *I'm sorry* were as much a part of her daily routine as *thank you* and *please pass the gravy*.

Reed hoped that slamming the truck door would alleviate his tension. It didn't. He was rigid as a fence pole, and feeling just as splintered and worn.

As he joined the solemn cluster around the porch, Shawna, who'd been hovering in the kitchen door looking frightened and confused, finally spoke. "Who are these people, Kate?"

Startled, Kate turned around and gave the teenager the first genuine smile Reed had seen since the arrival of her family. "I'm sorry," she said to no one in particular. "I seem to have forgotten my manners." She slipped an affectionate arm around Shawna's shoulders and began introductions in a posed but perfunctory manner. "This is Shawna Morgan, Reed's oldest daughter. Shawna, this is George MacGregor, my father—"

Shawna pulled away. "Your father?"

A hint of compassion softened Kate's eyes. She brushed a wayward strand of blond hair out of the girl's face. "We always knew that this could happen," she said softly.

"Yes, but—" A sheen of moisture brightened Shawna's pale eyes as she bit her quivering lip.

Kate hugged the girl fiercely, a surge of emotions contorting her features only for a moment before she regained her composure. "I'd also like you to meet Sylvia Mac-Gregor, my father's wife, and Steven Sebring, a friend of the family."

A friend of the family? Reed frowned, thinking that an odd way to introduce one's future husband, but before he could ruminate on the peculiarity, Kate was speaking again.

"Do me a favor, sweetie, and go tell your sister we have company." Kate stroked Shawna's cheek so sweetly that it made Reed's heart ache. "Perhaps we can make some coffee for our guests. I'm sure they've had a tiring trip."

Sniffing, Shawna followed Kate's lead, squaring her shoulders and responding with polite formality. "Maybe they'd like something to eat, too. That coffee cake you made yesterday morning turned out pretty well."

MacGregor's head vibrated with surprise, and although he refrained from comment, his wife exercised no such restraint.

Sylvia was outraged. "Working in the kitchen like a common housemaid? My God, Belinda."

To his credit, MacGregor silenced his wife with a reproachful glance. "Not everyone has the luxury of a full-time staff, Sylvia. Frankly, I'm quite proud that Belinda was able to help out."

Properly rebuked, the woman clamped her thin lips together while her eyes flashed green fire, and she offered no resistance when her husband descended the steps to clamp a firm hand around her elbow.

MacGregor ushered his wife to the kitchen door, which Shawna was holding open. "You and Steven go inside with Belinda," he told his wife. "Mr. Morgan and I have some matters to discuss."

Peeking through the kitchen door with an expression that conveyed her distaste, Sylvia MacGregor stepped inside warily, hugging her handbag as if expecting a mugger to leap from the pantry.

Sebring followed without hesitation, although Reed noted that the man basically ignored Kate, showing considerably more interest in his surroundings than his newly recovered fiancée. "Very interesting," he mumbled, glancing in the direction of the kitchen sink, which Reed suspected was still heaped with breakfast dishes. "Quaint and, er, homey."

Kate, whose eyes still held the glazed expression of a doomed deer caught in headlights, made no response to Sebring's comment as she disappeared into the kitchen, beyond Reed's view. Shawna, however, rolled her eyes with the silent disdain that adolescents muster so effectively, then heaved a pained sigh and left the back door ajar as she went into the house.

It was Kate about whom Reed was most concerned. There was a dazed quality to her expression that reminded him of the disorientation she'd exhibited when he'd first found her. She looked numb, and that worried him deeply. Reed had brought the MacGregors here because he hadn't believed that he had the right to keep Kate from her family. Now he realized that allowing them to appear without adequate warning had been a mistake; he hadn't considered the possibility of psychological trauma. Reed could have kicked himself for not having insisted that Doc Stivers be consulted before Kate was confronted by a past she might not have been ready to accept.

Dear God, what had he done?

A frisson of fear propelled him forward, but as he started up the porch steps, MacGregor stopped him with a firm hand on his shoulder. "Our family owes you a tremendous debt of gratitude, Mr. Morgan. If you hadn't contacted the authorities, God knows how long it might have been before we found Belinda."

"Hmm?" Preoccupied by his own somber thoughts, it took a moment for Reed to realize that MacGregor had pressed a slip of paper in his hand. He looked up quizzically.

"It's the reward you were promised," MacGregor replied, giving Reed a jovial slap on the back. "I hope the amount is adequate compensation for your effort."

Still confused, Reed vaguely recalled Sebring mentioning something about a reward while they'd all been at the sheriff's station, but at the time he hadn't paid much attention.

It certainly hadn't occurred to him that Sebring had been discussing money, just as it didn't occur to him now that his conversation with MacGregor was being monitored.

Inside the kitchen door, Kate was watching. And listening.

"Here, Molly. Sweet baby, come on...that's good, that's my girl." The mare's soft lips tickled as she gently removed the carrot nested in Kate's palm. "Good girl," Kate crooned, stroking the shiny white star between the animal's wise eyes. "That's yummy, isn't it? I know, sweetheart, I know."

A warning prickle on Kate's nape alerted her to Reed's presence. She continued to caress Molly's muscular neck, suppressing an urge to turn around. Instinctively she felt Reed hang back, and imagined him tucking his thumbs into his jeans pockets, or rearranging the brim of his hat the way he always did when he was unsure of himself.

He cleared his throat. "Your folks have come a long way to see you."

Kate responded by digging another piece of carrot out of her pocket and silently holding it out to the mare. She felt Reed move closer.

"Shawna said you walked from the kitchen straight through the living room and out the front door without a word to anyone."

Since that was exactly what she'd done, Kate felt no need to expand on it. Besides, she didn't want to talk about the people inside the house, particularly not now, when she was mesmerized by the tender softness of the mare's mouth nuzzling her palm.

The heat from Reed's body was now radiating against Kate's back. Still she refused to face him.

"Your family is anxious to speak with you."

Kate reached into her pocket, found it empty and sagged against the fence rail, propping her body weight on her forearms. She sighed. "I don't want to speak to them right now."

"Why not?"

Although Kate detected a slightly hopeful tone in Reed's voice, she ignored it and responded only to the question. "Because I don't know what to say."

Reed came up beside her, hooking an elbow over the rail and propping his hip against a wooden post. "They aren't angry with you, if that's what you're concerned about. They understand that the memory loss was caused by an accident at the chapel."

Frowning, she angled a tilting glance in his direction. "It was?"

"Don't you remember?"

"No. That entire day is a blur," she whispered, absently scratching a bent nail head protruding from the fence. "I don't remember anything that happened before I got into Pastor Hargrove's car." The image of a weathered face and smiling eyes brought a lump to her throat. "He was such a good man."

"He still is," Reed said. "Phil came out of the coma last night. He's going to be fine."

"Oh . . ." Kate steadied herself on the fence but couldn't stop the rush of grateful tears. "Thank God," she murmured. "I thought I'd killed him."

Reed's jaw drooped. "Lord, honey, why on earth would you think that? It was an accident—"

"No, you don't understand." Covering her face with her palms, Kate took several deep breaths. When she spoke again, her voice quivered with emotion. "We'd been driving for hours, and I think I fell asleep. Then suddenly the car started to jerk wildly, and when I woke up, the pastor was slumped over the steering wheel. His face was gray. I . . . I was so scared. I should have just steered to the side of the road and flagged down help." She pressed her palm against her ips to bury a sob. "But I panicked and yanked the steering wheel too hard and—oh, God, it was all my fault."

"Oh, honey." Reed embraced her tenderly, stroking her wet cheeks and pressing her into his warmth. "It wasn't your fault. None of it was your fault."

Kate clutched at his flannel shirt, pressing her face against his strength. "I left him there. I just walked off and left him there."

"You were hurt, too." Stroking her hair, Reed brushed his lips across her forehead. "You didn't even know where you were, honey. There was nothing you could do for Phil, because at that moment, you didn't remember being with him or that an accident had even happened, did you?"

"No, not until I saw the pastor's photograph at the Hargrove house." She wiped her eyes roughly. "Nothing makes sense. If my memory loss took place at the chapel, why wouldn't I have remembered everything that happened afterward, including the accident?"

"I don't know, Kate." A glance upward confirmed that Reed's lips were pursed thoughtfully. "Your memory came back while we were at Patty's?"

She pulled away, leaning against the fence to study a few blades of sturdy green grass poking through the cold, wet ground. "I remembered getting into the pastor's car," she said quietly. "And I recalled what happened right before the accident. The memories frightened me so much that I managed to convince myself they weren't real. I guess they were, though."

"I guess they were."

Still staring at the ground, Kate whispered, "Pastor Hargrove *is* going to be all right, isn't he? I mean, you wouldn't make something like that up?"

"He's fine, Kate, honest to God." Since Reed's arms were now empty, he folded them, following Kate's gaze to the smattering of new grass at her feet. "We'd never have found out who you were if he hadn't come to and started asking about you."

A leery prickle slid down Kate's spine as she recalled the conversation she'd overheard between Reed and her father. "So it was the pastor who told the authorities about me?"

When he didn't answer immediately, Kate angled a glance in his direction. He answered without looking at her. "Yes, it was the pastor."

That's when Kate saw it, the vague flare of his nostrils followed by an almost imperceptible vibration. Her gaze narrowed. "So Phil Hargrove simply woke up asking about a woman named Belinda MacGregor, and the sheriff coincidentally picked up the telephone to call you, even though he had no reason to believe that you had ever met me. Is that about the size of it?"

"Ah, yeah, that's about it." Reed covered a cough with his fist, but not fast enough to conceal the tiny tremble at the base of his nose.

He was lying, and Kate knew it. "I'm not a complete fool, Reed."

Busted, he dropped his hand to his side. "It's not like you think."

"What I think is that you promised not to turn me in, but you went ahead and did it anyway." When he started to respond, she silenced him with an upraised hand. "It doesn't matter, Reed. What's done is done."

"I was only trying to help you." Frustrated by the telltale nose quiver, he kicked the dirt and swore. "All right, yes, I was also protecting my family."

If Kate hadn't been leaning against the fence, she would have been physically staggered, not only by the realization that Reed had contacted the authorities because he'd wanted to be rid of her, but also by the blatant reminder that Reed counted her on one hand, and his family on another. No matter how much she'd tried to delude herself, he'd never considered her to be a part of his family, of his life. And he never would. "I see."

"No, I don't think you do." Reed yanked off his hat, slapping it against his knee in frustration. "Okay, I admit that I went to the sheriff the day after you arrived—"

"Please, Reed. I don't want to hear about this." Understanding his motivations did little to ease the pain of realizing that he'd felt it necessary to protect his children. From her. "It doesn't matter," she lied. "Flashes of my memory were already coming back. Sooner or later, I would have remembered who I was, and where I came from."

What Kate didn't say was that she wouldn't have willingly returned, because she'd have never given up the life she'd found on Morgan Ranch.

Beside her, Reed's shoulders sagged but he simply nodded and made a production of tugging his hat back down over his forehead. He sighed, glancing back toward the house. "Your parents seem nice."

"My father's a very nice man. My stepmother, well, she's very different from my real mom. I never understood why my father married her."

"Perhaps for the same reason that Sylvia married your father."

Kate knew Reed was referring to love, but she dismissed that out of hand. "Sylvia married my father to get her hands on my mother's money, pure and simple."

"That sounds a little harsh."

"Truth hurts, doesn't it, Reed?" When he had the grace to look away, Kate's anger softened. "The fact is that my father came from a typical, middle-class working family. When he married my mother, he became CEO of the import-export firm that my grandfather had built into one of the largest in the world. But money had nothing to do with their relationship," she added quickly. "My parents were very, very much in love. When Mama died, I didn't think Daddy would survive the grief."

"But he did survive," Reed reminded her, with a compassion in his eyes that reminded Kate of his own loss. "And he found Sylvia."

"Yes," Kate whispered, her jaw aching. "He found Sylvia."

Reed's smile was sad. "You don't care for her. That's too bad."

"Trust me, the feeling is more than mutual. Sylvia has always resented the fact that Mom left the lion's share of the family fortune to me instead of Daddy."

"To you?"

Under other circumstances, Kate would have been amused by Reed's astonished expression. At the moment, however, she was merely irritated, and considering he'd already been paid a reward that she suspected was rather hefty—her father had never been a tightwad—Kate was more than a little skeptical of his motivation to feign surprise. She skewered him with a direct gaze. "On my twenty-fifth birthday, I'll inherit the trust my mother set up for me, which includes enough company stock so that Daddy won't be able to control the board without my vote."

"Well," Reed murmured, plainly surprised, "what do you know about that?"

Kate's anger died as suddenly as it had erupted. Drained, she turned away, embarrassed and feeling shy. "It was Daddy's idea," she explained. "He didn't want his daughter to ever be dependent on the generosity of a man, even her husband."

At the word "husband," Reed's features hardened. He folded his arms again, tighter this time, and cleared his throat with more force than necessary. "Your, ah, fiancé is an interesting young man."

"Yes."

That wasn't the answer Reed had been hoping for. He glanced away. "How did you meet him?"

Kate gazed across the pasture, to where Spot was grazing beneath a gnarled oak. Snapshots of her childhood flashed through her mind. Steven had always been there. His father's stable was barely a mile from the MacGregor mansion. Of course, Kate had never thought of her home as a mansion—it was all she'd ever known, after all—but the townsfolk had always referred to it as such, and sheltered little Belinda had been in high school before she'd learned that the mansion label had been applied with envy rather than respect.

Steven had always understood that. For most of Belinda's life, he'd been her only friend because they'd shared the curse of wealth that walled them off from their peers.

"Steven and I grew up together," Kate said quietly. "His father's Thoroughbred farm was right down the road. I spent most of my childhood there, because I loved the horses so much. Charles Sebring was almost like a second father to me."

"But Steven wasn't like a brother, I take it."

The bitter edge on his voice surprised Kate. "Actually, he was. At first, we had a lot in common."

"Did that change?"

"I suppose it had to. We're very different people, after all."

"In what ways?"

Uncomfortable in discussing her relationship with Steven Sebring, Kate tried to shrug Reed's question aside. "The usual ways, I suppose. Steven was outgoing and ambitious. I was bashful to the point of pain. He loved the fact that being wealthy made him special. I just wanted to be like everyone else. But both of us were basically ostracized by other children, and we each had, well, problems at home."

Reed frowned. "You mean your relationship with your stepmother?"

"Yes, and Steven didn't get along with his father, so you see, we were bonded by commiseration."

Kate smiled sadly, shaking her head as fuzzy memories became more focused in her mind. She remembered being confused by Steven, because he'd loved wealth and privilege, yet had resented his father's obsession with the Thoroughbreds that had made that life-style possible. She also recalled having discovered how dark that resentment truly was on the day Steven had learned that his father had no intention of sharing that wealth with his only son and heir. He'd never profit from the stable until after his father's death, and only with the condition that he continue the family tradition of breeding the top-quality animals that Steven quite frankly loathed.

Kate recalled that Belinda had felt sorry for Steven but hadn't understood his fury. After all, the money belonged to his father. In her mind, Steven was young and bright, able to carve out his own niche in life but a few months ago, when Belinda had verbalized her feelings, things had suddenly turned ugly.

"Kate?" It was Reed's voice.

She knew she should answer, but memories were flickering through her mind, a script so vivid and yet so frightening that she was mesmerized.

Kate remembered that Steven's face had gotten all red, and he'd screamed terrible things about how lucky Belinda was because her mother had not only set her up with a trust worth millions, she'd also had the common courtesy to die while Belinda was young enough to enjoy the money.

Belinda had been as frightened by Steven's transformation as she had by his horrible words. She'd tried to get away from him, but he'd grabbed her, babbling wildly about how it wasn't fair for a silly mouse like Belinda to have a fortune while he was left penniless and beholden to a father he despised.

In Kate's mind, she saw the argument evolve between Steven and Belinda as if she were watching from a distance. She could taste Belinda's fear, feel the frantic pounding of her heart, yet was estranged from the situation, an interested observer from another place and time.

From her safe vantage point, Kate saw Steven's eyes turn cold as he told Belinda that after they were married, things would be different. He wouldn't have to beg his father for every dime. He'd have his own money, and people would have to respect him.

Belinda's voice had quivered with weakness. "I loved my mother more than anything in the world. How dare you imply that her money is more important than her life?"

"Money *is* life," he had snapped. "After we're married, you'll understand that."

For the first time in her life, Belinda had straightened to her full height and stared Steven Sebring directly in the eye. Kate was proud of her.

"I wouldn't marry you if you were the last man on the planet," she had shouted in a voice that finally showed some gumption. "I hate you, Steven Sebring. *I hate you!*"

"Oh, you'll marry me, all right," Steven replied with a manic expression that even frightened Kate. "Terrible things happen to people who break their promises."

That's when Belinda had pulled away and run to hide in the expansive stables where she'd spent so much of her childhood, the place that Steven hated with such passion and where young Belinda had found so much solace and joy.

But at that moment Belinda's joy had been replaced with terror as she'd dashed past the tack room, past dozens of stalls bedecked by framed photographs, championship rosettes. And as she'd cowered in the corner, a shadow fell into the corridor.

The voice had been deep, soft. Chilling. "I know you're there. You can't hide forever."

Kate shuddered, recalling the memory snippets she'd relived weeks earlier in the tiny Morgan stable. She'd been so very frightened then, unable to recall details yet feeling as if that moment had been a turning point in her life.

It hadn't been, of course. Her chagrined fiancé had been sick with remorse, apologizing profusely for his behavior. Because they'd been friends for so very long, and because Belinda truly cared for Steven, she'd put the unpleasant incident behind them. From that moment on, he had treated her with the utmost courtesy and respect.

Still, months later, the memory of how Steven had stalked Belinda in the stable gave Kate goose bumps.

"Kate?"

"Hmm?" Blinking, she looked up and was swallowed by Reed's dark gaze.

"I know what you're thinking, and I want you to understand how terribly sorry I am."

Kate stepped back, bewildered. "Sorry for what?"

He licked his lips, tossing a helpless hand toward the house. "If I'd known, I'd never have—I mean, God, you must hate me."

"I could never hate you, Reed." *I love you,* cried her heart. *How could you not know that by now?*

But he responded only to her words, and not to her heart. With a shuddering breath, he laid his hands on her shoulders, tenderly, without passion. "What happened between us was my fault, Kate. I'd give anything in the world if it hadn't happened."

Suddenly Kate felt as if she'd been kicked in the stomach. Reed was talking about the night they'd made love, the night that she'd offered him everything she had and shared with him the essence of her very soul.

And he'd give anything in the world if it hadn't happened.

Apparently Reed misunderstood her grief-stricken expression, because he tightened his grip on her shoulders and moaned. "I'll talk to Sebring, if you want me to. I'll explain that it wasn't your fault, that I took advantage—"

Swiftly raising her arms, Kate knocked Reed's hands away. "Don't," she whispered. "Don't ever speak of this again, not to Steven, not to me."

Reed stepped back, stricken. "All right, if that's what you want."

Kate closed her eyes, reaching out to steady herself on the fence rail. She couldn't have what she wanted. Not now. Not ever. At that crushing moment, Kate realized that Reed had never really loved her.

To his credit, he'd never said that he did; she'd simply assumed, because he'd made love to her with such aching sweetness—

But he regretted that, of course, now that his wish to be rid of her had come true and he had a fat reward check in his pocket.

Spinning around so quickly that she stumbled, Kate lurched toward the driveway. She'd barely gone two steps when Reed stopped her. "Wait... please, we need to talk."

"We've been talking," said a bashful voice from the past. It was Belinda's voice, apologetic and whispered, quivering and shy. "I do appreciate the courtesy that you and your lovely family have shown to me, Mr. Morgan."

Reed's hand dropped from her elbow to dangle at his side like a broken gate. "Kate—"

"Please say goodbye to Shawna and Rory," she murmured to his shirt. "I'd also appreciate it if you'd be kind enough to inform my family that I'll be waiting in the car."

Reed's perplexed gaze bounced from the rental car to the top of Kate's head, which she'd bowed as if in prayer. "But why, Kate? I don't understand."

"I need to go home now," she whispered, staring down at her beloved Christmas sneakers. "It's where I belong."

Chapter Fourteen

"Dad, Rory hid the remote control again. Make her give it back!"

As Reed closed the front door, his shoulders sagged under the thick pall of anger shrouding his once-happy home. He said nothing, and not just because he didn't trust his voice. His daughters were bickering so loudly that any attempt to communicate at a volume short of a shout would have been fruitless.

"Shawna's been hogging the TV all afternoon," Rory hollered. "It's my turn."

The teenager's eyes narrowed into furious slits. "Give me that remote right now or I'll knot your arms to your legs and turn you into a human Nerf ball."

"Oh, yeah? You and who else?" Instantly Rory was on her feet, shoulders squared, arms straight, hands extended in a Bruce Lee caricature. "E-ee-ya!"

"You are such a brat!"

"Yeah, well you're a grumpy, rotten old...um...cow plop."

Shawna's eyes bulged. "Why, you little—"

Reed snagged the teenager's arm just as she lunged for her sister, who'd leapt into a defensive stance and was swishing her stiff hands through the air screaming "Hai!" at the top of her lungs.

"Give it a rest," Reed snapped. "Both of you are behaving like children."

"We *are* children," Rory reminded him, still glaring at her furious sibling.

Shaking loose from her father's grasp, Shawna pinned the younger girl with an eat-dirt-and-die look. "Speak for yourself, you obnoxious little dung beetle."

Rory poked her thumbs into her ears, wiggled her fingers and stuck out her tongue.

Frustrated, Shawna spun around, shaking an accusatory finger toward the younger girl, who was gleefully whispering "cow plop, cow plop" under her breath. "You see what I have to put up with, Dad? She's like that all the time. Ever since Kate left—" At the mention of Kate's name, the fire evaporated from Shawna's eyes and Rory fell silent.

Reed, feeling as if his heart had been squeezed by a giant hand, somehow managed to keep his composure. He had to, for his children's sake. If he allowed himself to think about Kate, about all that she'd given to them and all that she'd taken away, he wouldn't be able to bear the pain.

And Reed understood that he wasn't the only one in pain. By acting out, his daughters were expressing their own heartbreak and anger. They loved Kate, too, and felt betrayed by her absence.

All Reed could do was help them cope. That wouldn't be easy, since he could barely cope with his own feelings. It hardly seemed worth getting out of bed to face a day without Kate's radiant smile and wacky humor. The world was a colder place now; winter had settled in Reed's heart with an icy grip that chilled him to the marrow.

If he couldn't deal with losing Kate, how on earth could he expect his children to deal with it?

Finally he cleared his throat and decided to broach the problem directly. "I know you miss Kate," he told the girls quietly. "I miss her, too. But Kate is safe and sound with people who love her. She's happy now, and that should make us happy." Even as he spoke, a small voice in the back of his brain reminded him that she was also surrounded by comforts and luxuries that he could never have provided for her. Since Kate deserved the best, he took some solace from that. "What do you think Kate would say if she saw you two acting like this?"

A sudden anger darkened Shawna's eyes. "Who cares?"

"That's a mean thing to say!" Rory jammed her hands on her chunky hips and stuck out her chin. "Kate was really nice to you."

"She had to be nice," Shawna muttered. "Or we would have thrown her out."

"Uh-uh, no way!" Tears spurted from Rory's red little eyes. "I wish we could throw *you* out! You're the meanest, most hateful sister in the whole entire world!"

"Yeah, we'll you're nothing but a—"

"Stop it right now," Reed growled, stepping between the feuding youngsters. "Rory, turn off the television and go start your homework."

She folded her arms, sulking. "I don't have any."

"Then why did your teacher call me this afternoon and say that you haven't turned in an assignment all week?"

Staring at her shoes, the child gave a listless shrug.

Reed sighed. "Look, punkin, your teacher is concerned about you, and so am I. You've been doing so well, then all of a sudden you just stopped trying. You even failed to-day's spelling test, didn't you?"

"The words are too hard," she mumbled, wiping her wet cheeks. "Besides, spelling is dumb."

"All of your schoolwork is important, even spelling." Reed laid a gentle hand on his daughter's quivering shoulder. "I want you to make an effort, Rory. I want you to do your best."

Sniffing, Rory managed a thin nod, so Reed turned his attention to Shawna, who was sullenly staring at the floor.

"I know things have been difficult," he told her. "Maybe I depend on you too much because you're the oldest, but hopefully the new housekeeper will be able to take over most of those responsibilities so you won't feel so pressured. Which reminds me . . ." Frowning, he glanced around, irritated that the woman hadn't put a stop to the girls' squabble before it had escalated into a near-brawl. "I'd like a word with her. Where is she?"

"She left an hour ago," Shawna said, folding her arms. "I think she quit."

Reed groaned, wiped his face with his hands and peered over his fingertips. "Why, pray tell, did she do that?"

Shrugging, Shawna's gaze darted everywhere but toward her father. "Who knows? Maybe she found a better job."

"Or maybe," Rory added coyly, "she got mad when Shawna flushed her hamburger-macaroni stew down the toilet."

Reed's stomach sank to his knees. He gave Shawna a pleading look. "Oh, Lord, you didn't."

"The stuff stank," she mumbled, scratching a blemish on the thigh of her jeans. "And there was all kinds of disgusting junk in it, like canned tomatoes and some kind of boiled green garbage. I wouldn't have fed it to Gulliver."

Yanking off his hat, Reed raked his hair in utter frustration. "For crying out loud, Shawna—"

"It's all your fault," Shawna blurted at her shocked father. "We wouldn't need some dumb old housekeeper if you hadn't sent Kate away."

The accusation staggered him. "Kate simply decided to go home, Shawna. I had nothing to do with that."

"Kate loved us!" Shawna shouted, tears streaming down her cheeks. "She didn't want to leave, I know she didn't. Those people took Kate away, and the only reason they could do that is because *you brought them here!*"

Choking back a sob, Shawna whirled around and dashed into her room, slamming the door.

Reed stood there, stunned, even though he understood his daughter's fury. In a sense, Shawna was right. From the very beginning, Reed had done everything wrong. Not only had he broken his promise by notifying the sheriff of her mysterious arrival, he'd even gone so far as to confiscate a fingerprinted glass like some kind of pathetic James Bond wannabe.

If all that hadn't been bad enough, he'd added insult to injury by handing Kate over to her family without question, as if returning a lovable stray that had been hanging around long enough to become a nuisance.

Yes, Reed could definitely empathize with his daughter's anger. The worst part, however, was that he'd do the same thing all over again, because he loved Kate too much to do anything else. She deserved so much more than Reed could ever give her. Even if he could put aside the matter of her wealthy, virile and depressingly handsome young fiancé, there was no way Reed could have ever asked Kate to give up riches and luxury for life on a struggling ranch that was teetering on the brink of bankruptcy.

Despite the pain of loss, Reed still felt blessed by the time Kate had shared with them. Loving her had been the simplest, most natural thing in the world. She'd brought immeasurable joy into their lives, and for that he was deeply grateful.

As for his own grief, he'd simply lock it away in the secret painful room of his heart and pretend that everything was normal. It wasn't normal, of course. Nothing would ever be normal again. Reed's world had lost its luster. Without Kate, the sky seemed pale and faded, the sun had cooled, and stars that once glistened like diamonds on velvet were no more than drab, colorless dots splattered over a dreary black canvas.

The joy had seeped out of his life. Reed would never be the same.

From the parlor window, Kate gazed out at acres of manicured lawn, which were outlined by formal brick planters. In the warmth of summer, a profusion of colorful flowers would blossom forth, but now the planters were barren except for hardy evergreens and a few impatient daffodil shoots breaking the earth's chilly crust.

Inside, a crackling fire cradled the massive room in superficial warmth, along with a scent of pipe tobacco and disappointment hanging heavily in the air. The rhythmic click of fashionable high heels on the parlor's polished cherry wood floors announced Sylvia's arrival. "Steven will be dining with us this evening," she announced.

Kate continued to gaze silently out the window. Behind her, a newspaper rustled as her father shifted in his favorite Louis Quatorze wing chair.

"That's nice, dear," he said. "We'll have a lovely evening, won't we, Belinda?"

Kate didn't want to respond; Belinda, however, had been well coached on the conversational niceties expected in polite society. "Yes," she murmured without conviction. "We'll have a lovely evening."

Another rustling sound, this one lasting long enough to suggest that her father was indulging his habit of folding the newspaper to fit neatly in the hand-carved magazine holder beside his chair. "Perhaps after dinner, we'll have an opportunity to talk about, ah . . ."

When he paused, Kate imagined that he was gazing quizzically at Sylvia, silently requesting his wife to complete the statement. Her father did that a lot, Kate realized, particularly when the subject matter was even slightly distressing.

It struck Kate as odd that a man considered one of the most decisive and savvy in the corporate world would falter so miserably with his family life, but he'd always been that way: hardheaded in business, softhearted at home. When it came to sensitive matters, George was relieved to have his wife take the heat.

Strangely enough, Belinda had never recognized that side of her father, and had been willing to lay blame on Sylvia for situations that Kate now realized had not been entirely of the woman's choosing.

As Kate expected, her stepmother took over the conversation. "We must discuss wedding plans, Belinda. Steven hopes that the ceremony can be rescheduled for next month—"

"No." The calm refusal sliding over Kate's tongue would have shocked spineless Belinda, who'd always dutifully complied with what was expected of her. But six weeks ago on a rural Northern California highway, mousy Belinda had died and in-your-face Kate was born.

Pushing aside the final remnants of the person she'd once been, Kate turned to face her stunned parents. "I'm not going to marry Steven."

Her father's brow furrowed into a perplexed frown, but Sylvia, who'd blanched visibly, clutched her chest as if warding off a seizure. "That is utter nonsense. Of course you'll marry Steven. It's been arranged."

George MacGregor laid his pipe in an antique crystal ashtray and leaned forward, regarding Kate thoughtfully. "Have you and Steven had a quarrel?"

"No, Daddy, we haven't quarreled." Kate didn't bother to point out that she and Steven had barely spoken since her return last week. In fact, they'd barely spoken throughout the past year, and it had occurred to Kate that outside of obligatory discussions concerning wedding arrangements, she and Steven Sebring had absolutely nothing to say to each other. "It's just that Steven and I want very different things out of life. I don't think we can make each other happy."

"Happy?" Incredulous, Sylvia dropped into a nearby armchair, fanning herself with her hand. "My God, what nerve. What about your father's happiness? Doesn't that mean anything to you?" The woman leaned forward, her eyes flashing with fear and fury. "How can you be so selfish, Belinda? You know what this marriage means to us... to your father. Why, the merging of the MacGregors and the Sebrings would create an economic dynasty of epic proportions. No one would dare deny us the respect we deserve, and yet you'd throw it all away because you're afraid you won't be *happy?* I've never heard—"

"That's right," Kate snapped, allowing years of suppressed anger to bubble into righteous fury. "You've never heard anything except the sound of your own voice. Certainly, you've never listened to what I had to say."

"How dare you take that tone with me?" Furious, the woman turned to her husband for support, but found that he was watching Kate with an expression of curiosity mingled with surprise, and perhaps even a touch of admiration.

"We're listening to you now, Belinda," he said quietly. "Please, go on."

Kate swallowed hard, staring down at her knotted fists. "Ever since I can remember, it's been understood that Steven and I would marry, yet I don't recall anyone asking me if that's what I wanted."

George's frown deepened. "I assumed...I mean, you never said otherwise."

"No, I didn't, and that's my fault." She took in a deep breath, holding it for courage, then expelled it all at once. "I always knew that there was something expected of me. I didn't understand until that day at the chapel exactly what it was." Looking up sadly, Kate saw confusion on her father's face and fear on Sylvia's. "I wish you'd just told me what you wanted, Daddy. I would have signed over my shares of stock as soon as the trust issued them to me. You didn't have to make me marry Steven to get them."

Clearly flabbergasted, George vibrated upright as stiffly as his portly frame would allow. "What on earth are you talking about?"

Kate rubbed her eyelids, willing herself not to cry. She'd hoped that her father wouldn't deny the betrayal. But plainly he'd been denying it for years, and old habits die hard. "When you showed up at the ranch last week, all my memories came back," she said slowly. "Except for the day of the wedding. All I recalled of that day was being driven to the church in the morning, then climbing into the pastor's car that afternoon. Everything in between was blank... until yesterday."

George issued a supportive nod, but seemed otherwise unmoved by the revelation. "Well, now that you've remembered everything, that's good, isn't it?"

"Not really." She looked away. "The truth is, I wish those hours had remained buried forever."

"Why, child?" he asked softly. "What could possibly have happened that was so unsettling to you?"

Sylvia spoke up, plainly rattled. "Leave her alone, George. Can't you see that she doesn't want to discuss it?"

"Oh, but I do," Kate said coolly, staring until her stepmother avoided her gaze. "I saw you, Sylvia, you and Steven. I heard you arguing."

"You don't know what you heard," Sylvia replied stiffly. "You were obviously quite confused."

"Not so confused that I couldn't understand Steven's distress because he hadn't received the power of attorney that I was supposed to sign before the nuptials. You, Sylvia, were assuring him that Daddy would take care of it."

Sylvia stood, clasping her hands. "I don't have to listen to this."

"Sit down, Sylvia." George spoke to his wife without looking at her, then rested his chin on his steepled fingers. "Go on, Belinda. What else did you hear?"

Kate waited until her subdued stepmother was seated. "I heard enough to understand that Steven had been promised complete control over my trust fund in exchange for his co-operation in signing my shares of company stock over to you, Daddy." Despite her resolve, hot moisture seeped into her eyes, betraying the depth of her pain. "I don't understand," she whispered. "You always told me that you wanted Mom to split her stock between us. Why did you say that if it wasn't true?"

"It was true, Belinda, and it still is." If her father wasn't completely bewildered by her revelation, he certainly was an impressive actor. "I have no idea what you're talking about, but I can assure you that I know nothing about any deal with Steven Sebring. Good Lord, the stock I already own is worth more than one man could spend in a lifetime. Why on earth would I want any more?"

A shudder from across the room drew his attention and Kate's. Sylvia was sitting there, her head bowed and propped on her closed fist.

After a moment, she lifted her chin, regally crossing her hands in her lap. "It wasn't the money." The soft response was issued directly to Kate. "Your father has given his life to that company. He took a moderately successful little business and turned it into a corporate giant, but was he given the recognition he deserved? No, he was not. Instead of a lucrative retirement and a seat at the head of the board table, he was expected to work for his own daughter."

George went white, but Sylvia continued speaking to Kate as if her husband weren't even in the room.

"You don't understand what it's been like for him," she said. "The constant pressure of running that abysmal place was making him ill, but you never seemed to notice, Belinda, because you were always holed up in your room, or off in some dream world of your own making. But I saw the grayness in your father's face each night when he was so exhausted he could barely speak. He was killing himself and I simply couldn't bear to see that happen. I knew that with your shares of stock added to his own, he'd have enough power to take over the board, then he could hire others to work themselves into an early grave."

"Sylvia." George covered his eyes with his hand, shaking his head.

Unblinking, Sylvia never took her eyes off Kate. "Yes, I made a deal with Steven, but your father knew nothing about it. Please don't blame him for something that was entirely my doing."

Rocked by what she'd heard, Kate could barely find her voice. She wanted to believe that her father hadn't betrayed her, yet the memory of what she'd seen at the chapel was all too vivid. "I saw Daddy come in while you and Steven were talking. He handed Steven an envelope and said, 'This is what you've been waiting for.'"

George looked up, gaping.

"That was the marriage certificate," Sylvia replied. "After your father left to see if you were ready for the ceremony, Steven opened the envelope and was very disappointed. I was trying to convince him that the other documents would be forthcoming when George ran out of the bridal chamber shouting that you were gone."

"Oh, Sylvia," George moaned. "How could you have done such a thing?"

A heavy silence hung in the air. "I wanted you to live," she said simply.

Reed buried the ax blade in the chopping stump, wiped his brow and cast a skeptical glance at the morose figure slumped against the pasture fence. "Rory, have you finished cleaning out the stalls?"

The child poked a dried leaf with the toe of her sneaker. "I don't feel good."

"What's wrong?"

She shrugged.

Reed crossed the yard to lay a concerned hand on her forehead. "You don't have a fever. Is your stomach upset?"

"Maybe." Peeking up from beneath a thick fringe of stubby lashes, she fixed her father with a guileless gaze. "I should probably stay home from school tomorrow. I might be contagious or something."

"I see." Reed pursed his lips, observing the subtle twitch of her rigid little jaw. "Aren't your past-due homework assignments supposed to be turned in tomorrow?"

She shrugged again, lowering her gaze to the ground.

Before Reed could pursue the matter, his attention was diverted by a cloud of dust at the end of the long, winding driveway.

Rory looked up as an unfamiliar vehicle cruised toward the house. She recognized the driver the same moment Reed did. "Kate!" she squealed happily. "Daddy, it's Kate!"

Dashing across the yard, Rory skidded into Kate with such a frantic hug that they both nearly fell over.

"Ohmigosh," Kate exclaimed, half laughing and half crying. She cradled the child's flushed face in her hands. "I don't believe it. You've grown at least an inch in the past week."

Rory grinned. "I knew you'd come back. Shawna said you wouldn't, but I knew you'd miss us too much to stay away."

Kate bit her lip, waiting until her throat spasm eased before testing her voice. "You were right, sweetie. I missed you so much, I couldn't even eat a chocolate brownie."

"Wow." The girl's eyes widened in awe. "Chocolate brownies are your favorite. You musta been really sad."

"I was," Kate whispered, hugging her fiercely. "I've never been more sad in my whole life."

Stepping away, Rory wiped her damp eyes. "Me, too."

A movement caught Kate's eye. She looked up, and the breath caught in her throat. "Hello, Reed."

For a moment, Kate feared he wouldn't respond. He just stood there, expressionless and immobile, like a gorgeous statue. Then he nodded an acknowledgment. She wanted to say more, much more, but Rory was tugging on her sleeve.

Kate glanced down, then followed the child's gaze to the front porch, where Shawna was hovering like a sullen bumblebee. The teenager glared silently for a moment, then sauntered down the steps with a don't-give-a-spit demeanor that sliced Kate to the core.

Stopping well out of reach, Shawna eyed Kate's imported sports sedan. "Nice wheels. Did you come back just to show off?"

Rory stiffened, and looked about ready to pop her sister in the nose except that Kate laid a restraining hand on her shoulder. "I came back because I wanted to see you," Kate said gently, noting the obvious hurt in the teenager's eyes. "I, ah, brought presents."

Clearly that was the wrong thing to say. Shawna's eyes narrowed. "Golly, aren't we lucky?"

Rory jammed her fists on her hips. "You are so hateful," she muttered to her sister. "Can't you at least pretend to be nice?"

Blinking away a sheen of moisture, Shawna focused directly on Kate. "You didn't even say goodbye."

"I couldn't," Kate whispered, fighting a surge of emotion. "Saying goodbye was like admitting that I was going away forever, that I'd never see you again. That would have killed me, because I love you all so very, very much."

Shawna quivered as if shaken by a giant hand. Tears spilled down her face, flowing freely as she chewed her lip, plainly torn between giving in to her emotions and protecting herself from another disappointment.

Understanding that, Kate simply opened her arms and waited. In less than a heartbeat, Shawna flew into her embrace, sobbing pitifully. Kate hugged her desperately, kissing her wet cheeks and smoothing her silky blond hair. "Oh, sweetie, if you only knew how much I've missed you. I'm so sorry I hurt your feelings. I never meant to." Sniffing, Kate stepped reluctantly back, still brushing strands of hair from the girl's damp face. "Mentally, I was a real mess when I left. I had a whole bunch of stuff jumbled up inside me, and I had to sort everything out to figure out who I really was."

A deep male voice responded. "So, did you figure things out?"

Kate met Reed's eyes, and her knees nearly buckled. "Yes, I did. Maybe we can talk. You know, later. When you have time."

His gaze drilled straight to her soul, but he said nothing. Not that he had a chance, because Rory had stuck her head inside Kate's car and was eyeing a pair of parcels on the front seat.

She looked over her shoulder, grinning. "Didn't you say something about presents?"

Kate chuckled, Reed laughed, and even Shawna cracked a grin. The ice had been broken.

For the next few minutes, Rory bounced with excitement over her new monogrammed book bag, and Shawna seemed genuinely thrilled by an illustrated needlecraft encyclopedia. The girls oohed and ahhed, as they'd done on Christmas, and for those few blissful moments, it was as if the past week had never happened.

But it had happened, and deep inside, Kate was terrified by the possibility that in the end Reed would still reject her.

Her fear intensified when he sent the girls into the house and turned to Kate, his expression serious. "So, Kate...or should I call you Belinda?"

"My name is Kate now."

"All right, then." He folded his arms, gazing out over the pasture. "I take it that you and your family have gotten things ironed out?"

"Yes, I think so." Inside her, Belinda cringed like the coward she'd always been, and pleaded with Kate to run away before she could be hurt again. Kate was sorely tempted to do just that. Instead, she ignored the frightened voice from her past and faced the future head-on. "Now it's our turn, Reed. We have some things to iron out, too."

His eyes darted sideways, angling a quick glance at her before refocusing somewhere in the distance. "The oaks are budding. It's going to be an early spring."

"I've learned a lot about myself," she said quietly. "About the person I used to be, and the person I've become."

"The alfalfa crop will be good this year. That'll bring the price down some."

Kate reached out and took Reed's hand. He didn't look at her, but she felt him squeeze her fingers. They stood silently for a moment, then she took a deep breath and spoke in a halting voice, telling him everything she'd remembered, including the incident at the chapel that had started her on a journey that had forever altered the course of her life.

"I never loved Steven," Kate said finally. "Of course, he never loved me, either, only neither of us was bright enough to know that, because we were both entrapped by own suffocating little world. One of Belinda's problems was that she'd rather live with her head in a sand dune than risk confrontation. That's why she was willing to marry a man she didn't love—"

When Reed released her hand, she skimmed a glance at his rigid jaw, then looked quickly away.

After a moment, she continued. "That, and the fact that Belinda had no clue what love really was. Sylvia considered her to be selfish, and she truly was. She'd managed to build a huge wall around her heart, and she let no one inside, not even her father.''

Reed touched Kate's cheek, turning her face toward him. "Why do you refer to Belinda MacGregor as if she's a person outside of yourself?"

"Because in a sense, she is. I don't like her very much. She's a major wimp with no sense of humor and she has this annoying habit of running away from her problems, and making erroneous assumptions without seeking out truth. Which is," Kate added, rubbing her moist palms together, "one of the reasons I'm here."

A glimmer of suspicion was reflected in his dark eyes. "To run away from your problems?"

"To seek the truth."

Reed considered that. "All right, then. Seek away."

Nervously coughing away a throat tickle, Kate reached deep inside herself for courage. Somehow she found it. "First of all, the only reason I left is because I thought you wanted me to."

"I never—"

"Shh." Kate touched his lips softly. "Please, let me finish. Maybe then I'll gather enough strength to hear what you have to say."

His eyes widened, but he fell silent.

"I could have accepted you contacting the sheriff about me because you had your children's safety to consider, and for all you knew I could have been an escaped felon, or something equally unpleasant. In fact, I recall wondering the same thing myself." Kate took a deep breath, forcing herself to go on. "And I'll admit that I was deeply hurt when I learned you'd gotten a reward for turning me in, but—no, don't say it."

Shaking his head, Reed shifted miserably and propped a fist on his hip.

Kate continued. "Anyway, I think I'd have gotten over that because I know how much you need the money, and besides, you'd already spent a small fortune feeding me and putting clothes on my back. But when you told me..." When her quivering voice gave way, she struggled to regain at least a modicum of composure. A deep breath helped. "When you told me that you regretted our lovemaking, I couldn't deal with that."

"Oh, God, Kate, I never meant it that way." Reed closed his eyes and seemed to be fighting for control. When he finally was able to look at her again, she was stunned by the pain she saw. "Is that why you left?"

"Yes."

He started to say something, then thought better of it. After a moment, he sighed. "Then I guess I don't understand why you came back."

"Several reasons," she said carefully, retrieving a fistful of scraps from her jacket pocket. She handed them to Reed. "These represent one of them."

He frowned at the remains of the torn check nested in his palm.

"My father said that you never accepted the reward, that you immediately tore the check up and stuffed the pieces into his shirt pocket. I figured that if I'd been wrong about the reward, maybe I was wrong about other things, too." She paused a moment. When Reed made no effort to either confirm or dispute that, she went on. "Daddy also told me that at first he'd thought you were upset that the check wasn't big enough, but when he offered more than the original ten thousand, you got so mad that he was afraid you were actually going to take a swing at him." Kate regarded Reed thoughtfully, noting the embarrassed flush creeping up his throat. "Why didn't you take the money, Reed? You deserve it, and God knows, you could certainly use it."

"Thanks for the reminder." He flung the check scraps on the ground. "I don't want your damned money."

"Well, that's tough, because you promised me a partnership in the ranch as soon as I could afford it." She batted her eyelashes. "Guess what, Reed? I can afford it."

"No way."

"You promised."

"That doesn't count," he shouted in frustration. "I only made that promise because there wasn't a snowball's chance in hell that you'd ever have more than two dimes to rub together. How the devil was I suppose to know that a woman who was all thumbs in the kitchen and couldn't turn on a vacuum cleaner without instructions would end up to be a freaking heiress?" When his anger was greeted by a muffled giggle, Reed's eyes glazed and his jaw slackened. "What's so damned funny?"

"The male ego," she replied, pausing for a chuckle. "You really do love me, don't you?"

He blinked at her.

"Oh, I know you never said as much, but that's all a part of the ego thing, isn't it?" Before he could so much as open his mouth, Kate was talking again. "Here I thought that you couldn't wait to get rid of me because I was a pain in the butt, and all the time you'd labeled me a bubble-brained airhead who wanted nothing more from life than a snazzy car and a closet full of designer dresses. Strange, isn't it, that two people could know so little about each other and still be so crazy in love? And you do love me, Reed Morgan, don't you dare try to deny it. Belinda would let you get away with that stuff, but I won't. I want you to admit it right here, right now."

Looking like a man who'd just been gut-punched, Reed barely had the breath to speak. "Kate, I—"

"Wait a minute. I want to watch your nose." She adjusted his face, then stepped back. "Okay, carry on."

The poor guy looked so bewildered that Kate's heart went out to him. He extended his hands, palms up, in a gesture of helpless frustration. "I don't know what you want me to say."

"The truth," she murmured. "I have to know the truth."

Reed sucked in a breath, tugged down the brim of his hat, then placed his hands on his hips and stared at the ground. "All right, the truth is that I probably fell in love the first time I laid eyes on you, while I was still wiping mud off your nose and pulling twigs out of your hair." He shifted his gaze upward. "You're the most beautiful woman I've ever known, not to mention the kindest, most compassionate, quirkiest, most frustrating and downright funniest. A man would have to be crazy not to love you, Kate. I'm not crazy."

As a giant weight lifted from her shoulders, Kate issued a silent prayer of relief and gratitude. She would have kissed him then, except he stepped back, turning away.

"But life is tough," he said, refusing to look at her. "Love just isn't enough, Kate, and I have nothing else to offer."

"Nothing to offer?" She shook her head, astonished, and gestured expansively. "You have everything I want, Reed, everything there is. All I want is to love you and your children and, God willing, the children that we'll have together. All I want is to be part of your life, Reed. Is that too much to ask?"

When he stood there, hesitant and unyielding, she stepped forward and slipped her arms around him. "All right, then. I can see this is a decision you're unwilling to make, so I'll do it for you. If you want me to leave, Reed, you'd better say so in the next five seconds. Otherwise, I'm going to haul the suitcases out of my trunk and the only way you'll get rid of me is to drag me away, kicking and screaming."

The corner of his mouth twitched. "Well, if you're going to be pesky about it, you might as well earn your keep. As a matter of fact, we do happen to have a job opening."

Kate's heart swelled. "The yarn shop still wants me to give lessons, but I insisted on only morning hours because I was hoping you hadn't hired a new housekeeper—"

"Actually, I have. Three in the past week." He heaved an exaggerated sigh, ignoring her crushed expression. "The thing is, I thought you might be interested in a more permanent position. The pay is awful, the hours are ridiculous and you'd be supervising a rather difficult staff."

"Sounds challenging," Kate murmured. "Tell me about the boss."

"Why, you'd be the boss, Kate. Everyone knows that the wife is always in charge."

"Mr. Morgan," she whispered, draping her arms around his neck. "You've got yourself a deal."

Epilogue

Spring really did come early that year, and that was good, because of the wedding and all. Rory had never been a bridesmaid before. Neither had Shawna, even though she acted real prissy about it, as if it were no big deal. Rory had pretty much ignored her sister's silliness, because she knew that deep down Shawna had been real nervous about standing up in front of a whole church full of people.

Rory hadn't been nervous at all. Well, she might have been a teeny bit worried about tripping on her dress, on account of she didn't like dresses much in the first place and she'd never, ever worn one with a big fat skirt that flooped all the way down to the floor.

But she hadn't complained or anything, because Kate had worked so hard sewing all the dresses for her and for Shawna and Gramma Sylvia, who got to be the matron of honor. The dresses were made of pretty blue satin that was all shimmery, with puffy sleeves and tons of ruffles. Shawna and Gramma Sylvia thought they were neat, but Rory didn't like ruffles much, and the humongous bow on her butt made her look like a total dweeb.

Rory liked Kate's wedding gown a lot better. It had puffy sleeves, too, but there wasn't any big bow. Kate said that she'd run out of fabric, but she was grinning like a weasel in a grain bin, so Rory figured that Kate probably hated butt-bows as much as she did.

But other than that, the wedding turned out swell. Everyone was real happy, and people kept walking up to shake Daddy's hand. Rory thought her dad looked a bit peaked at first, but when he saw Grampa George walking Kate down the aisle, his eyes got all glowy and stuff, so Rory figured he must be feeling better.

It was still a little weird though, because halfway through the ceremony, Gramma Sylvia started crying. Since she was standing right beside Kate, everyone in the whole church heard her blowing her nose behind the bouquet. Rory thought it was all pretty gross, but everyone else just kinda smiled, so she figured that blowing your nose at a wedding must be an okay thing to do.

Later, Rory heard Gramma Sylvia tell Kate that she'd cried because she was so happy, and also because she was sad that they'd wasted so many years without knowing that they could have been friends. That made absolutely no sense to Rory, but Kate had just given Gramma Sylvia a really big hug, which seemed to make both Daddy and Grampa George real happy.

In fact, everybody was real happy, even Grampa and Gramma Morgan, who drove all the way from Florida and stayed for a whole week in a great big motor home that Rory thought was the neatest thing she'd ever seen in her whole life. It had nifty chairs that swirled around in circles if you pushed the floor with your feet, and a teeny-weeny television set, and a shower so bitty that even Gulliver would have trouble fitting inside.

Anyway, Rory thought the week of Kate and Daddy's wedding was just about the most exciting time of her whole entire life—except for when she heard Kate and her daddy arguing about Kate's money. That got Rory real scared, but Shawna said it was no big deal. She said that Daddy had already agreed to let Kate set up something called a "trust fund" so Rory and Shawna could both go to college—although Rory wasn't sure she liked that idea much. Shawna also said that Kate had agreed to let Grampa George invest the rest, except that Kate wanted to buy new cherry trees. That's when Daddy's face got all screwed up like he'd stepped in cow stuff or something.

But the very next week, a big truck rolled up and unloaded about a million baby trees.

Afterward, Grampa and Gramma Morgan went back to Florida, and Grampa George and Gramma Sylvia flew off to Europe for something Kate called a second honeymoon. Rory wasn't exactly sure what a honeymoon was or why anyone would need two of them, but Kate had just laughed and said that nobody could ever have too many honeymoons. Then Shawna asked how come Kate and Daddy weren't gonna have one. Daddy and Kate just kind of looked at each other all gushy and gooey-eyed and said that they had a honeymoon every day of the week.

Rory didn't get it, but Shawna turned all red and sputtery, which made Kate and Daddy laugh real hard. After a couple minutes, Shawna started to giggle, so Rory had laughed, too. She still couldn't figure out what was so funny, but it didn't much matter because everybody laughed for no real reason whenever Kate was around.

And Kate was going to be around forever and ever. Rory knew that because Daddy had said so, and his nose hadn't twitched even a little. That suited Rory just fine, and since there'd only been one person in the whole world who'd known what she had really wanted for Christmas, Rory sat down to write one last thank-you note right after the wedding.

Dear Santa,
As you can see, my spelling is alot beter now . . .

* * * * *

Watch for A HERO'S CHILD, *the next installment of Diana Whitney's charming* PARENTHOOD *miniseries, coming March 1997 from Silhouette Special Edition.*

Silhouette®

SPECIAL EDITION

COMING NEXT MONTH

#1075 A LAWMAN FOR KELLY—Myrna Temte
That Special Woman!
U.S. marshal meets gal from the wrong side of the law. Result?
Arresting display of sparks until that special woman Kelly Jaynes
finally gets her man—handsome lawman Steve Anderson!

#1076 MISTAKEN BRIDE—Brittany Young
Kate Fairfax had always had a troubled relationship with her identical
twin. So when her sister asked her to be at her wedding, Kate was
happy to attend. But she *never* expected to be so attracted to the
groom...or that the upcoming wedding would be her own!

#1077 LIVE-IN MOM—Laurie Paige
Love was in the air the moment Carly Lightfoot and Ty Macklin set
eyes on each other. Ty had a ranch and a son to look out for, and
didn't have time for romance—that is, until Ty's son decided Carly
would make a perfect mom and schemed to get her together with his
dad....

#1078 THE LONE RANGER—Sharon De Vita
Silver Creek County
Texas Ranger Cody Kincaid had come to Silver Creek to get the job
done—protect widowed Savannah Duncan and her son from someone
trying to scare her off her land. But he didn't bargain on getting so
attached to the sexy single mom and her mischievous child. Whether
Cody knew it or not, this lone ranger needed a family....

#1079 MR. FIX-IT—Jo Ann Algermissen
Finding themselves working side by side was an unexpected bonus
for Brandon Corral and Molly Winsome. Her broken heart needed
mending, and "Mr. Fix-It" Brandon was sure he was the man for the
job....

#1080 ALMOST TO THE ALTAR—Neesa Hart
Elise Christopher and Wil Larson had almost made it to the altar years
ago. Now, fate had unexpectedly reunited them, giving them a chance
to recapture their romance. But would they make it down the aisle
this time?

FAST CASH 4031 DRAW RULES
NO PURCHASE OR OBLIGATION NECESSARY

Fifty prizes of $50 each will be awarded in random drawings to be conducted no later than 3/28/97 from amongst all eligible responses to this prize offer received as of 2/14/97. To enter, follow directions, affix 1st-class postage and mail OR write Fast Cash 4031 on a 3" x 5" card along with your name and address and mail that card to: Harlequin's Fast Cash 4031 Draw, P.O. Box 1395, Buffalo, NY 14240-1395 OR P.O. Box 618, Fort Erie, Ontario L2A 5X3. (Limit: one entry per outer envelope; all entries must be sent via 1st-class mail.) Limit: one prize per household. Odds of winning are determined by the number of eligible responses received. Offer is open only to residents of the U.S. (except Puerto Rico) and Canada and is void wherever prohibited by law. All applicable laws and regulations apply. Any litigation within the province of Quebec respecting the conduct and awarding of a prize in this sweepstakes maybe submitted to the Régie des alcools, des courses et des jeux. In order for a Canadian resident to win a prize, that person will be required to correctly answer a time-limited arithmetical skill-testing question to be administered by mail. Names of winners available after 4/28/97 by sending a self-addressed, stamped envelope to: Fast Cash 4031 Draw Winners, P.O. Box 4200, Blair, NE 68009-4200.

OFFICIAL RULES
MILLION DOLLAR SWEEPSTAKES
NO PURCHASE NECESSARY TO ENTER

1. To enter, follow the directions published. Method of entry may vary. For eligibility, entries must be received no later than March 31, 1998. No liability is assumed for printing errors, lost, late, non-delivered or misdirected entries.
   To determine winners, the sweepstakes numbers assigned to submitted entries will be compared against a list of randomly pre-selected prize winning numbers. In the event all prizes are not claimed via the return of prize winning numbers, random drawings will be held from among all other entries received to award unclaimed prizes.

2. Prize winners will be determined no later than June 30, 1998. Selection of winning numbers and random drawings are under the supervision of D. L. Blair, Inc., an independent judging organization whose decisions are final. Limit: one prize to a family or organization. No substitution will be made for any prize, except as offered. Taxes and duties on all prizes are the sole responsibility of winners. Winners will be notified by mail. Odds of winning are determined by the number of eligible entries distributed and received.

3. Sweepstakes open to residents of the U.S. (except Puerto Rico), Canada and Europe who are 18 years of age or older, except employees and immediate family members of Torstar Corp., D. L. Blair, Inc., their affiliates, subsidiaries, and all other agencies, entities, and persons connected with the use, marketing or conduct of this sweepstakes. All applicable laws and regulations apply. Sweepstakes offer void wherever prohibited by law. Any litigation within the province of Quebec respecting the conduct and awarding of a prize in this sweepstakes must be submitted to the Régie des alcools, des courses et des jeux. In order to win a prize, residents of Canada will be required to correctly answer a time-limited arithmetical skill-testing question to be administered by mail.

4. Winners of major prizes (Grand through Fourth) will be obligated to sign and return an Affidavit of Eligibility and Release of Liability within 30 days of notification. In the event of non-compliance within this time period or if a prize is returned as undeliverable, D. L. Blair, Inc. may at its sole discretion award that prize to an alternate winner. By acceptance of their prize, winners consent to use of their names, photographs or other likeness for purposes of advertising, trade and promotion on behalf of Torstar Corp., its affiliates and subsidiaries, without further compensation unless prohibited by law. Torstar Corp. and D. L. Blair, Inc., their affiliates and subsidiaries are not responsible for errors in printing of sweepstakes and prizewinning numbers. In the event a duplication of a prizewinning number occurs, a random drawing will be held from among all entries received with that prizewinning number to award that prize.

SWP-S12ZD1

5. This sweepstakes is presented by Torstar Corp., its subsidiaries and affiliates in conjunction with book, merchandise and/or product offerings. The number of prizes to be awarded and their value are as follows: Grand Prize — $1,000,000 (payable at $33,333.33 a year for 30 years); First Prize — $50,000; Second Prize — $10,000; Third Prize — $5,000; 3 Fourth Prizes — $1,000 each; 10 Fifth Prizes — $250 each; 1,000 Sixth Prizes — $10 each. Values of all prizes are in U.S. currency. Prizes in each level will be presented in different creative executions, including various currencies, vehicles, merchandise and travel. Any presentation of a prize level in a currency other than U.S. currency represents an approximate equivalent to the U.S. currency prize for that level, at that time. Prize winners will have the opportunity of selecting any prize offered for that level; however, the actual non U.S. currency equivalent prize, if offered and selected, shall be awarded at the exchange rate existing at 3:00 P.M. New York time on March 31, 1998. A travel prize option, if offered and selected by winner, must be completed within 12 months of selection and is subject to: traveling companion(s) completing and returning a Release of Liability prior to travel; and hotel and flight accommodations availability. For a current list of all prize options offered within prize levels, send a self-addressed, stamped envelope (WA residents need not affix postage) to: MILLION DOLLAR SWEEPSTAKES Prize Options, P.O. Box 4456, Blair, NE 68009-4456, USA.

6. For a list of prize winners (available after July 31, 1998) send a separate, stamped, self-addressed envelope to: MILLION DOLLAR SWEEPSTAKES Winners, P.O. Box 4459, Blair, NE 68009-4459, USA.

EXTRA BONUS PRIZE DRAWING
NO PURCHASE OR OBLIGATION NECESSARY TO ENTER

7. The Extra Bonus Prize will be awarded in a random drawing to be conducted no later than 5/30/98 from among all entries received. To qualify, entries must be received by 3/31/98 and comply with published directions. Prize ($50,000) is valued in U.S. currency. Prize will be presented in different creative expressions, including various currencies, vehicles, merchandise and travel. Any presentation in a currency other than U.S. currency represents an approximate equivalent to the U.S. currency value at that time. Prize winner will have the opportunity of selecting any prize offered in any presentation of the Extra Bonus Prize Drawing; however, the actual non U.S. currency equivalent prize, if offered and selected by winner, shall be awarded at the exchange rate existing at 3:00 P.M. New York time on March 31, 1998. For a current list of prize options offered, send a self-addressed, stamped envelope (WA residents need not affix postage) to: Extra Bonus Prize Options, P.O. Box 4462, Blair, NE 68009-4462, USA. All eligibility requirements and restrictions of the MILLION DOLLAR SWEEPSTAKES apply. Odds of winning are dependent upon number of eligible entries received. No substitution for prize except as offered. For the name of winner (available after 7/31/98), send a self-addressed, stamped envelope to: Extra Bonus Prize Winner, P.O. Box 4463, Blair, NE 68009-4463, USA.

SWP-S12ZD2

As seen on TV!
Free Gift Offer

With a Free Gift proof-of-purchase from any Silhouette® book,
you can receive a beautiful cubic zirconia pendant.

This gorgeous marquise-shaped stone is a genuine cubic
zirconia—accented by an 18" gold tone necklace.
(Approximate retail value $19.95)

Send for yours today...
compliments of ❤ *Silhouette*®
™

To receive your free gift, a cubic zirconia pendant, send us one original proof-of-
purchase, photocopies not accepted, from the back of any Silhouette Romance™,
Silhouette Desire®, Silhouette Special Edition®, Silhouette Intimate Moments®
or Silhouette Yours Truly™ title available in August, September, October, November and
December at your favorite retail outlet, together with the Free Gift Certificate, plus a
check or money order for $1.65 U.S./$2.15 CAN. (do not send cash) to cover postage and
handling, payable to Silhouette Free Gift Offer. We will send you the specified gift. Allow
6 to 8 weeks for delivery. Offer good until December 31, 1996 or while quantities last.
Offer valid in the U.S. and Canada only.

Free Gift Certificate

Name: _____

Address: _____

City: _____ State/Province: _____ Zip/Postal Code: _____

Mail this certificate, one proof-of-purchase and a check or money order for postage
and handling to: SILHOUETTE FREE GIFT OFFER 1996. In the U.S.: 3010 Walden
Avenue, P.O. Box 9077, Buffalo NY 14269-9077. In Canada: P.O. Box 613, Fort Erie,
Ontario L2Z 5X3.

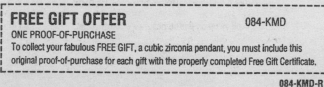

FREE GIFT OFFER
ONE PROOF-OF-PURCHASE   084-KMD

To collect your fabulous FREE GIFT, a cubic zirconia pendant, you must include this
original proof-of-purchase for each gift with the properly completed Free Gift Certificate.

084-KMD-R

The collection of the year!
NEW YORK TIMES BESTSELLING AUTHORS

Linda Lael Miller
Wild About Harry

Janet Dailey
Sweet Promise

Elizabeth Lowell
Reckless Love

Penny Jordan
Love's Choices

and featuring
Nora Roberts
The Calhoun Women

This special trade-size edition features four of the wildly
popular titles in the Calhoun miniseries together in
one volume—a true collector's item!

Pick up these great authors and a chance to win
a weekend for two in New York City at the
Marriott Marquis Hotel on Broadway! We'll pay
for your flight, your hotel—even a Broadway show!

Available in December at your favorite retail outlet.

NEW YORK
Marriott ®
MARQUIS

HARLEQUIN® ® ❦ Silhouette® ™

NYT1296-R

You're About to Become a *Privileged Woman*

Reap the rewards of fabulous free gifts and benefits with proofs-of-purchase from Silhouette and Harlequin books

Pages & Privileges™

It's our way of thanking you for buying our books at your favorite retail stores.

PROOF OF PURCHASE
SSE-PP20
Offer expires March 31, 1997

Harlequin and Silhouette—
the most privileged readers in the world!

For more information about Harlequin and Silhouette's PAGES & PRIVILEGES program call the Pages & Privileges Benefits Desk: 1-503-794-2499

Silhouette®

SSE-PP20